"Is this your j

Jackson, half-smili
froze at the sight o
An array of emotio   ms lace,
making Emalea regret the question.

Returning the pictures to the table, she
went into the kitchen, immediately noticing
his white-knuckle grip. *Tread carefully*, she
cautioned herself. *This might be a subject that
makes him angry.*

"Sorry. I didn't mean to pry."

"Of course you did. But it's okay. They died,
back in Chicago two years ago, car accident."

"I'm truly sorry. I didn't know."

He was quiet and she thought the conversation
had ended.

"It should never have happened. It was my
fault."

The words were spoken so softly Emalea
wasn't sure if she'd actually heard them. If she
considered what he said through the filter of
her own past, she would run out the door. But
she didn't. She realised she desperately wanted
Jackson not to be like other men she'd known.

A Different Kind of Man

SUZANNE COX

*First published in Great Britain 2006
Silhouette Books, Eton House, 18-24 Paradise Road,
Richmond, Surrey TW9 1SR*

© Suzanne Cox 2005

*ISBN-13: 978 0 373 78064 8
ISBN-10: 0 373 78064 8*

38-1206

*Printed and bound in Spain
by Litografia Rosés S.A., Barcelona*

Dear Reader,

Life in small Mississippi River towns has been fodder for books since Mark Twain wrote his stories about Tom Sawyer and Huckleberry Finn. Throw in the spice and character of Louisiana's Cajun culture and you have a setting that simply asks for a story. This is what led me to create the town of Cypress Landing. I hope Louisiana residents will forgive any geographical liberties I have taken for the sake of this story and *laissez les bon temps rouler!*

I've always been awed by people who freely give of their time and talents to help others in distress. That's why I wanted to tell the story of volunteer search and rescue member Emalea LeBlanc. Like many of us, her life hasn't always been a bed of roses. But I hope that, like Emalea, we can learn there's still a lot of good in the world and a lot of love. We simply have to learn to look for it without trying to paint everything with colours from our past. People sometimes ask if the things I've written are based on my life, and I have to admit that I only wish I were as capable as Emalea. I never did learn to ride the Harley by myself and although I can scuba dive, I'm not nearly as fearless as she is. The only true adventures are those of the real Jade, my sister-in-law's cat, whose real-life exploits are quite bookworthy!

I hope you enjoy my first book. It's been a long but thrilling ride to get here. I'd love to hear from readers. You can e-mail me at suzannecox@ suzannecoxbooks.com, or by post at Suzanne Cox, PO Box 18836, Hattiesburg, MS 39404, USA. You can visit me on the web at www.suzannecoxbooks. com or at www.superauthors.com.

Hugs,

Suzanne Cox

A Note from the Author

I wrote my Dear Reader letter nearly three months before life in south Mississippi and New Orleans was irrevocably changed. My editor was kind enough to let me squeeze in this last piece. I hope you find the chapters in this book bring to life the image of small-town life, which I found greatly tested in these times. In the most frightening early days when water, gas and food were in short supply for many, those in the smallest communities depended on the help of their neighbours, churches and friends for survival and recovery. At the moment the chapters set in New Orleans are the most heartbreaking for me because we are yet to know what direction this beloved city will go. I am certain by the time you read this great strides will have been taken to restore the things along the Gulf Coast and in New Orleans that we loved most to something we will love even more. I am in even greater awe of the real-life heroes seen during this time, from the search-and-rescue teams to the everyday citizens who held out their hands to help one another. And again I say, *laissez les bon temps rouler!* For I know they will. It is the spirit of the people.

To my husband, Justin,
for believing and being perfect without fail.

To my mom for all the reading.
I know you'll always be my biggest fan.

To Lisa White, for the critiques that helped me get here.

To Jan Sears and Stephanie Buhrer, for all your help, support and trips to Maria's.

To Kathy Harvey, for all your support over the years.

CHAPTER ONE

THUNDERING MOTORCYCLE ENGINES caused Jackson's beer mug to vibrate on the smeared copper bar. He twisted the frosty glass, then took a swig. Someone put money in the jukebox, sending an old Guns n' Roses tune blasting. For a biker bar, Sal's was all right.

From the road, it appeared to be a quaint restaurant, with French doors across the front and back walls. Maybe the place had once done time as a fine dining establishment, but now it was more of a beer, pizza and burger joint.

Outside, someone whooped as the definitive thump, thump of another arriving Harley-Davidson filled the air. Jackson glanced through one of the open doors just in time to see a motorcycle come to a stop in the parking lot. He sat up straighter, staring. Royal-blue paint etched with a red scrollwork design covered the gas tank and fenders. The rest of the bike sparkled with shining chrome. Who-

ever owned that bike certainly hadn't purchased it straight from the store. At the moment, the owner, or at least the rider, of that
racy machine claimed his undivided attention.

"Definitely, a custom job," Jackson said
under his breath.

"Doc ain't gonna ride nothin' but."

He jerked around to see the large, burly
bartender standing across from him. The guy
scratched his ragged beard then leaned
nearer. "I guess you were talkin' 'bout the
motorcycle. But now, Doc's a custom job
herself." He winked then clomped to the
other end of the bar to wait on someone.

Jackson couldn't help but be captivated
by the driver of the flashy motorcycle. She
settled the kickstand in place and slung her
leg over the bike. There was absolutely nothing but legs, forever. Bare legs. Her cutoff
denim shorts were short. Not indecent, he
had to admit, but really short. Underneath
her thick leather jacket, he saw flashes of a
blue-and-red shirt with the same design as
the motorcycle. He wasn't surprised at all to
see that the bandanna tied around her head
also matched the paint job.

Realizing he hadn't breathed for a moment, Jackson gulped in air followed by beer.

Checking out women was not why he was in this bar. He'd planned to ride his Harley and investigate his new hometown. Cypress Landing, Louisiana, was a far cry from Chicago, but it was just what he needed. Sitting high on the east bank of the Mississippi River, it was a place where people seemed to be able to know their neighbors. Calm and quiet, that's what he wanted. Chicago held nothing but a life and memories better left behind.

The woman, along with the other riders, crowded inside, shoving tables together as the waitress chatted with them. The biker girl pulled off her jacket, dropping it on the back of her chair, then tossed her thick brown braid across her shoulder. Legs weren't all she had going for her. She definitely had plenty of curves in all the right places. His hand tightened around his glass when a pair of almond-shaped green eyes caught him staring. Jackson realized he had spun sideways on his stool to watch her. Now, he was busted.

He could vaguely remember when he'd found it easy to attract a little female interest. What would it hurt to practice some of those old charms? He met her stare for a few seconds then gave a slow smile inclining his head. The green eyes narrowed, and the biker girl—Doc—frowned before dropping into her chair. Turning his back to their table, Jackson grabbed a handful of peanuts from a bowl on the bar. Possibly, his charms had rusted like an old lawn mower left neglected in the rain.

Using the mirror on the wall, he studied the small group directly behind him. A few of the other patrons in here appeared to have been straddling a bike since they were old enough to walk, and they sported the tattoos to prove it. With their clean-cut looks and expensive leather, Doc's group obviously didn't fall into that category. Much like himself, they had become representative of the new breed of motorcycle enthusiast, the middle-to-upper-class, college-educated biker. A friend in Chicago had convinced Jackson the bike could make a difference in his life. He guessed in a way it had. He'd decided to move here not long after the purchase.

He spotted the restroom sign over a hallway into which the jukebox had been shoved. He sighed. Attempting to exorcise the past from his mind every day exhausted him. He left his stool and headed to the restroom, squeezing by the big jukebox.

In the worn but decently clean bathroom,

Jackson washed his hands without looking in the spotted mirror. A pair of shining green eyes would be all he saw and his eyes were brown. It was that woman. Why had her image locked itself in his mind? He hadn't thought twice about a woman in years, not since Christa.

He rolled his shoulders to loosen a bit of tension at the base of his neck, then shoved through the door as though hurrying would clear his head. Just as he reached the end of the hallway and prepared to squeeze by the jukebox, a figure in blue turned the corner. He tried to slow down and even made a grab for the glass in her hand, but he'd been traveling with much more purpose than he'd realized. The woman called Doc bounced off his chest and banged against the wall, her drink soaking the front of her shirt while her handful of coins clattered to the floor. Jackson gripped her shoulders in an effort to steady her. Even before he met her eyes, his body tightened in a gut reaction. Some kind of soft powdery scent, mixed with fresh air from her ride, floated around him. This woman had a presence. That was for sure. Their surroundings seemed to shrink into the background when he finally focused on those eyes.

Beneath his fingers she quivered like a

scared puppy for a moment, then she wrenched from his grasp with a force that surprised him. The liquid remaining in her glass landed on the floor.

"What the hell is wrong with you? You could hurt somebody barreling down the hallway like that. Why don't you watch where you're going?"

"I'm sorry, I didn't see you." He squatted to round up her change. The bartender appeared beside them, and Jackson thought the guy smiled before he handed her a towel.

He frowned at Jackson. "You need to be more careful, big fella."

"Thanks for the towel, Mick," Doc called as the man lumbered away.

"Look, I'm sorry, I didn't see you. I didn't mean to make you spill your drink."

"Or knock me into the wall?"

"No, I didn't mean that, either." He didn't know what else to say. It had been an accident. She scrubbed at her wet shirt while Jackson wondered what to do next.

"I'm really sorry."

"You said that already."

He had, but she hadn't accepted it.

"Why don't you go and cause someone else trouble?"

Did bumping into someone always make

her this mad? Of course, her soaked shirt wouldn't help her mood and she might even have a lump on her head, considering how hard she'd banged it against the wall. "You didn't hurt yourself, did you?" He lifted his hand in an attempt to check her for injury.

She jerked away, her arm raised defensively. "Don't touch me."

He took a half-step back. "I'm just concerned. I'm not trying to hurt you."

"Yeah, well, just give me the money."

Her voice carried in a temporary lull in conversations and a few people looked their way. She scuffed the toe of her boot almost self-consciously and stuck out her open hand.

Jackson quit any attempts to respond and emptied the coins in her palm. What kind of person went berserk when someone bumped into her? She began dropping coins in the jukebox. He had to wait until she finished because he couldn't get past her without knocking her into the machine. The idea was tempting after her rudeness, but she remained stiff, tense, as though waiting to spring into action if he should try to get past. That's when he noticed it. Her fingers trembled slightly each time they deposited money into the slot. When the last coin dropped, she left.

He returned to his seat hoping there wouldn't be more trouble from her friends. He didn't know how or why he'd upset her. But he had.

In front of him, the bartender set a fresh beer on the counter. "Looks like you need this."

What was the guy's name? Rick? No, Mick. "Mick, I didn't mean to cause trouble."

"Aw, Doc ain't hurt. She'll get over it. She just gets a little wired up over some stuff."

"I'd like to buy her another glass of whatever she's drinking, since I spilled most of the one she had."

"That ain't gonna help. 'Sides, I took her one already."

"Yeah, well, what else can I do?"

Mick shrugged then filled a glass with soda and left the bar. In the mirror, Jackson saw him place the glass on the table with a few words. The woman only shoved the full glass to the center of the table. He couldn't be sure why he felt disappointed. The whole jukebox thing was a misunderstanding and he didn't like being misunderstood.

When the bartender returned, Jackson reached for his wallet.

"Don't worry, her drink's on the house. And don't leave yet."

"Why?"

Mick bent to rinse a glass, using a clean towel to pat it dry. "The races will start in about an hour."

"What races?"

"Every Saturday afternoon folks show up here with their bikes and race on the old highway, just the other side of the store. Sometimes there's even a little friendly betting."

Motorcycle races sounded interesting. What else did he have to do but go stare at half-unpacked boxes?

EMALEA LEBLANC TRIED to appear unperturbed. Her table was quiet. Probably had something to do with her reaction and the fact that guy nearly had her cowering.

"Big klutz," she said with a forced grin.

Her friends laughed and everything was back to normal again. Sort of. She half listened to what was going on around her as she watched the back of the man sitting at the bar. Her head ached a bit from its brief encounter with the wall. Guys like that thought they could push people around, run over women. Not her.

He'd made her lash at him like a bullwhip. She hadn't done that in a long time. Her ranting had managed to attract the attention of the whole bar. She pressed a finger to her forehead to slow her runaway thoughts. *Accident, Em.* The guy hadn't attacked her, but when he'd put his hands on her shoulders, she'd felt the need to get away and had ended up embarrassing herself. That part wasn't his fault, but if he hung around long enough she might give him a turn at looking silly, just for fun. She tried to read the faded lettering on the back of his shirt. Was that FBI? Yeah, right. Like that thug was ever in the FBI. More likely wanted by the FBI.

"You all right, Em?"

Emalea broke her gaze from the man's back and focused on her friend. "Fine, Lana. Why?"

"You're awfully quiet. That guy wasn't rude, was he? Or I guess I should say, was he any more rude than you?"

Emalea's mouth dropped open. "You think I'm rude?"

"You didn't exactly sound as if you were applying to be Ms. Manners."

"He should be more careful. He practically bounced me off the wall."

"It highly resembled an accident to me. You could at least have accepted the soda he sent over."

Rubbing at the sweat on the glass of soda, Emalea sat quietly for a moment not bothering to respond to her friend. Lana was right. What about this guy had set her off? Was it the hungry look he'd given her when she'd come in or was it that slow sexy smile? Maybe she just flat didn't like him. She took a quick drink. Yep, that was it. She didn't like him, no particular reason needed.

From the corner of her eye, she noticed Lana still watching her. "I'm not accepting the soda." Emalea knew she sounded childish, but she couldn't help that. "I don't want to encourage him."

"One day you're going to run off the perfect guy."

Em rolled her eyes. "Lana, there is no perfect guy."

Lana reached beside her to pat her husband's thigh. "Sure there is. I found mine. You'll find yours." Lana continued to run her hand farther along her husband's thigh until he turned to look at her and raised his eyebrow, then winked.

Emalea snorted. "You know, you two have been married seven years. When are you going to stop all that? Anyway, I don't expect I'll find Mr. Perfect bashing me into the wall at Sal's."

Lana touched her arm lightly. "It could happen, Em."

Emalea pretended to study the view of the Mississippi River through the French doors that lined the back wall. Who did it happen for? Maybe women like Lana. But did it happen for women like her mother? Like herself? Never. Em downed her drink to wash away the beginnings of the lump growing in her throat. Lana didn't understand. She tried to, God bless her, but she just didn't.

The waitress placed Emalea's hamburger and French fries on the table. Grabbing the ketchup, she began shaking a large puddle onto her plate.

Not willing to be thwarted yet, Lana leaned closer. "You have to admit this guy has potential."

The ketchup bottle banged as Emalea set it back on the table.

"Potential for what? To be arrested in the next five minutes?"

"Come on, Em, he's practically sizzling."

Emalea peered at the man. Jeans hugged massive thighs and a rear that could have been carved from stone. A well-trimmed goatee surrounded lips that weren't too full, weren't too thin, but were, well, inviting. The black bandanna tied around his head gave him a roguish pirate appeal. She shook her head, not a pirate—an ex-con or a mafioso hit man.

She squinted at Lana. "Are we talking about the same person? Lana, the guy's a thug." Best not to give Lana any ammunition by agreeing the man could be model material.

Lana picked up a fry, chewing thoughtfully. "You're covering."

"Excuse me?"

"You're covering. You think the guy's attractive. I mean, who wouldn't? So you're pretending not to be interested."

With a quick shake, Emalea dumped hot sauce into her ketchup and stirred the concoction with a fry. "Could we please move on?"

Lana grinned. "Whatever."

Biting into her hamburger, Emalea ignored Lana. What else could she do? Her friend seldom let things go easily. Especially when it concerned Emalea and a man.

Muscles bunched under the tight, dark T-shirt. She shivered, realizing she had been staring at the thug again. It would be better for her to think of him that way, even though Lana was right. The guy had a look that wasn't all bad. In fact she needed an extra amount of self-control to keep from staring at him constantly. She wondered briefly what color his hair was. His mustache and goatee were dark, so his hair was probably brown or black. He had chocolaty-brown eyes. She did love chocolate.

Dropping the burger onto her plate, she wanted to kick herself. Was she drooling over ex-cons now? So maybe he wasn't an ex-con. In truth, there was a stiff, almost Dudley Do-Right aura about him. But in the middle of her chest—or maybe it could have been her stomach—she got the feeling he could be trouble. The image of him towering above her made her queasy. Not many men could look down on her five-feet-nine frame. But this one had, easily. He was a bull of a man. And he likely had the temperament to match. She shivered again and this time it wasn't from admiring his physique.

She had spent a big part of her life learning the hard way about men like that. Her own father had given the very first lessons. They should be required by law to have Keep Away stamped on their foreheads. But since they didn't, she'd learned how to spot them. Lately, the bad ones seemed to be everywhere. But for some reason, she couldn't quite get a fix on this guy's personality, something she could usually do in minutes. Perhaps that was why he kept drawing her attention, like she was searching for the missing piece to a jigsaw puzzle.

EMALEA PATIENTLY WATCHED the man as he stood next to his motorcycle on the edge of the old section of closed highway. Up and down the asphalt, bikes roared as people took their Saturday off to become the decadent bikers they secretly dreamed of being while sitting behind their desks. Her plan to embarrass this guy had formulated in her mind while she ate. It had become her quest for the day, even though she realized he might not deserve it. She felt driven to show him, to prove to him... something. She just wasn't sure what. The need to prove anything to a stranger was ridiculous and she knew it. She tried to suppress the idea that she was actually attracted to him—better not to dwell on such things now.

With a toss of her head, Emalea slipped away from her friends and started down the path of a woman bent on revenge. She strolled toward him as seductively as she could in her dusty leather boots. He noticed her and visibly stiffened. She met his gaze head-on. *Mmm, chocolate.*

Giving herself a mental shake, she ran her hand across the seat of his bike. "So you're the one riding this piece of junk."

The chocolate became brown granite. "Lady, don't start with me."

Emalea heard footsteps on the gravel behind her, but chose to ignore them. She figured it was only Lana, who wouldn't be too happy when she heard what was coming next. Emalea refocused on the man in front of her.

"What? You think you've got something special here?"

"I think it's a lot better than that flashy girl bike you're on." He tried to look serious but couldn't quite hold it, so he grinned instead.

She tried not to smile with him. She had a mission. She wanted to embarrass him a bit, and maybe show him what this "lady" was made of, all in the name of fun, naturally. "I imagine I could blow you and this piece of junk straight off the road with that girl bike."

He paused in the middle of digging his key from his pocket and swiveled his head around, his mouth partially open in amazement.

"Are you trying to say you want to race me?"

"That's exactly what I'm saying."

"Em, for heaven's sakes." She heard Lana's voice behind her but waved her hand.

Mr. Thug grabbed on to his handlebar and straddled his bike, his brawny thigh bumping into her. She swayed for a moment and clutched his shoulder to keep from falling.

"I'm not racing you." He had a hand on the key to his bike, and Emalea realized she still had a fistful of his shirt.

She unclenched her fingers and wiped her palms on her shorts. "Oh, come on, we'll make a little bet. It'll be fun."

"A bet, huh? What will we be betting?"

"You say whatever you want then I'll decide something for myself."

"Really?" His eyes narrowed as though he didn't believe her or maybe he was really intrigued. She should have been able to tell, but a fog kept obscuring her senses.

"In that case, I'll do it. If I win you'll go to dinner with me tomorrow night."

Emalea's heart surged into her throat for a moment before breaking into an erratic rhythm. Trying to make a valiant recovery, she tossed her braid over her shoulder. He caught her fluttering fingers between his and grinned. "What do you think?"

She pushed her feet solidly into the ground, using all her determination to keep from turning tail and running. The scent of him—leather, beer, man—filled her nose, causing a certain amount of dizziness. Her hand was already starting to burn. She wanted to blame that heat on the late evening sun, but she knew exactly where it was coming from. She was attracted to him. It was a mind-numbing realization.

She put the brakes on her runaway feelings. She wasn't going to lose. Pinning him with a sweet smile, she said, "I'll take that bet."

They shook hands. He had a nice laugh and for a minute she felt a little guilty about what she was going to do. Just a little joke and she'd clear it up tomorrow, right?

She put her hands on her hips. "Well, when I win, I want your bike, to keep. As in, you give me the papers."

The thug flinched. "Have you lost your mind?"

Emalea felt a bump at her side. Lana hovered next to her shoulder. "Please excuse her, sir. She seems to be having an attack of pure insanity."

Lana tugged at her arm. "Stop it!" Emalea hissed. "I know what I'm doing."

"I doubt that," Lana said, but let go, retreating a half step.

"You better listen to your friend."

She widened her eyes innocently. "You're not afraid you're going to lose, are you?"

Jackson frowned. The woman just didn't know when to quit.

"We'll run this strip like everyone else. The first one to pass the orange stripe at the end of the road will win."

He gritted his teeth. "Is this something you do on a regular basis, challenging people to races for their bikes?"

The shorter woman moved forward. "No, she does not." She glared at her friend. "She needs to reconsider what she's doing."

The woman—Doc—pushed her friend to the side. "I know what I'm doing."

He glared at the two of them. So what? He'd race. When he won, he'd tell her to forget about the dinner. Part of him still wanted to go, but that wasn't a part he needed to be thinking with. Good sense was beginning to tell him this might not be the type of woman he needed to spend time with or even let know where he lived. Images of mad stalkers and pet rabbits in cooking pots flashed in his mind.

He twisted the key, then thumbed the start switch. "Get on your bike, honey. Let's do it."

When he pulled onto the road she was

right behind him. The asphalt stretched before him into the distance. The small crowd that had gathered to watch the races didn't seem especially interested. Though, at the moment, they didn't know what was at stake.

For a second, he considered backing out. What was he thinking? This was not the way he had imagined he'd start life in his new town. She raced ahead of him, and he gunned the engine to pull alongside her. She needed to learn a little lesson. Now was as good a time as any. With a wave of her arm, she began to slow, then came to a complete stop.

Beside them, Mick had come to be the official race starter, leaving someone else in charge of the bar. Jackson revved his engine. He was way too old for this. Doc rolled her motorcycle into position and he did the same. The dark shades she wore hid her eyes, leaving him wondering if a hint of worry might be lurking there. Probably not. She was a little too cocky for that. He adjusted his own sunglasses, then faced forward, twisting the gas, his engine roaring.

Mick raised a towel into the air as Jackson had seen him do several times already for other races. Before he could reconsider, Mick brought the cloth down with a flourish.

The race was on. Jackson's lips twitched

upward slightly as his front wheel inched past hers, then half his bike was ahead. He could just imagine her desperation, now that she was beginning to realize she would lose. A full bike length ahead, his mouth curved into a victorious smile.

A thundering noise exploded next to him and his hands nearly slipped off the rubber grips. A flash of blue streaked past him, a long braid blowing in the wind. His wrists flexed as he begged his machine for more speed. But it was completely spent. The wind whistled in his ears, and he felt a little sick.

JACKSON SLAMMED HIS FIST on the seat of his Harley. Or was it her Harley? "What kind of motorcycle is that you're riding? You shouldn't challenge someone to a race when you're on a souped-up machine."

The long-legged witch grinned at him as she stuffed the keys to her motorcycle in her pocket. With a deft move, she straddled his bike. Her friend ran up.

"Em, you're not really going to take this guy's bike, are you?"

"Of course I am. If he had won I'm sure he'd have collected on his bet." She regarded him disdainfully. "You can just leave the papers at the bar. I'll come for them later. I know you won't try and shirk on this bet, not with all these witnesses."

The other woman stepped back from the motorcycle, giving Jackson a brief but worried glance. "You need to admit yourself for therapy, Em. Enough is enough. Now end this little joke and give him the bike back." She stomped over to him. "I'm sorry. I don't know what's gotten into her today. But she'll give you your bike back, I'm sure."

He could barely hear her, as Doc or Em or whoever she was revved his motorcycle. He wasn't so sure he'd ever get it back. She gunned the engine one more time then roared onto the highway. A moment later she disappeared from sight. He stood there, stunned.

"I'm Lana."

The woman standing next to him held out her hand. If he hadn't been so angry he'd have laughed. He grasped her hand. It really wasn't her fault, anyway. "Well, Lana, your friend should be locked in a padded room somewhere."

"She's really a nice person. She's never done anything like this."

"So what are you saying? She suddenly developed a split personality?"

Lana tucked her hair behind her ear. "I

don't know." She pulled on the arm of a man who had been at the table with them earlier. "This is my husband, Lance. Lance, tell him how Em is usually not like this."

The man put an arm around Lana. "Em's not usually this bad."

Jackson fumed. "Yeah? Well, looks like she chose today to be off-the-chart bad."

"How will you get home?"

He eyed Lana. Now there was the question of the hour. "I guess since your friend took the keys to her bike I won't be riding it."

A large, rough hand hit him on the shoulder. "Come on, man. I'll give you a ride home in my truck. Somebody'll cover for me in the bar."

He squinted at Mick's smiling face then nodded. Jackson followed the beefy man to a dilapidated blue truck. The passenger door squeaked in protest when he opened it. He tried to get comfortable in the worn seat while the truck rumbled down the road. Somehow his plan to explore his new neighborhood had gone seriously awry.

"Take a right, Mick. It's only a few miles."

Mick pulled at the steering wheel, following his directions.

"What do you know about the woman who took my bike?"

The big man gave him a sidelong glance. "You mean the woman you lost your bike to in a bet."

"Yeah, yeah, okay. But do you know her?"

"Known her all her life."

Jackson's elbow slipped off its resting place on the edge of the window. "And you didn't see fit to warn me that she was crazy."

"Doc's not crazy," he said with a grunt. "But I ain't never seen her do nothin' like this before."

Resting his elbow back on the window, Jackson wanted to spit. "What do you call her Doc for? Is she a doctor? Turn here."

Mick hit the brakes then pulled on the steering wheel. "Not no medical doctor, but she has papers that say she should be called a doc. She's a head doctor. You know, talks to people about their problems and stuff."

"A psychologist?"

"Yep, that's it."

Where had he moved to? A psychologist with a Ph.D. had raced him for his motorcycle. Worst of all, she had won.

"This is it." He pointed to the driveway ahead of them.

"You're on the old Wright place."

"Yeah, I'm just renting for a while until I can find something for myself."

The ragged truck veered into the gravel

lane that led to his new home. He'd been here for a week. Talk about getting things off to a good start.

"Uh-oh." Mick hit the brakes on the truck. "Looks like the law's at your place."

Jackson ignored the car with the emblem painted on its side and shifted in the seat with something akin to embarrassment.

"That would be my car, Mick. I'm the new investigator for the parish and the coordinator for Cypress Landing's volunteer search-and-rescue unit."

Mick stared at him for a moment then gave a deep belly laugh that continued until Jackson thought the man would start crying. He slammed the truck door behind him then leaned into the window. "Thanks for the ride, Mick. I really appreciate it."

The big man wiped a hand over his beard. "Man, this just keeps gettin' better and better."

Jackson had to jump to keep the tires from crushing his feet as Mick gunned the old truck back down the driveway. Yeah, he guessed it probably didn't look too good that the newest employee of Cypress Landing's sheriff's department had just lost his Harley on a bet with the local psychologist. Or maybe it just meant he was going to fit in really well.

CHAPTER TWO

"WHAT'S THIS I HEAR about you and some guy's motorcycle?"

Emalea chewed on a beignet without looking at her uncle. The sweet white sugar melted against her tongue as she breathed in the rich coffee-scented air. With her elbows propped on the counter, she twisted on the small stool. News sure traveled fast and to the most unwanted places. She'd only exacted her revenge late yesterday evening. But she did live in a small town. Cypress Landing was an hour and a half away from New Orleans and a stop off for tourists or anyone needing a ride across the river on the car ferry. She had heard the town called *quaint, historical,* even *an arts-and-antiques mecca,* whatever that meant.

Overhearing the question, her aunt Alice stopped to lean across the counter, ignoring the bustling workers behind her as they hurried to get orders for the diner's early morning customers. John and Alice Berteau had raised Emalea since she was twelve. Truthfully, she'd spent a big part of her first twelve years with them, too. They weren't going to like this.

"I won a bet, that's all." She met her aunt's gaze for a second and caught a flash that could have been a smile but it never reached her lips.

"Emalea, you got no business doin' any bettin'. What kind of lady does that?" Alice stepped away from the counter, putting her hands on her hips. Her Cajun accent always thickened when she was upset. "This is your fault, John. You got her on those motorcycles and such. She's goin' to bars with all those biker people. You better be settin' her straight, now." She stood in front of Emalea and her husband for a second longer, then wiped her hands on her white apron and disappeared into the kitchen. The idea that a thirty-year-old woman would be "set straight" by her aging aunt and uncle would have been laughable to some. Not Emalea. Aunt Alice and Uncle John were two of the most important people in her life; if they thought she needed to change something, she would give them her utmost consideration. They deserved that from her. Besides, she respected their opinions and they were usually right.

Emalea stared past her uncle to the window at the front of the diner, known simply as Main Street Coffee Shop. Naturally, the place sat at the end of Cypress Landing's Main Street, next door to her uncle's equally successful garage. He was a gifted mechanic, working on cars as well as motorcycles. Together, her mother's brother and his wife did very well and that's exactly how they did everything. Together. As a team. Unlike Emalea's own parents, Aunt Alice and Uncle John kept life running smoothly by pouring on plenty of love. They were the lucky ones.

"See now, Emmy, you gone and got me in trouble with your aunt Alice. I didn't build that bike for you to run around racing."

She turned her attention back to her uncle while trying to figure how she could squirm her way out of this. "What makes you think I was racing?"

John scratched his head. "Em, how long you been livin' here? You know good and well what happened yesterday was gonna be prime gossip this morning."

The edges of her napkin fluttered in the breeze from the air-conditioning and she smoothed it unconsciously. "I guess I was hoping at least a day or two would pass before that story made it here."

When she finally got the nerve to face her uncle, he was frowning at her. "So, what you doin' with this fella's bike?"

"Teaching him a lesson." She lifted her coffee cup then put it back on the counter without taking a sip.

"You got no business teachin' anybody in a bar a lesson. What do you know about this man? He could do anything to you. Maybe he decides to come take his bike back and teach you a lesson while he's there."

Emalea's gut instinctively tightened at the thought.

"I don't mean to scare you, but you take the bike back to Mick and see that he gets it to this fella. You don't need that kind of trouble."

"You're right. I'll take the bike back after our search-and-rescue team meeting."

Gulping her now lukewarm coffee, Emalea brushed the napkin across her mouth to clean off the last bits of sugar.

"I've got to go. The school's hired me to counsel students and their families. I have a couple of appointments this morning." Sliding off the stool, she kissed her uncle on the cheek.

He patted her on the shoulder. "All right, girl. Oh, that fella who likes you came by here yesterday."

Emalea paused. "You mean Paul Jones?"

"That's the one. He said he was through this way on business and stopped by for breakfast, but he was askin' for you. I don't know why you want to be seein' that guy."

Paul Jones was a sales rep for a pharmaceutical company and traveled to various doctors' offices and pharmacies in the area. She had been avoiding him lately. She wasn't sure why, because he was a nice man. "What's wrong with Paul, Uncle John? I thought you liked him that day I met him here for breakfast."

"I like him fine, but he's not for you, Emalea. I don't know why you keep dating these men that are nothing like you."

That stopped her in her tracks. Her uncle seldom commented on the men she dated, probably because they were few and far between. "What does that mean?"

Her uncle sighed, catching her hand between both of his.

"Ever since you had all that trouble with Jean Pierre, you've been seeing this kind of guy. Mr. Jones, he's…" Uncle John let go of her hand and grabbed the half-eaten beignet from his plate. "Like the beignet before you cook it, just so much dough in the bowl. But you, you're the finished one, light, airy, coated with sweet sugar. Quite a treat, eh? When are you going to date a man to appreciate that?"

"I think you might be the only one to see it that way, Uncle John."

He thumped his hand on the counter. "No, one day you'll find the man who sees it that way, too. Then you better not be runnin' him off."

She laughed. "I'll try to remember."

He patted her cheek. "You take care of this little situation with the motorcycle, you hear."

"I hear," she replied, halfway to the door. Why her uncle had to mention Jean Pierre was beyond her. Most days she chose to forget that part of her life. She'd misjudged a man, just as her mother had. Only she'd had sense enough to get away before it was too late.

She smiled at her uncle's comparison. Maybe that was why she wasn't that interested in Paul. The description had been almost too exact. He could definitely be considered bland, but he was safe. He certainly would never raise a hand to hurt her.

Squinting against the sun, she stood on the sidewalk. Her uncle made sense. She needed to get the motorcycle back. But for some reason, every time she tried to clear her mind, the image of broad shoulders towering above her surfaced. Except this time he was flashing a smile at her, similar to the one he'd worn when she'd first caught him watching her in the bar. She doubted if he'd smile at her that way now. She tried to ignore what felt a lot like disappointment.

JACKSON GROANED, letting the shovel he'd been using drop to the ground. He recognized the driver of the red truck immediately. This was just what he didn't need. His new boss must have heard about the episode at the bar yesterday.

Jackson had to admit he'd gone a bit too far. Matt Wright might be a fair man and a good sheriff, but he wouldn't expect to find his newly hired investigator racing motorcycles and betting. The truck stopped at the end of the driveway.

Sweat ran down the side of his cheek, and Jackson dragged the back of his hand across his forehead, taking a deep breath as the sheriff of Cypress Landing strolled across the yard, coming to a stop in front of him.

"I can explain," Jackson began, then paused. Could he? Maybe that wasn't the best way to start this conversation.

"Don't worry about it," Matt responded quickly.

Almost too quickly. "Really? You're not going to bust my butt?"

Matt laughed. "You've got to be kidding. I should have done it myself a long time ago. But I just don't have the knack."

Jackson pushed the shovel with the toe of his boot. Something wasn't right. "I guess I don't, either."

Matt motioned toward the strip around the house where Jackson had been planting shrubbery. "Seems like you're doing a good job to me. I told you to do anything you wanted to the house. Keep the receipts and I'll take it off the rent."

He didn't know. Jackson wasn't sure whether to be relieved or sick. Maybe Matt would never find out. Jackson glanced at the Indian hawthorn he'd just put in the ground. He'd turned yard work into his way of dealing with the weight of the memories that sometimes threatened to bury him.

Matt was waiting for him to continue the conversation. He'd give it another day and if Matt hadn't heard by then, he'd tell him.

"I… Yeah, I'll let you know how much it cost. I worked with a landscaping company when I was in college, just something I learned how to do."

Matt crossed his arms across his chest. "It sure helps the old place. Anyway, I came by to remind you we've got that volunteer search-and-rescue meeting today. I know you don't officially start work until next week, but I'd like you to come by and meet everyone tonight."

Jackson picked up the shovel. "I've got it written on my calendar."

"It's not the whole group, just the leader of each team. It'll be a good chance for you to get into town and maybe start meeting the feminine side of Cypress Landing. We've got quiet a few head turners here."

Jackson tried not to cringe. The last thing he needed was Matt matchmaking. He'd already had one bad experience with the "feminine" side of Cypress Landing. He wondered what would constitute a head turner in this town, other than the one he'd already met, then decided he probably didn't want to know.

"I'm not interested in dating right now, but I'll keep that in mind."

Matt kicked a clump of dirt and Jackson

tried to give a name to the expression on his face. Uncomfortable. That was it.

"How's everything else going? I mean… you haven't had any other problems here, have you?"

Jackson wanted to look away but made himself stay focused on Matt. It was a fair question. "If you're trying to ask if I've been in any fights since I've been here, the answer is no."

"I'm not trying to make this an issue. I just know that a big change like you've had, leaving the bureau and moving here, can be tough."

Sweat beaded above his eyebrows and Jackson wiped at the moisture. "I've gotten control of the problem I had in Chicago. And I didn't just leave the bureau, we both know that."

"They made you an offer. You chose not to take it."

Jackson's mouth twisted. "That wasn't an offer. It was a sentence."

Matt shrugged. "Okay, then." He began to walk toward his truck. "I'll see you tonight."

He should have told Matt what had happened at Sal's. Keeping secrets from his boss wasn't a good way to get started. Besides, he respected Matt. Cypress Landing's sheriff's department might be a far cry from the FBI, but the sheriff could have held his own with any agent Jackson knew. Matt had taken a chance giving him this job after what had happened with the bureau. They'd met five years ago, when he'd been here as an FBI agent on a case involving missing children. He and Matt had become friends and stayed in touch over the years. Matt had been supportive during some of his hardest times. When he'd needed to make a change in his life, the small-town sheriff had been there with an offer. Maybe it was the streets lined with live oaks, their branches dripping Spanish moss or the antebellum homes scattered throughout the area that sometimes made him feel like he'd stepped into a different time. It was fate that Cypress Landing needed a new investigator just when he wanted a new job. Chicago had become an ugly reminder of everything he'd lost. For two years he'd tried to keep going on with his life.

But he'd been living a lie. Gripping the handle, he jammed the shovel into the ground, his teeth jarring as he hit a rock. Lifting the blade, he knocked away a clump of dirt. The sun flashed on the metal, reminding him of a pair of flashing green eyes he was doing his best to forget.

Why was she constantly in his head? Maybe it had something to do with the fact that she now owned his most prized possession. Sliding his hand along the shovel, he could almost feel the skin of her hand beneath his fingers. The shovel thudded against the ground when he dropped it again. This kind of fantasizing would get him in a world of trouble. With the pieces of his life only recently jammed back together, he didn't need that woman scattering them all around again.

"What's been going on, Kent?"

The thin, gangly boy shrugged his shoulders and shoved an unruly clump of black hair from his forehead. Emalea wondered when he'd last washed his hair. A good kid at heart, he just needed a little guidance. Too bad he wouldn't be getting any on the home front. His mother shunned Emalea's attempts at family counseling but had finally agreed to let Kent have sessions with her. The boy's father didn't know. The man didn't seem the type to allow any weakness in his family.

Biting back a sigh, she regrouped. "How's your art class?"

"It's great." He brightened considerably and Emalea made a mental note.

"So what's happening in there?"

"Mrs. Wright is really cool. She's letting me and Megan Johnson help her paint a mural at the first and second grade building."

"That's quite an honor. I told you when I first saw some of your drawings that you had talent."

Kent played with the hem of his shirt. "I guess my stuff's okay, but Megan, she's gonna be a big artist one day. She even works in Mrs. Wright's shop part-time."

"Is that the blond girl I saw you talking to last weekend?"

He nodded, staring at the wall just past her shoulder.

"She's very pretty."

His bony shoulders rubbed the back of the chair. "She's Gary Johnson's cousin."

Emalea tried not to frown. "Gary still giving you problems?"

"Not so much anymore. He found another kid to stuff in the garbage can."

"Just remember, guys like Gary have a lot of issues to deal with, too. That tough-guy act won't get him very far in life."

"Yeah, well, I don't think it's an act." He glanced at the clock. "I've got to go now. It's time for me to be home. I'll see you next week."

She held out her hand to the boy who grasped it, giving a quick shake, before sliding from the chair and disappearing through the door.

The school had scheduled Kent for tutoring in the afternoon, but he actually met with her. A tenth-grader didn't need the school bully to hear he was seeing a head doctor, as Kent often referred to her.

Kids could be so mean to each other. She knew only too well the whispers, the looks, the cruel remarks. Some you tried to ignore. Others cut you to the bone and sent you off to lick your wounds. Maybe Kent would make it through intact. She had, if you could call her life intact.

For some reason, the idea of her life being intact brought to mind the incident at Sal's. So maybe the guy wasn't an ex-con, but she wasn't interested in his type. Pure animal power had oozed from every pore. The very type of man she'd learned to avoid. She wouldn't be repeating any mistakes, not her own and definitely not her mother's, no matter how much the guy kept intruding on her thoughts.

With a snap, she closed her notebook, dropped it into her briefcase and studied her calendar. A psychologist in a town that had one main street and three stoplights wasn't going to get rich. But making money wasn't the reason she lived here. Over the past few years she'd established herself with a few businesses in the area that used her as part of their employee assistance program and the paper mill usually sent a number of clients her way. The state prison had also hired her to counsel inmates and conduct psychological evaluations.

She stretched her legs in front of her and leaned her head back against the chair. Sometimes the idea of working at the prison was like a joke, but she'd never actually found the punch line. It was ironic that in all the years her father had been alive she'd never gone to the prison. Now, fifteen years after his death, she went there several times a week. Could she have taken the job if he'd still been living? It was a question she was glad she didn't have to answer.

One counselor had told her the only way to make a full emotional recovery was to forgive her father. It had been her last visit with that particular therapist. Maybe she could come to terms with what her father had done, but the word *forgive* stuck in her throat.

She pushed to her feet, smoothed her

khaki pants and straightened her black cotton blouse. Too much rehashing of the past wouldn't do her any good. She had just enough time to get to the search-and-rescue meeting. Briefcase in hand, she locked the counselor's office behind her.

IN THE SCHOOL HALLWAY Kent paused, breathing heavily, then hurried for the exit and home. Not that he really wanted to go home but some things you just had to do. Talking to this lady would be a big waste of time. She asked questions. He answered. She didn't need to know anything about his life. He double-checked his watch to make sure he wouldn't be late. The walk would be a long one. The counselor had said she would wait and take him home after he talked to the head doctor, but he'd lied and told her he had a way home. He didn't need her at his house, didn't want her even to pull into the yard. If his dad knew about this, there'd be heck to pay. This whole counseling thing would lead to nothing but trouble and he knew it. He left the streets behind and struck out at a brisk walk along the side of the highway out of town.

"YOU ARE NOT GOING TO BELIEVE the new guy. I mean, Em, he's beyond description. I wouldn't have thought the bald look was so hot."

Emalea rested her hip on the corner of the younger girl's desk. Dana had been working at the sheriff's office since she'd left high school and, even though that had been five years ago, the girl remained as boy crazy as a teenager.

"Have you asked him for a date yet?"

Dana rolled her eyes. "He's a little too old for me. I'm thinking you can go after him."

Emalea grimaced. "Gee, thanks. Leave all the old geezers for me."

"He's not that old."

"But you said he was bald."

Dana put her hands on her hips. "I know what I said. I meant that he's shaved bald, like by choice, in that male-model kind of way. And he's got this goatee." Dana smacked her lips. "Delicious."

She had to laugh then. Dana was obviously smitten. "Well, lucky me, I get to work with him, don't I?"

"You sure do. Since you guys are doing that training course for new SAR members."

Standing, Emalea made exaggerated moves at smoothing her long brown hair. "I guess I better go and meet this wonderful male specimen."

"They're all in the conference room." Dana rubbed her hands together. "I'll go with you just in case you faint when you see him. I can catch you."

They both giggled while Dana followed Emalea to the conference room. At the door she stopped to glance around the table. She could feel Dana at her shoulder, pressing her forward. Her muscles froze and her stomach flipped completely then maintained a steady quiver. It wasn't possible. She'd pulled one crazy stunt and the stupid thing kept coming back to bite her in the rear. The warm brown gaze that locked on her registered shock. Her shaking middle knotted with sheer dread. What was he doing here? He didn't belong here. He was… He was… Good grief, he *was* gorgeous.

The sheriff motioned to an empty chair directly across from the man she'd robbed of his motorcycle. "Come on in, Emalea. We're ready to get started." When she still didn't move, he just kept talking. "Emalea Le-Blanc, this is Jackson Cooper, he's our new investigator. He'll also be working directly with the SAR team."

Obviously, neither Matt nor Dana had heard the story. But she could tell by the half grins and smothered coughs that they were the only ones in the room who hadn't. Gritting her teeth, Emalea marched to the chair and fell into it. She peered at the man across the table, her heart pounding, from the shock, of course, not because she was actually seeing him again. Even without the bandanna tied around his head, he was quite an eyeful.

The silence finally penetrated her thoughts, and she realized the whole table was waiting for her to say something. Had they asked her a question? If so, she hadn't heard it. Her gaze centered on Jackson Cooper and she couldn't break away.

"You... You don't have any hair."

No one even tried to hide their amusement. Probably, this wasn't her best moment. Even Jackson Cooper grinned. He rubbed his hand over what appeared to be the beginnings of a five o'clock shadow...on his head.

Matt took his seat, watching the two of them.

"Ms. Leblanc and I met already. I'll tell you about it later," Jackson said to Matt.

Someone in the room coughed a little too loudly while Emalea tried not to bang her head against the table. She'd taken the motorcycle of a former FBI agent. Could it get any worse? He should have given her a hint as to who he was. Matt continued his introduction of Jackson Cooper, who would be the SAR team's official contact at the sheriff's office, but Emalea barely heard because she was starting to seethe. This only proved her point. Jackson Cooper was not a man to be trusted. But then what men could you trust? In her mind's eye, the man in front of her morphed into some of her most horrific memories. He could snap her in half if he wanted. Her fist gripped the wooden arms of the chair, while her throat constricted. She couldn't seem to get enough air.

Stop! Loosening her grip on the chair, oxygen filtered into her lungs as she took a slow calming breath, forcing the panic to subside, while the others carried on a meeting oblivious to her emotional state. This man, a stranger, wasn't her father or Jean Pierre. There was no relationship to bind her to him and she certainly didn't have to depend on him for anything. He was just another employee of the sheriff's office. She only had to work with him occasionally. As soon as she returned the motorcycle, she'd never have to see him again, except officially and around town. A groan rose in her throat but she squelched it.

FIVE, FOUR, THREE STEPS then she'd be at her truck. Almost there, almost ready to reach for the door handle. Then fingers wrapped around her arm and she couldn't ignore the shouted "Hey, Emalea," anymore.

She spun around, twisting the offending fingers loose. "What? If it's about your bike, I'm on my way to take it to Mick right now. I only did it as a joke."

Jackson Cooper paused for a moment with his mouth half-open. "I was actually going to say that I hoped we could work together without too many hard feelings. I know we've had a rough start, but life will be a lot easier if we aren't at each other's throats all the time."

"I'm not the kind of person to be at anyone's throat."

He folded his arms across his chest. "Really?"

"Really," she replied, trying to unclench her teeth.

He was quiet for a moment and Emalea was more than a little afraid of what he might be thinking. His fingers moved to stroke the goatee around his mouth, and muscles in his forearm undulated. Standing this close, Jackson Cooper was discomfiting.

Her own fingers itched to grab the door handle of her truck and escape.

"If you're really planning on giving my bike back, I'm sure we can work something out so neither one of us has to go to the bar."

Emalea's head bobbed slightly but she was only half listening. How did his T-shirt fit him like a second skin without being completely indecent? That gave him such an unfair advantage over women. He could do or say anything and a woman might never really hear it because she'd be so fascinated by his body. Some women, but not her; she wasn't into that.

"So, what do you think? Will that work for you?"

The sun caught the gold flecks in his eyes that she hadn't noticed before. "Mmm… Yeah, that's fine."

He seemed to relax and she thought he might smile.

"Do you need directions?"

The last rays of the evening light began to feel a little warm on the back of her head. Wait, what had she agreed to?

"Directions for what?"

He frowned.

"Directions to the house I'm renting from Matt. If you really don't mind bringing the bike there, I'll be glad to drive you back home."

The keys in her pocket bit into her hand as she clamped her fingers around them. Is that what she had agreed to do? She chewed at her bottom lip. Time alone with Jackson Cooper, not exactly what she'd been planning for the evening. But taking the bike to his house would be much easier since the only house Matt had to rent wasn't that far from hers. She could handle it, didn't want to, but she could.

"I know the way." She opened the door of the truck and slid behind the wheel. As she tried to pull the door closed, she felt resistance. Jackson held the door, peering in at her as if she had grown a second head.

"What?"

"Tell me this isn't your truck."

Typical stupid male reaction. Just because it wasn't a girlie ride, except for the glossy pearl-white paint job. "Of course it's mine."

He stepped back, pulling the door open wider. "A 1968 Ford step side in mint condition. That's unbelievable."

"It's a sixty-six."

He stared at her in amazement. "How do you get all this specialty stuff? I mean, the custom motorcycle, this truck. Are you a collector, or just really rich?"

She had to laugh then. "I'm really spoiled."

Jackson tilted his head to one side, giving her a questioning look.

"My uncle John is a master mechanic. He rebuilt my motorcycle when I bought it secondhand. This truck——" she skimmed her fingers around the smooth steering wheel "——he found rusting in a field. He and I worked on it for a few years before we got it to this point."

"I'd like to meet your uncle."

Her heart skipped a beat as panic hit her. All she needed was for Jackson Cooper to talk to Uncle John. How long would the conversation go before he uncovered her story? What would he think? With her past, he'd wonder how she was allowed to counsel anyone. His first trip would likely be to the sheriff's office to dig up the old files and there he'd find her whole ignoble past. But why should she care what this guy thought?

"I'll see you in an hour." Yanking the door out of his hand, she slammed it shut. She could have made it home and back to his house in less time, but what was the sense in rushing? When she got to his house, she could mention an early appointment that she didn't actually have, then he'd have to bring her right home. Of course, she was sure he'd be more than happy to get rid of her just as quickly.

CHAPTER THREE

THE LOUD RUMBLING of a Harley broke the silence. A smile tried to work its way onto Jackson's face, but he managed to battle it down in favor of a more nonchalant expression. A woman who drove a truck like Emalea's and rode a custom Harley was something of a mystery to him. One he couldn't afford to ponder, no matter how badly he wanted to, or at least that's what he kept telling himself when he bothered to listen.

From the front porch, he watched her come up the driveway. A tightening below his belt called to his attention the fact that parts he'd thought were dormant had suddenly decided to make themselves known. Even though, when he'd first seen her, he'd imagined he could have a fling with a wild biker girl, that idea hadn't survived long. Besides, Emalea wasn't exactly a wild biker girl looking for a fling. She didn't seem to be looking for anything, which was good because he had nothing to offer.

"Hi!" She stopped at the bottom of the porch steps, the corners of her mouth lifted slightly skyward. She'd changed into jeans with a bright red T-shirt.

He fumbled for a moment over what to say next. "I, uh, have some sweet tea if you'd like a glass before I take you home." He sometimes wondered at his own stupidity. He didn't know why he'd asked such a thing. She only raised an eyebrow.

"What does someone from Chicago know about sweet tea? I thought you'd only know two kinds of tea, hot and cold."

He rocked back on his feet. "I'm originally from Arkansas so I know exactly how to put the sugar in the tea when I make it."

Her laugh was low and soft, not what he expected, but it made him eager to hear more.

"Tea would be good. But I can't stay. I've got an early appointment in the morning."

He started toward the door. Just a quick drink, then they would leave. "If you'll come in for a minute, I'll get my keys, while we have some tea."

The polite thing would have been to ask if she wanted to join him for dinner. But she'd already said she had to get back home, so he wasn't being completely inhospitable. He should have been angry with her after yesterday, instead of wondering if he was being a good host. Somehow the whole thing only made him want to grin. A good sign that he'd put all his pent-up anger behind him. He placed her glass of tea on the bar while he admired the way loose strands from her ponytail framed her face. His fingers itched to pull the elastic band off to see how far her hair fell down her back.

He poured tea in his own glass while giving himself a mental butt kicking. He'd known this woman for less than forty-eight hours. In two years he'd never been tempted to cross the line he'd drawn in the sand. He certainly wasn't going to start now.

"So how does an Arkansas boy, turned Chicago dweller, end up in Cypress Landing, Louisiana?"

He smiled—though he imagined it looked a little forced—while he made a decision only to give her the basics. She didn't need to know how rough the road was that had brought him here.

"When I first started at the FBI I worked on missing children cases. I came here to help with a string of abductions that were happening."

"Of course, I remember you. Or at least I remember FBI agents being here. I was new in SAR back then, and I didn't work on those cases. I guess I never met you."

"You might have. I had hair back then and no goatee. Right after that I made a move from missing children to working organized crime." He didn't mention that after his daughter had been born he couldn't take seeing what often happened to children who were abducted. "Anyway, I worked organized crime a couple of years then decided to leave the FBI. Matt and I had become friends when I was here and he offered me a job. I really liked the town and I didn't want to go back to Arkansas." That would have been too much like hiding, and he didn't want to have any slipups with his selfcontrol in his own hometown. "So, here I am."

She nodded, and he tried to let go of the breath he felt like he'd been holding. Obviously, the flimsy story made sense to her.

The phone rang, startling Emalea. She'd been trying to remember Jackson being in Cypress Landing, but that had been years ago. He stepped to the counter to get the phone, while she continued to sip her iced tea. So far so good. He hadn't made any references to yesterday. As a matter of fact, he was being absolutely cordial. Kind of odd after the way she'd behaved at the bar.

Standing in the kitchen with him while he was on the phone almost felt like eavesdropping, so she wandered through a wide archway into the next room and paused in front of a small mahogany table with several pictures on it. In the other room Jackson ended the conversation and she heard drawers opening and closing.

"I'll be ready in a minute," he shouted. "I need to find a phone number and make a quick call."

Emalea didn't respond but stood staring at the pictures in front of her. The first silver frame held a photo of Jackson with two men and a younger girl. The resemblance was too strong for them to be anyone other than his brothers and sister. A wistful smile drifted along her lips. Two more pictures framed in silver caught her eye.

"Do you know where the SAR training will be held?"

Emalea jumped at the question. He hadn't looked up from the drawer he was digging in. She continued to stand by the table. "I'm not sure."

He must not have thought her mumbled response unusual, because he continued plundering in the drawer. She lifted the pictures from the table. One was Jackson with a beautiful blond woman and an equally beautiful blond little girl. The other was of the woman and the girl alone.

Her breath caught in her throat. She'd never considered that he might be married. Not that it mattered to her, but why weren't they here? Maybe they were coming after he got settled.

She glanced back toward him. "Is this your family?" No reason to beat around the bush; if the guy was married or divorced or whatever, he ought to let someone know.

Jackson, half smiling, turned to answer, but froze at the sight of the pictures in her hand. An array of emotions contorted his face, making Emalea regret the question. He strode to the sink—his back to her—and stopped to grasp the edge of the counter.

Returning the pictures to the table, she went in to the kitchen, immediately noticing his white-knuckle grip. *Tread carefully,* she cautioned herself, *this might be a subject that makes him angry*. She didn't want to make him angry with her, not while they were alone at his house. Although this time, her usual flash of fear was absent. The sickly mask of stone that had settled onto him concerned her more.

"Sorry. I didn't mean to pry."

"Of course you did. But it's okay. They died, back in Chicago two years ago, car accident." He slowly relaxed his grip.

"I'm truly sorry. I didn't know. I didn't mean to bring up a bad memory."

He nodded, still gazing out the window as though he might see something in the darkening sky. "You're lucky if you haven't had to deal with losing someone in your family."

"My mother was killed in an accident when I was twelve." Emalea fought the urge to slap her hand over her mouth. Why in heaven's name had she said that? He didn't need to know about her past. An accident? What a stretch.

"I'm sorry for your loss. Were you not able to stay with your dad? Is that why you went to live with your aunt and uncle?"

She wondered if she could say she had to go to the bathroom, then just never answer his question. "My dad was… Well he wasn't around after my mom died."

Jackson didn't respond, seemingly satisfied with her rough interpretation of the truth. His fingers tapped absently on the counter.

"It's still not like losing your wife and child, though. I'm sorry."

He was quiet and she thought the conversation had ended.

"It should never have happened. It was my fault."

The words were spoken so softly Emalea wasn't sure if she'd actually heard them. If she considered what he said through the filter of her own past, she'd run out the door. But she didn't even feel the fear that had once resided constantly inside her. Even though he appeared physically capable of doing whatever he wanted, he didn't seem to have that spark of pure meanness that could make men dangerous. He didn't notice that she stared at him, and she was glad because she couldn't stop. She realized she desperately wanted Jackson not to be like other men she'd known.

"I guess I better get you home." He stepped away from the sink, grabbing a set of keys from the bar. "You want to go in my truck or on the motorcycle?"

"Truck," she responded quickly. An image of being on the motorcycle with her arms wrapped around him was too much.

"What about the phone call you needed to make?"

He shook his head. "It can wait."

CLASSIC ROCK MUSIC HID the fact they weren't talking. She had only spoken to give him directions, and Jackson easily found her small house at the end of a short driveway. Huge live oak branches hung low in her yard. The whole scene sent waves of peacefulness washing over him.

"Live here by yourself?"

"Yeah, my aunt and uncle live just around the corner from their shop in town but I like it here."

He rubbed his hand across the dashboard. "It's been quite a change for me from the city. I'm enjoying the solitude, most of the time anyway. I appreciate your bringing the bike and having tea with me."

It was true, even though he'd had to speak of his family. Something he was always loath to do, though what had he expected when with the pictures were sitting in plain sight? Normally, he was able to discuss the horror of two years ago without all the emotional upheaval he'd felt tonight. He should have told her the whole story. But what was the point?

She was out of the truck, waving goodbye before he realized she had opened the door.

"Umm. Thanks for the ride, and no hard feelings about the motorcycle thing, right?"

"None at all. I said so earlier, remember. Everybody has to let their bad side loose once in a while." He smiled but she appeared to be less than congenial. She seemed… well, scared. There was no other word for the way her eyes rounded and her breath seemed to come in gasps. He'd seen plenty of people afraid—he'd been the cause of it many times—but he certainly hadn't expected to see this woman afraid of anything. The worst thing was he didn't know what had caused that expression.

She was on her front porch and in the house before he could say anything else. Stepping on the accelerator, he headed toward the highway. He hadn't really had a good chance to tell her how his family had died, had he? But then again, why bother? It wasn't like he was going to be asking her to dinner or spending long hours cuddling on the sofa with her, although just the thought of it made him want to give it a try. He shook his head. No way. He'd have to help with the search-and-rescue team, it was part of his job, but helping didn't mean getting involved with Emalea.

He wasn't going to have a relationship with a woman again. Being a magnet for death and destruction wasn't conducive to happily ever after. That's what he was, a death magnet. The loss of Christa and Connor had proved that.

The charred ruins of Christa's car hung in his memory like the black smoke that had poured from the wreckage. Just another job for one of the men hired by the Mafia family he'd gone undercover to investigate. That assignment had ended his world and sent him, two years later, to live in this small town, far from the greedy fingers of organized crime. He'd never again let himself have so much to lose.

THE BEEPER IN EMALEA'S PURSE hummed as she finished her notes on Kent's session. Her last for the day, thank goodness. Something was bothering the boy. Though he'd been gone for nearly an hour, she was still struggling with the feeling. Hints of violence at home had Emalea doing a very personal check. She didn't want to miss any abuse that should be reported, nor did she want to read something into the situation because of her own experiences. Another session, then maybe he'd begin to trust her more. All she really wanted to do now was go home and soak in the tub for, oh, maybe an hour.

Her lips thinned and her pulse quickened to a rapid pace. Finding the number for the sheriff's department on her beeper wasn't usually a good sign. Putting her pen and notebook aside, she found her cell phone and called the number.

"Dana, it's Em. What's up?" Emalea tapped her finger on the desk hoping someone had dropped a boat motor in the river and needed help locating it.

"Thank goodness I got you, Em. There's been a shooting at the boat launch at Red Bluff Road."

"A shooting? What do you mean?"

"I mean someone's been shot and killed. The body's still there. Jackson thinks the shooter might have tossed the gun in the water. Matt wants you to get your gear and come have a look-see."

Emalea groaned inwardly. "I'm on my way."

Diving in the river was something she absolutely hated, though she'd never admit it. The water was muddy and she was never sure just what she might find in the heavy silt.

Leaving the school behind, she tried to keep herself calm. She hadn't even asked who'd been shot. People just didn't get shot in Cypress Landing. Unless you counted the time Ole Sebe's hunting rifle had gone off and the bullet had grazed Grady Redding's arm. Unfortunately, working search-and-rescue meant seeing some ugliness firsthand. She generally ended up knowing way more about crimes in the community than she wanted. This was definitely going to be one of those times.

THE SCENT OF MUDDY WATER, crushed grass and car exhaust was thick in the air as Emalea sat on the tailgate of her truck tugging her wet suit on over a bright blue swimsuit. The water wouldn't be cold, but she liked the protection of the wet suit, and if the search took very long, even the warmest water could begin to chill.

She watched the deputies keep back a few nosy onlookers. With its grassy parking area and shade trees, Red Bluff boat launch was a more likely place for a picnic than a shooting. The launch itself was at the bottom of the hill and not quite as picturesque. The current here didn't make it a very good place to launch a boat, so few people used it, but the parish kept it in working condition as best they could, though she remembered hearing that it was underwater only a few weeks ago.

With her weight belt fastened and her tank secured to her buoyancy compensator vest, she was ready to go. The buoyancy compensator, or BC jacket, could be inflated with air to keep her from sinking to the bottom of the river once she was underwater. The regulator she would breath from was also attached to the tank and swinging near her arm. With fins and an underwater metal detector in hand, she set off in a cumbersome gait to the river's edge.

"Em, sorry I had to call you." Matt took off his shades to wipe the sweat from his eyes. "I tried Bud and Cody, but they were both working out of town."

The wet suit was making the heat feel oppressive, and Emalea took a deep breath. "No problem, I can do it. Was the victim someone from around here?"

Matt shook his head. "No. He had an Illinois driver's license."

A large body appeared between Emalea and the river. "What are you doing?"

Her mouth was dry, and she had to wet her lips with a parched tongue before she could speak. "I'm searching for the gun you think is in the river." She flapped her fins against her leg. "Kind of obvious I would think."

Jackson turned to Matt. "Absolutely not. She's not doing this. If there's no one else, I'll do it."

Matt winked while attaching a safety rope to the front of Emalea's vest. "She's doing it, Jackson. You're the investigator. I need you up here coordinating. She's the search-and-rescue diver. This is what she does."

Jackson didn't move for a moment, then his fingers closed around her upper arm.

"No. It's too dangerous. The current's fast, and who knows what could be down there."

Emalea made a half step but the restraint at her arm tightened and she jerked to loosen his grip. When he wouldn't let go, she felt a little sick. She twisted roughly away from him, nearly upending herself. Matt held her shoulder to keep her from falling.

"Enough already. We did handle things before you got here." The sheriff glared at Jackson.

Bossy, and overbearing, that's what he was. She poked his arm with the metal detector. "Don't worry, boss, I can handle it." She moved away from him and waded into the water.

Following her, he caught her upper arm again but this time with less force. She noticed Matt still watching them. If Jackson planned on manhandling her, he'd have a huge fight on his hands. Instead he helped her balance, as she lifted one foot then the other to slide her fins in place. When she reached for her mask, he still held on.

"I'll be needing that arm."

He tightened his grip. "Be careful. If something doesn't feel right, I want you back here immediately, understand?"

"You act like the shooter's sitting on bottom waiting for me."

"I don't want you sitting on bottom."

"Not gonna happen."

Grabbing the slate and pencil hanging from her BC, he jotted compass coordinates. "Use your compass and work this grid. I don't know how deep it is here but don't go deeper than fifty feet."

Emalea flashed him a thumbs-up then settled her mask on her face. She placed the headphones attached to the metal detector over her ears before wading into the murky water. Her first thought was how many times she'd have to wash her hair to get rid of the gunk.

Two flicks on the hose had the air adjusted in her BC jacket and she turned on her headlight. Now she was ready to work. Kicking hard, she made her way around the river bottom in small squares as Jackson had planned. Nothing but thick brown water swirled around her while the staccato beats of the metal detector sounded in her ears. The darkness began to close in and her chest tightened. She forced herself to breathe slowly and repeat, "Stay calm, this is important." Her pulse slowed and she began the painstaking process again.

With only one small section of her search incomplete, Emalea had nearly decided the gun wasn't there. Then the beeping of the machine changed. Her hand plunged into the mud, fingers connecting with something solid. Even through her gloves, she could tell it wasn't a gun. Probing farther, she realized it was a heavy cloth, probably a bag that had fallen off someone's boat.

She grasped the strap of the bundle, but it was wrapped around what she thought was a tree limb. Giving the bag a jerk, she sent silt swirling into the cone of light from her lamp. The thing felt as if it weighed a ton. Whatever it was would be the devil to get to the bank. Her fins planted in the mud, she hauled at the object. Something was coming toward her. It was... Oh God, a man's face. And most of the flesh was missing from one side.

Letting go, she pushed for the surface. At the first brush of late evening sun on her skin, she flung the regulator aside sucking in the warm thick air. When she exhaled, the scream that had been bubbling all the way from her toes went with it. In her peripheral vision she saw Jackson shove the deputy holding her safety line to the ground. Then he grabbed the line himself and pulled until she was at the bottom of the launch. Her legs wouldn't seem to work so she stayed on her hands and knees, gasping.

A huge pair of hands jerked her gear off and carried her to the back seat of the sheriff's cruiser. Jackson swept scraggly wet hair away from her cheeks, until she could at last get her eyes to focus.

"Everything's fine, Emalea. Just relax, then tell me what happened."

Those brown eyes should have revived harrowing images of surging, dirt-filled water, but they didn't. She could have happily, peacefully drowned in these depths.

"It's... There's another body."

Jackson shot a look at Matt, who leaned into the car.

"I found something that felt like a bag. I think the arm of whoever it is might be tangled in the strap. When I yanked it really hard, a corpse floated right here." She held a hand in front of her face, her body shivering uncontrollably.

Her wet suit would soak Jackson's clothes,

but the thought of protesting never crossed her mind when he pulled her close. She was beyond questioning why.

"Get someone in here to recover that body before the current takes it," Jackson said to Matt.

"No, I can do it." Dragging someone else in to finish her job wasn't an option.

Arms tightened around her. "You're not going back down there."

She pushed him away. "Of course I am. I know where to find the body. Send me with an extra line and I'll tie it off. You can pull in the body and the bag."

"I've got another line in my trunk," Matt said and headed for the back of the car.

Jackson moved with a swiftness Emalea hadn't expected of such a big man. With one hand to the shoulder, he spun Matt around. "I said she isn't going to do it."

Matt spread his feet and stared. Jackson's hands were clenched into fists, and she waited for him to take a swing. But Cypress Landing's sheriff wasn't one to back down, even when he was outsized. Matt continued to stand his ground.

Where was the man she'd shared a glass of tea with just a week ago? She'd been right to be afraid when he'd mentioned people letting loose their bad side. Emalea shivered and this time not from the cold water or the thought of the dead body she'd pulled from the mud. Jackson's face was tight and the anger in his eyes seemed to have a life of its own.

Finally, Matt spoke, his lips thin and voice tight. "This is Emalea's job as part of the SAR team. She said she's willing to do it, so she will." He paused for a moment. "I thought you told me you had a handle on this."

Jackson's whole body seemed to droop as he looked away. He strode quietly to the river as if he'd forgotten both of them. Had a handle on what? she wondered.

Matt retrieved the rope from the trunk and handed it to her. "He has a problem with his temper, so you steer clear." He stood in front of her for a moment before going to answer a call on the radio. He didn't bother to explain what had just happened, but one thing was obvious. She couldn't risk getting to know Jackson Cooper.

As she pulled on her gear, Jackson appeared beside her. She would have preferred to ignore him, but he seemed intent on trying to help her.

"I'll tie the bag and the body to this extra

line, then you can pull both to the bank," she told him.

He took the rope from her and knotted it to her vest. "This is the kind of stuff that will give you nightmares," he said in a gruff whisper. His breath was warm against her ear. She hadn't realized he was standing so close.

"They'll have to get in line." Their breath intermingled, and Jackson leaned toward her then blinked and quickly straightened. Emalea waded into the murky river again. More afraid of what was on the bank than what was in the water.

Using her compass as a guide, she went immediately to the spot where the body had been. Of course, the current had shifted it. As the minutes ticked by, she was certain the men on the shore were getting more anxious. She wasn't exactly thrilled with the slow pace.

Just when she was beginning to think she'd never find the bag or the body, she felt something. This time, she grasped a pant leg. Continuing to delve around the muck, her hands landed on the bag. She found what felt like the handle and ran her extra line through it. Now for the worst part. Locating the leg again, she inched her hand along until she found a belt loop. Not allowing her brain to dwell on exactly what she was doing, Emalea knotted the line onto the loop then swam away. She surfaced and waved to the men.

As she started toward the boat launch, she felt herself being propelled through the water. Glancing ahead, she saw Jackson pulling at the safety line hooked to her vest while a few feet away deputies hauled in the body and bag. With his help, she was on the bank in a matter of seconds.

"Thanks," she mumbled, taking off her gear.

He stepped forward to help her but she waved him off.

"I've got it. I just want to get this stuff off me. I'm sure they need you over there." She tipped her head toward the bank where the body was lying.

He took a step away, then paused. "I'd like to see you before you leave."

She frowned. "Sorry, but I'm going straight home to bathe for an hour or three. I imagine you'll be tied up here a while."

For an instant Emalea thought she heard him sigh. But he left without another word. Struggling to her truck, she dumped her gear in the back and slammed the tailgate. She'd spend the first hour washing the dirty water from her diving equipment. As the truck rumbled down the road, she wondered if anything would wash from her mind the image of the body floating in front of her.

CHAPTER FOUR

JACKSON PUT ON LATEX GLOVES before grasping the handle of the muddy bag. So much for a calm job in a quiet town. He'd come here expecting a less stressful life and all he seemed to find was more confusion. Two dead bodies, one with a bag full of who knew what, only promised trouble for the folks of Cypress Landing.

He tugged at the sludge-covered zipper with one hand while scraping mud from its path with the other. Someone had made a hasty exit to leave this behind.

When he finally opened the bag, he cursed. He hadn't expected this. Drugs, yes. With the city of New Orleans not far away, it would only stand to reason that a certain amount of drug trade would be happening in the smaller surrounding towns. Drugs could be quick money, dangerous but quick.

A canvas bag full of guns was another matter entirely. Guns were one of the favorite items of trade for the Mafia family he'd investigated while still part of the FBI. Just when he thought he'd be tracking down stolen boats and lost hunting dogs, he'd found a bag of guns. And these weren't destined for the local deer hunter, either. Right at the top were two assault rifles. If a sportsman planned on landing a trophy buck with this, he'd sure taken a risk.

"Do you think these two were together?" Jackson recognized Matt's voice above him and looked to see the sheriff motioning toward the first body they'd found on the riverbank.

Jackson lifted one of the assault rifles turning it slowly from side to side. "My guess would be yes, although we'll know more when we get the autopsies and some of the forensics back."

"No serial number." Matt pointed to the gun before Jackson dropped it back in the bag. "That could have been made in somebody's own makeshift gun factory or else there's a gun maker doing a few illegals. Either way we can't track guns without serial numbers."

"Let's hope they're not all like that." Peeling off his gloves, Jackson got to his feet. The scenery was different in Cypress Landing, but that might end up being the only difference if his cases continued to be like this one.

"I'm going to talk to the guys collecting evidence."

TEN MINUTES LATER Jackson had three men helping the state crime lab officials scour the area for pieces of evidence as he leaned against the sheriff's car writing notes on a pad. Nearer the river, Matt stood in the glare of car lights and battery-powered spotlights they'd set up to help them work into the night. Beside him a slim woman with long black hair squatted fingering the dirt before making marks on a piece of paper she had fastened to a clipboard. Jackson returned to his own notes only to look up fifteen minutes later and see her still there, moving about in an ever-widening circle. Every few steps she would pause, look at the ground, scratch on her clipboard or shuffle through the papers. Several times, she touched the ground or picked up a piece of dirt and held it to her nose. After thirty minutes of this, he couldn't stand it any longer. He had to know what she was doing. Besides, she was stomping around in his crime scene, even if she did have Matt's permission.

"What's going on?"

Matt held up his hand to silence him and Jackson crossed his arms and sighed impatiently. Several more minutes passed before the woman stopped in front of them.

"Finished?"

"I'll need a bit longer then I'll type it up for you if you like."

Jackson stared at the two of them as they ignored him.

"Good." Matt nodded. "Remember, give it just to me." He glanced at Jackson.

The woman smiled. "I know, it's all unofficial." She stuck out a slightly grimy hand. "Hi. Brijette Dupré. Matt called me in."

Jackson shook her hand "What exactly are you doing here?"

"Brijette's on the search-and-rescue team. You didn't get to meet her the other day, but she's our tracker."

He gave a quick glance at Matt. "As in she follows human tracks?"

The woman gave a soft laugh.

"How exactly is that supposed to help us?"

"Brijette, why don't you give Jackson here your brief first impression so far." Matt winked at the girl and Jackson felt like he was missing the joke, but then there wasn't a lot of call for trackers in Chicago.

"This is what I can see." She started walking, with Jackson and Matt following close behind. "Four guys got off a boat or boats here." She pointed to the ground where Jackson only saw a bunch of footprints. "They all jumped off. One of them had something heavy, probably that bag you found. Then another person came from the parking area. He walked down here and at some point, the guy with the bag got back on the boat. Something happened, and they moved really fast from this spot. Possibly the shooting of the guy you found on the bank. The person who came from up the hill went back to his car and one of the guys from the boat went with him. The other got back on the boat in a hurry." She pointed to the edge of the water. "Someone slipped right here. I'll look some more and be more detailed in the written report."

Jackson shook his head. "You get all that from a bunch of footprints?"

She nodded then walked away, leaving him staring at Matt.

"You think she's got a clue about this?"

"She knows what she's talking about, I promise. It may not help us but I like to get a report from her and file it away. Just in case."

Jackson started to leave but Matt didn't move. The sheriff regarded him expectantly, and he knew why.

"Look, I'm sorry I lost my temper earlier. It won't happen again. I guess I just felt over-protective for a minute."

"Em doesn't need protecting."

Jackson wasn't sure if he wanted to argue with the man or just crawl in a hole. What kind of guy did Matt think he was?

"I know I have a bad history, with the fights and everything that happened back in Chicago, but you and your wife visited me when Christa and Connor were still alive. I was different back then. After they were murdered, I lost my head, but I don't think I've shown myself to be a threat to anyone, especially a woman."

"The bureau saw you as a threat. 'Out of control,' I think were their exact words. That was why they wanted to put you be-hind a desk."

The bureau had thought he was out of line following a Mafia guy whose uncle had paid for his quick release from jail. Jackson hadn't been able to prove it, but he was sure the man was responsible for his family's death. Of course, the beating he'd given the man once hadn't helped. He stuffed his hands in his pockets. "I couldn't be a desk jockey, pushing paper all day."

"I realize that. But you still have some problems. We saw that today. I want to hear you say it's going to get better, or at least it's not going to get worse."

Matt didn't know how badly Jackson wanted the whole thing to go away. He'd actually thought it had. But when he'd held Emalea close, it had affected him, even though she meant nothing to him. She'd been trembling, and he'd wanted to protect her from everything bad in life. In an instant, he'd been ready to stop Matt from sending her into the river again. Never mind that she'd been the one who'd volunteered to go. A few hours ago he'd have said he was over the issues he'd had with his anger, but now he wasn't sure.

"I won't make promises, because I doubt if you'd believe me, but I will honestly tell you that I'm doing everything I can to stay clear of situations that set me off."

"Good. I hope you include Em in that. You're not the only one with demons in the past, you know."

Dropping that bombshell, Matt strode away. Jackson realized he'd just lost some of Matt's respect. Since he'd already lost the respect of everyone in his office in Chicago, he wasn't going to let things get worse. He wasn't a monster who went around hurting people. He would be friends with Emalea and nothing more, then he wouldn't have to worry about protecting her from any danger that he might bring her. But first, he had to make sure she was all right.

EMALEA ROLLED OFF THE COUCH, her knee slamming onto the hardwood floor. Disoriented, her gaze flew from the window to the door, then finally to her watch. Good grief, it was eleven o'clock. She'd only planned to lie on the sofa for a minute and watch television. On the screen, Jay Leno was bantering with Jim Carrey. The noise that had awakened her rattled through the house. She clenched her teeth, her knee smarting as she scrambled to her feet. Whoever was banging on her door at this time of night had better have a good excuse. She lifted one slat of the blinds covering the French doors that led to her front porch.

"What the hell is he doing here?" she whispered. With a quick twist, she threw open the door, not bothering to hide her irritation. "I don't know how people conduct themselves in Chicago, but around here we don't go visiting in the middle of the night."

He took a half step back. "We just finished at the river."

"And what did you find?"

"A bag full of guns."

Emalea knew the shock had to have registered on her face.

"Not a normal occurrence in Cypress Landing, I guess."

"You'd guess right. Did Matt think the militia might be involved?"

"He did, but I'll have to do some research on that subject. I'm not very familiar with militia activity."

She leaned against the door frame, playing the possible scenarios in her mind. She could think of no plausible reason for guns to be in the river. After a few moments, she realized they were standing in her doorway staring at each other and saying nothing.

Jackson cleared his throat. "I'll be going then. I only wanted to make sure you were okay."

"And why wouldn't I be okay?"

"You seemed upset after you found the body. I...I don't know. I guess you're fine."

"Of course I'm fine. If I'd been a guy who'd found that body, would you have come by to check on me?"

His lips drew together in a thin line, and

she noticed a slight quivering just above his right eyebrow. "I might have, if he'd been as upset as you were. I really can't say for sure. After all, you're not a man. I didn't mean to disturb you."

One boot squeaked as he made his way back to the steps. Emalea bit her lip when she felt it move, as though she might tell him to stop or that she was sorry or some other foolish thing. She started to close the door but stopped when he reached the bottom step and turned back.

"Emalea, I don't know what you've heard about me but if you ever want to know the facts, I'll tell you myself. I've done things I'm not proud of. But I guess most people have. I'm not trying to hit on you or play games with you. I'm new here and it looks like we'll be working together. We obviously have the same interests, motorcycles, scuba diving. I'd just like to see if we could be friendly, if not actually friends. That's why I'm here."

His chest rose and fell visibly several times as though the speech had taken an immense physical effort. She wondered what he thought she might have heard about him. He took two strides toward his truck before her mouth got the best of her.

"Saturday morning, eight o'clock, in front of the library, we get together and go for a motorcycle ride once every other month. I... You're welcome to come if you want."

His expression was hard, yet sad, and a cold chill ricocheted along her spine. Then one side of his mouth went up in a tentative smile. "I'd like that. If I can get done at work I'll make plans to be there."

She slammed the door shut before she could get herself in more trouble. An emotion that might have been elation or despair swirled inside her. No reasoning in the world could explain why she'd invited Jackson to their Saturday ride. Such a nasty habit, this attraction she had for men who were so wrong for her. Maybe if he went along with her friends, she would be safe from making further mistakes and she wouldn't feel as if she were shunning a new person in town. Her aunt had raised her to be more hospitable than that. Inviting him had been the neighborly thing to do. She nodded to herself, trying to pretend she hadn't twisted logic to suit herself.

She pressed the off button on the television and made her way, in the dark, to her bedroom. Without turning on the lights she pulled back the cover and slid into bed, only then realizing that she'd answered the door in her favorite pajamas. She groaned and hugged a pillow to her. No wonder he'd looked at her with such a wide-eyed expression when she'd flung open the door. The nearly threadbare cotton top and matching bottoms trimmed in lace had seen better days. She had to admit the tank top revealed much more than she would have liked but, under the circumstances, what did the guy expect, showing up at her house in the middle of the night? She pressed her eyelids together, wishing for the deep sleep from which she'd been awakened. Instead, a wide chest seemed to be pressing against her, as though she were still in the back of the patrol car. Exasperated, she rolled over again, fairly certain that any dreams she had tonight involving Cypress Landing's new investigator would be anything but neighborly.

JACKSON TAPPED at the computer keyboard then sat pondering what he saw. What were Vincent Pendarius and Lawrence Relicut doing belly-up here in Louisiana? Pendarius had a petty rap sheet, but Jackson knew he did odd jobs for DePaulo, the nephew of the Mafia boss he'd investigated in Chicago—if you could call arranging payoffs to public officials odd jobs. Lawrence Relicut—the name sounded like it belonged to a high-society lawyer. High crime society was more appropriate. Lawrence had once been DePaulo's right-hand man. DePaulo had been doing everything possible to win his uncle's favor, including setting up gun sales. But he'd gotten greedy and taken a little extra money off the top and when DePaulo had been arrested, they'd all expected the old man to let him go to jail. In the end, the boss must have decided to have mercy on his sister's child and given DePaulo another chance, because their two main witnesses had developed amnesia when questioned on anything related to the guns or the Mafia. Jackson had lost Christa and Connor not long after that, and no matter how hard he'd tried, he couldn't tie DePaulo to it, except in his own mind.

Now he had the bodies of two of DePaulo's men lying in the local morgue. They'd had ID on them as if they'd not been the least bit worried about being identified. This town didn't need that kind of trouble.

A shadow loomed in the doorway, catching his attention.

"Hey, Pete." Jackson had only been here a short time but he'd already learned that

Pete Fonteneau, Matt's number-one deputy, had an ear in all the right places when it came to the town of Cypress Landing and the surrounding community. Thirty-one-year-old Pete had lived here his whole life and whatever information he didn't know would likely never be found out.

"Jackson, how's the investigation going?"

"We still haven't found the weapon used in the shooting at the river. And this militia thing, well, I've never dealt with that before."

Pete made himself at home in the chair across from Jackson. "The Acadian Loyalists have a Web site, hand out flyers and try to recruit people. They don't trust the government or much of anything else. I've heard hints that they're doing a pretty good trade in crystal methamphetamine, but we don't have hard evidence to support the fact."

Jackson fingered the brittle hair on his chin. "Do you have someone who gives you information on militia activity?"

"Do you mean an informant?"

"Yeah," he said with a slight chuckle. "That's what I mean."

Pete sat forward in his chair. "Ole Frances Bordeau is the best informant we could have."

Jackson scooted to the edge of his seat. He might make some progress with a man who could tell him something substantial. "Really? Is he a member of the militia or a plant?"

Across from him, Pete grinned. "Planted by us? Huh, not exactly. Frances is a retired tugboat captain. He spends most of his time on the river fishing or at the bait shop. But he's always listening and he doesn't mind passing on what he's heard when we have coffee at Haney's. You been there yet? They have a good breakfast and lunch."

Jackson eased his spine back against the cushion. He'd have to learn a whole new method of investigation if he was going to solve crimes in Cypress Landing. Two days ago he and Matt had gone to the little store just out of town for breakfast. The worn white building, with its extensive front porch, resembled a slightly run-down home, except for the two ancient gas tanks and the old men who met there religiously for a fierce game of dominoes. He'd certainly never expected the store to be home to an informant. He noticed Pete watching him. "Uh, yeah I've been there."

"Meet me there in the morning and I'll introduce you to Frances."

Jackson only nodded as Pete got to his feet. "Heard you got your bike back."

Dropping the pencil he'd been holding, Jackson began to wonder if he'd ever keep anything about himself private.

"Yep, I guess I won't be racing motorcycles again."

"You were at a disadvantage. No one would ever guess a woman would be riding a motorcycle like that."

"I sure didn't."

"Em rode a motorcycle long before it was a cool thing for a girl to do. And she can be kinda hard on men. I guess all that stuff with her parents, you know." Pete stepped through the door. "I'll be going now. See you in the morning."

Pete was gone before Jackson could tell him he didn't know Emalea's background or what had happened to her parents, but chasing gossip wasn't a good idea, especially if it concerned her. Nor would he use his access to police files and computers to check into her background. Right now getting interested in her was a very bad idea. He doubted he'd even go on the motorcycle ride Saturday. The girl was too prickly, too hard to get along with and just too much trouble, period. He'd wondered if a lighthearted relationship might help him ease back into a normal life, but Emalea was not a likely candidate. Still, he couldn't seem to get her off his mind, especially after seeing her last night, half-asleep and half-dressed. He'd been reining in that particular hunger from the time she'd opened the door until...well, honestly, until now. A relationship with her would be explosive in every sense of the word. He didn't want or need that, which was exactly why he should go Saturday. They could simply be friends. Then he wouldn't be feeling like this every time he thought of her, would he? Resting his elbows on his desk, he wondered exactly when he'd started thinking like this. First, he wasn't going. Then he was going. He went from one decision to the complete opposite in two seconds, using the most lame reasoning imaginable. Her fault, totally, he decided. The woman had caused his brain to shrivel into a barely viable organ.

EMALEA SHIFTED IN HER CHAIR, trying to find a more comfortable position as she watched Kent, who sat across from her mesmerized by the dusty green blinds. He seemed to have difficulty pulling his attention away from the unseen activity on the other side.

"I've been to see the mural you're helping with at the elementary school." She worried when he squirmed uncomfortably in the chair before speaking.

"You must be seeing students there."

"No, the only students I'm working with from there are seeing me in my office. I just ran by to see what the mural was like."

He stayed twisted in his seat for a second more. "Thanks," he mumbled. The gratitude on his face when he looked at her made the word seem like much more than the six little letters indicated. For a moment she felt guilty. She'd only run by briefly and the whole thing had seemed so minor she hadn't given much thought to how her visit would make him feel. He was starved for approval. Kent was one of those kids teetering on the brink of going down two different paths. She'd seen the guys he hung around with, cousins of his mostly, but they couldn't be described as anything more than a negative influence. Two of them had already had run-ins with the law. Kent wanted to do something, be something better, something more. The hunger for it shone in his eyes even now. She knew if he stayed with those cousins that light would be doused and he might not ever be able to re-kindle it.

THE LATE EVENING SUN heated the top of Kent's head as he hurried along the side of the road. Ms. LeBlanc wanted him to talk more, tell her more. Get his feelings in the open, she'd said. Going to see the mural had been a nice thing for her to do. He hadn't expected nice things from her, but then he didn't really expect them from anyone. If his feelings were the kind you could air out, he'd be talking to her for the whole hour. But that just wasn't what he was like. She didn't want to hear the real truth, his real feelings. He didn't want to have to hear them, either.

A truck rumbled alongside him and he smiled at his father's cousin, who sat behind the wheel. The vehicle pulled ahead slightly then stopped on the shoulder. A ride home, just what he needed, and with one of the few family members he actually wanted to be related to.

CHAPTER FIVE

WITH ONE LEG RESTING on the seat of her motorcycle, Emalea sipped at the cup of cheap cappuccino she'd bought at the gas station across the street. Counting herself, six riders sat on their bikes or stood next to them waiting to see who else would show for the ride. They didn't have a club, not an organized one, anyway. Of course, they didn't have an organized scuba diving club, either, but somehow everyone met periodically to eat dinner and each year a trip was planned.

This morning she'd been thirty minutes early, which had allowed her time to purchase the watery cappuccino. Rubbing her stiff neck, she gritted her teeth, trying not to fixate on what had caused her eyes to spring open an hour earlier than she had intended. She knew why it had happened, but as long as she didn't acknowledge the reason, maybe she could pretend it didn't exist.

A motorcycle engine hummed in the distance, and as she watched the figure approaching, she shivered. Today would not be her lucky day for pretending. Butterflies fanned her insides or possibly there were rocks shifting. Elation or aggravation, both were feelings she couldn't afford to have. Darn Jackson Cooper. Why did he have to keep showing up? She'd invited him, but he should have seen she'd only done it to be polite. He couldn't possibly think she'd want him to go.

Emalea thanked the heavens that Pete Fonteneau reached Jackson as soon as he swung off his bike and started introducing him to the other riders. Pete wore a huge grin when he stepped toward her with Jackson following him.

"I guess you two don't need to be introduced, especially since you've swapped motorcycles already."

Emalea glared at him. "Come on, Pete, that news is so old it's not even funny anymore."

"Besides," Jackson interrupted. "We didn't really swap motorcycles. Emalea had both of them."

Pete elbowed the big man. "It sounds much better for you if I say it the other way, Jackson."

"Truth's the truth, she won that motorcycle from me fairly. I'm just glad she decided not to keep it."

Emalea studied Jackson while trying to look as though she was watching the road for more riders. The guy didn't care what a woman beating him in a motorcycle race would do to his reputation? That alone didn't make him a good guy. He had his bad side covered for now, ready to be released when needed. Hadn't he told her that? Then she'd seen it firsthand that evening at the river. Men with things to hide could be like quicksand, dragging another person under before she realized what was happening. Even someone trained to recognize such behavior could be fooled, especially when other parts of her easily fell prey to such a man's attractions. She could feel him tugging at her, but Emalea refused to be sucked in.

Approaching engines averted any further conversation. She unclenched her fist, relieved as Lana and Lance Sanders rolled in next to them. Lana, sitting behind Lance, glanced at Jackson, immediately crinkling her nose at Emalea and mouthing, "What is he doing here?" She wasn't sure she could explain that one, even to Lana, who'd been her best friend since grade school.

Obviously, Pete had not heard the entire story, because he introduced Jackson to Lance and Lana. Not surprising that no one seemed to remember who all had been present to witness the show. Only the prime-time players, she and Jackson, had been good fodder for gossip.

Lance laughed and held out his hand anyway. "Yeah, we've met. I guess you'd say informally."

"I told him he should come and ride, since he had his bike back." Pete snickered and Emalea caught the glance Jackson sent her way.

So he hadn't mentioned to Pete that she, too, had invited him. That admission would have needed to be accompanied by an explanation of why and how he happened to be at her house the other night. She felt grudging gratitude for his keeping quiet. Most men would have been more than happy to let half the deputies know he'd seen her in way less clothing than she'd like. Jackson Cooper was beginning to be a mass of contradictions.

"Doesn't anyone want to know what I planned for our ride?" Emalea stopped her muddled thoughts at Lana's question.

"I'm almost scared to ask," Pete said, then turned to Jackson. "The last time Lana planned our ride, we got stuck in Lafayette, watching an opera in the park."

They took turns planning the day's ride throughout the year. With the variety of personalities in the group, Emalea had managed to see everything from musicals to mud wrestling. She grinned at Lana expectantly.

"It was a musical put on by the college and you have to admit the food was good."

"She's right," Pete agreed. "All you can eat crawfish, potatoes and corn is hard to beat. What will it be this time, Lana, a tour of the art museum?"

"I'm saving that for later. Today I want to go to New Orleans. We can eat an early lunch at Mother's downtown and go to the Aquarium of the Americas afterward."

Emalea nodded. "That's a pretty good plan."

"Yeah, this could easily make up for the music thing."

As the men strode to their bikes, Lana leaned toward Emalea. "Can you believe that guy is going on our ride? Will it be a problem for you?"

Emalea drained the last drop from her cup, feigning much more indifference than she felt. "He's not mad about the bike incident. It's no big deal."

"No big deal. Huh, very interesting."

The engine of Emalea's motorcycle roared to life with the tap of her finger. She could see Lana's mouth moving but twisted her hand on the gas, letting the roar drown out anything her friend might have been saying. Lana waved, completely undeterred. Emalea knew the girl would have her say, sooner or later.

Two and a half hours later, they rolled down the one-way street that ran next to Mother's. They had managed to stretch the one-and-a-half-hour trip to New Orleans into a much longer ride by following twisting back roads along the river whenever possible. By this point, Emalea had become quite adept at avoiding Jackson. At every stop, she raced to the bathroom or tried to appear engrossed in conversation with the nearest warm body. But he hadn't exactly been trying to get next to her.

When she settled in a chair at the restaurant, she had to convince herself she wasn't pleased to see Jackson's huge biceps bumping hers. Ignoring him, she ordered a shrimp-and-oyster po'boy and diet soda, then took an inordinate amount of time arranging her fork and napkin. In the end, her efforts got her in trouble. After moving the fork repeatedly, she knocked it on the floor next to Jackson's foot.

She sighed and, without a thought, went after it, but she had underestimated the distance, and her head bumped his knee. Above the table, a riot of laughter echoed and she paused. Part of her wanted to twist her head to see Jackson, but that would only make things worse as she realized the laughter was definitely directed at the ridiculous position she had assumed. The fact that she hadn't surfaced from beneath the table very quickly only made matters worse.

"Emalea, what in the world are you doing down there?"

She straightened to find every eye at the table on her and Pete more than happy to inflame the situation, one of his specialties.

"I dropped my fork." She held up the item as evidence.

Pete snorted. "Why didn't you leave it there? I don't believe for a minute you're going to use it after it's been on the floor. Either way, your fork retrieving sure put a smile on Jackson's face."

That brought Emalea's head around with a snap. Sure enough Jackson sported a huge grin, while trying to appear completely innocent. She vacillated between rage and delight. He had no right making her the brunt of a joke, even if she had pretty much put her head in his lap. On the other hand, his infectious grin tugged at a part of her she didn't ever want to let loose.

"That was just his wishful thinking. I certainly wouldn't be making any kind of advances toward a man who can't even hold his own in a race." She could almost see the sparks of anger flaring from her own eyes straight to Jackson's. Fine, she thought, go with the anger. A few people chuckled, but Emalea had no doubt her aggravation was evident to everyone. The others resumed their conversations, but she focused on Jackson.

"You're a complete jerk." The words nearly singed her lips.

"It was just a joke." His eyes clouded with confusion, evidently uncertain why his teasing had her bristling.

"You're not going to make a fool of me, ever. You'll be more than sorry for it, I promise."

His uncertainty slipped away and his expression darkened ominously. "No one's making you look foolish. Except maybe yourself, right now, by not being able to take a simple joke."

Her finger stabbed his chest. "I don't have to take a damn thing from you and you'd be well advised to remember that."

A viselike grip captured her wrist and her attacking finger was imprisoned along with the rest of her hand. She realized quickly she had gone too far. Jackson had decided to unleash his bad side and she wasn't prepared. He was strong enough to do whatever he wanted, shove her, hit her, drag her into the street. But she wouldn't back off. He'd find she wouldn't lie like a doormat ready to be stomped on. She shoved a stray hair from her face with her other hand, never breaking free of his icy stare.

Jackson leaned toward her until their noses were only inches apart. She waited for the onslaught of his anger.

"Emalea LeBlanc, you should be very careful who you go around poking with that finger of yours." His voice was barely above a whisper and Emalea waited for the panic to hit her, the fear, but it never came. Instead she inhaled his masculine scent and the shiver that rocked her had nothing to do with being afraid. Her arm seemed to be melting in his grasp and she studied it briefly to be sure it was still in one solid piece.

"You know what might happen if you stab the wrong person with that finger?"

She shook her head, totally hypnotized by his voice, his skin, hell, by everything about him. If he planned to do something horrible to her she was absolutely defenseless. For a moment she wondered if this was how her mother had felt, if this was why she could never leave her abusive husband. Emalea was certain, right now at this moment, she couldn't leave either.

Jackson straightened the offending digit with his free hand. A moment of panic hit Emalea as she imagined he might break her finger. It wouldn't be the first time a man had done that. Before she could complete the thought, he pressed her finger against his lips and another shock wave washed through her body. He tugged her fingers apart and planted another warm, damp kiss on her palm.

"I will attack back." He dropped her hand with a wink and leaned back in his chair.

Ice clinked in the glasses at another table but she couldn't speak, good grief, she could barely breathe.

"Okay, I'm separating you two since you can't play nice." Pete all but shoved Jackson out of the chair. "You go sit in my chair. Em needs a guy like me to sit by her. Someone who's still scared of her."

Emalea decided to keep quiet. Things just didn't go as she intended when Jackson Cooper was around. Across the table, Lana gave her a wicked grin. Everyone else seemed to think it had been another grand show between the two of them, but Emalea had never aspired to be an actress.

A SEVEN-FOOT REEF SHARK glided through the water effortlessly. Emalea stood a few feet in front of him and Jackson wondered if she could see his reflection in the glass. People moved around her but she remained motionless, appearing to be mesmerized by the sharks and rays swimming in the huge tank.

He glanced around the room but didn't see the others. They had scattered throughout the building housing the aquarium. Maybe a bit of guilt had kept him following Emalea, at a safe distance, of course. He wasn't sure what had set her off, other than the fact that he had embarrassed her. But the situation had been completely laughable when she dove under the table after the fork. It hadn't taken much from him, just a big smile and a little eyebrow motion, to get the whole table into hysterics. Unfortunately, Emalea hadn't thought it funny. Still, he hadn't expected such a personal attack. It was almost as if she wanted to show him he couldn't take advantage of her.

In front of him, she shifted her feet. Then as if awakening, she strode away from the tank toward the front exit. In his mind's eye, he saw her standing in the doorway of her house wearing nothing but those flimsy pajamas. If he'd ever been going to take advantage of the woman that would have been the time. The urge to drag her into his arms had nearly knocked him to his knees. Thankfully he'd controlled that emotion. She'd likely have cracked him over the head with her scuba tank. Emalea had something to prove. He wasn't sure what or why. But for reasons unknown, she seemed intent on proving that something to him.

He moved to follow her only to be stopped by a not-so-gentle tug at his arm. Lana Sanders gave him an impish grin.

"Don't worry, she's not going far."

"I don't know what you mean."

The brunette crossed her arms in front of her chest and shook her head. "Maybe it wasn't noticeable to anyone else, but I know good and well you've been keeping Em in your sights since the minute we got here. What I can't understand is why. She behaved like a pure butt to you back there."

Jackson tried to appear serious but this woman had his lips twitching in an instant. "I guess I'm waiting for a good moment to apologize for embarrassing her. I wouldn't have made the joke if I'd known she would get so mad."

"And I'm wondering why you care?"

He fingered the hair above his upper lip. Why indeed? "Lana, I wish I knew the answer to that one myself. When she's not busy trying to show how tough she is, she's one of the most interesting women I've ever met." He clamped his teeth together. He had no intention of trading secrets with Emalea's friend. This was beginning to feel like grade school.

"I bet you've met a lot of women."

Her statement caught him off guard. What was she digging for now? She made him sound like a man who hunted women for sport. Jackson scratched the back of his head. "I'm sorry to disappoint you. I married my high-school sweetheart and stayed happily married until two years ago when my wife and daughter were killed."

Lana's hand fluttered to her cheek. "That must have been awful for you."

Jackson stared past her into the shark tank. "They were my life and to say my life ended would be a huge understatement. I guess that's why I'm not pursuing your friend, no matter what. I had a good marriage, I don't imagine I'll find another."

She touched his arm. "Being alone isn't much fun, after a while."

He shrugged. "There are worse things than being alone, like losing everything that's really important to you."

She stepped in front of him, forcing him to meet her gaze. "That should make you all the more certain to treasure whoever and whatever you love."

Her persistence made him smile. "Are you a psychologist, too?"

"No, but my best friend is one, and I stayed at a Holiday Inn Express last night."

Jackson laughed at her rendition of the popular television commercial and nearly dropped the cup of soda he'd been drinking. He straightened as Lance crossed the room toward them.

"Just think on what I said."

He met her friendly glance with a smile. She made it difficult for anyone to get mad at her. "I'll keep it in mind."

She disappeared around the corner with her husband in tow while Jackson strode to the front exit and onto the plaza that extended to the riverbank. He spotted Emalea, leaning against the railing, watching the dark water below. He took a deep breath to prepare himself for what could easily become a nasty encounter, before striding across the brick-and-granite courtyard.

He leaned his arms on top of the rail, discreetly studying her. Where to begin? She reminded him of a spiny sea urchin with pointy quills ready to stab the foot of some unaware wader. Why he wanted to make amends was beyond his own comprehension. He tried to blame it on his need to do the right thing, by everyone, including Emalea. She projected an image of toughness, but he detected something else, a hint of frailty, the need to be protected. Was he the only one sensing that?

"I'm sorry for how I acted in the restaurant. It's not you personally."

Jackson was speechless. He hadn't expected an apology from her. "That's good to know. I felt like I had missed something. I've been trying to apologize to you since we got to the aquarium. I'm sorry if I made you mad but when you went under the table it was just too easy. If I've done wrong by you in some other way, I wish you'd let me know."

She continued to gaze across the water. "There's nothing to tell. Like I said, it's not you personally."

Emalea wanted to end the conversation there. He could tell, but he couldn't let it go. "If anything, I should be mad at you because of that whole motorcycle thing. I don't think I have a second personality that materializes while I'm asleep and runs around harassing innocent women to the point they think I'm a monster."

"Don't you?" She nearly spit the words, which were accompanied by a disdainful look.

Unsure how to respond, a coal of anger started to burn in his chest, but he refused to give in to the emotion. He'd never been so completely painted as a bad guy by anyone, unless he was undercover and wanted to be. Looking the part of a hard, cruel man wasn't difficult. Acting like one was something that didn't come naturally.

"You've lost me, I'm afraid. If you really want an answer to that question you'll have to explain."

She continued to keep her attention focused on the water. Her distaste replaced by a mask of indifference. "I don't need an answer."

He put a hand on her shoulder, pulling her around. "Well, explain anyway. I'd like to know."

She frowned and he thought she just might tell him to take off. "Look at you. You've got to be at least six-four and weigh a good two-fifty."

"Hey, you're right on the money." Jackson grinned. "You should hire on with a carnival. Oh, and that's all muscle you know, the two-fifty."

Her lips twitched, helping her to lose much of the seriousness that appeared to overwhelm her. Relief flowed through him. He hadn't intended this to be a heart-to-heart kind of thing, just the offering of an apology.

Managing to control her smile, she continued. "You're a tough guy. It's written all over you and, believe me, I know all there is to know when it comes to tough guys. You think you can push people around and get what you want, especially women. You're bigger than most, which means you believe everyone is beneath you and they should stay there. If they don't, you'll put them in their place. Tell me you don't see yourself in that description."

She watched him for a moment, then, as if the sight of him was more than she could stand, she turned her head to follow the movement of a passing tugboat. For several seconds, her nostrils continued to flare, her features taut, as though she were fighting for control. He might not have known her long but he could see that this lady had a problem that went way beyond him. Digging any deeper meant getting to know her, getting her to trust him. It stank of a relationship. He couldn't go there. No matter how much he wanted to pull her into his arms and take care of her. And he did want to. The little girl who needed to be protected and kept safe stood quivering right in front of him wearing a facade of false bravado. But he couldn't protect anyone. The task was too much for him, too much for his heart. He had a quick premonition of falling for this woman—definitely an emotional quagmire he wanted to avoid at all cost.

But she was wrong about him. She wanted him to be a round little peg that fit in a round little hole, because she said he should. If they were going to be working together, she'd see just how wrong, but not now.

He put a hand on her shoulder. "You don't know me. You presume to, but you don't. Those three letters behind your name don't mean you're never wrong. This time you are."

Forcing his fingers to let her go, he made himself step away. He'd gone only a few feet when the whisper of a voice stopped him.

"Jackson."

He turned toward her.

"Thank you, for the apology."

He nearly went back. A huge magnet seemed to be drawing him. But she had no interest in him. That was obvious. Besides, there was safety in walking away.

"My pleasure," he said and headed off to join the rest of the group, trying not to drag his feet as he went.

CHAPTER SIX

JACKSON SCRUTINIZED the pieces of golden, breaded meat skewered onto a thin wooden stick.

"Tell me again what this is."

Emalea snickered as she pulled pieces of meat from her own stick. "Fried alligator, it's good."

"And why is it on a stick?"

"Because you're in the South, and we deep-fry everything and put it on a stick. It's a cultural thing."

"Sounds like a heart-attack thing."

"Yeah, well, that, too. You just shouldn't indulge very often."

Jackson slid a piece from the stick, popping it in his mouth while all the time watching Emalea. She was right; it was good. A truce seemed to have been called when they'd left the aquarium for the French Market. He hadn't been sure what to expect, but the market was actually a long row of covered buildings open on the sides and both ends. Vendors sold everything from apples to jewelry to sunglasses. The scent of spicy foods had hit him the instant he'd swung off his bike, making him hungry even though lunch had only been a few hours ago. The riders had spread throughout the market to browse and he'd ended up with Emalea. He'd fully intended to keep his distance, but the lure of spending time in her company pulled him closer.

"What are these things between the meat?" He fingered more fried food of undetermined origin.

"Onions and dill pickles. If you don't like the pickles, give them to me, they're my favorite."

"Dill pickles, you've got to be kidding?"

She took the object in question from his stick and gobbled it up like a delicacy. "What did I just say? South, everything fried and on a stick, what part of that is difficult for you?"

He laughed. "Most of it, and remember I'm from the South, too. I've just been living a really long time in a place where they don't serve everything on a stick."

She laughed with him and Jackson made an immediate decision that this Emalea could be much more of a danger to him than the one who kept all her claws exposed. He reminded himself of his earlier decision to keep an emotional distance and not get involved. Friends, yes. More, no. It was very simple. They stepped away from the busy market aisles to eat. He'd finished all of his skewered alligator before she spoke again.

"How are things at the office?"

He squinted at her and snorted, while she only smiled.

"You make me sound like a stockbroker."

"Well, you're definitely not one of those." She took a long drink of her soda and he had to admire the skin on her throat, as he tried to keep up his end of the conversation.

"I guess you really want to know the latest on the shooting. The truth is we haven't learned much."

She went to toss her empty soda can in the garbage, glancing back at him as she spoke. "I wouldn't be surprised to see the militia tied to this."

He shrugged. "That's one avenue we're examining. But anytime you deal with illegal gun sales, the investigation can get frustrating. A large majority of guns that end up in the hands of criminals were actually purchased legally by someone who reports the gun stolen or can't seem to find it when questioned. That's what we've been up against so far. The only effective way to stop the flow of guns is to find out how they're being moved. Without the right breaks, that can be a long, slow process."

Emalea kicked the toe of her boot against the asphalt, frowning. "I hope you clear it up soon, our town isn't exactly used to dead bodies lying around."

He passed her two dill pickles he'd pulled loose, then broke the stick in half. "I know. That's why I came here."

"Really, the life of high crime in the FBI get to be too much for you?"

It was an innocent question, but Jackson chose his next words carefully. He had no intention of discussing his personal life with her, even if he felt the weight of it bearing down on him. A few minutes of friendliness didn't make Emalea a confidante. Besides, confiding meant taking a step in a direction he'd prefer not to go.

"I just needed a change. After Matt got married, he and his wife visited me in Chicago and I came back here a couple of times. I liked Cypress Landing, liked the quiet, the river. It seemed like a good place." He'd left out a lot, like how much trouble he'd had his last two years at his old job and how he'd told

Matt on more than one occasion that he felt lost in the city. That was more than she needed to know. It was her turn to give up a little information. He turned to her and smiled. "How'd you end up in Cypress Landing?"

The wall that slammed between them was tangible. Jackson knew whatever answers he got from her after this would be carefully guarded.

"I grew up there, of course, but I moved to New Orleans when I finished school and worked at a couple of hospitals. I made good money." She paused, staring at the tie-dyed dresses in a vendor's booth fluttering on their hangers in the afternoon breeze. He wondered if this would be where the story ended. Emalea appeared to be far away, reliving another time that had sent her running back to Cypress Landing. Jackson gave himself a slight shake. His imagination had begun to run amok. For all he knew, she could have happily decided to go home.

At last she looked at him with a faint smile. "I just got tired of the city and the noise, so I went home."

His first assumption had been right. He nodded at her and pretended to study the crowd around them. He'd become too adept at reading people to believe her going home had been a happy time. The skill also made him certain he wouldn't be getting the real answer from her today.

"I'm going to look at those dresses."

He watched her thread her way through the other shoppers to the booth. He really wanted her to buy one of the brightly colored dresses, a completely absurd thing to want. She fingered a couple, but moved on and he tried not to be disappointed. With no real plan in mind, he went into the booth and found himself holding the same dresses. The vendor pointed to a few she recommended, and he finally chose a green one that matched Emalea's eyes.

After handing the woman his money, he all but ran back to his bike, stuffing the rolled up dress in the zippered storage bag at the back of his seat. Getting caught with the dress would be inexcusable. There would be absolutely no way he could explain it to someone else. He couldn't really explain it to himself, except that he thought having a peace offering on hand might be a good idea.

Back in the market aisles in record time, he breathed a sigh of relief and began to thumb through a rack of leather belts before moving to a table loaded with wallets. He decided he might need a new wallet, so he began rummaging through the display. A bump against his arm made him move closer to the table. The next bump was hard enough to make him drop the wallet he'd been holding. Spinning around, ready to give a rude shopper an ugly look, he came chest to face with Lana. That is, her face hit him at the middle of his chest. She wore her usual grin.

"Don't worry, your secret is safe with me."

He narrowed his eyes at her, wondering if she'd lost her mind. "What secret is that?"

"The dress you bought. I won't tell anyone. It's for Emalea, isn't it?"

Damn, how could she have seen him? He'd been really careful. "It's for my mother."

She hooted with laughter. "I bet your mother would have a stroke if you gave her that dress, or didn't you notice it doesn't have a back."

Jackson could have kicked himself. Why hadn't he said he'd bought the dress for his sister? Lana wouldn't have had a thing to say then.

"I promise not to tell and I'll stay completely out of it. Unless you think my telling Em what a great guy you are would be bad."

He dropped another wallet he'd just picked up. "When did you do that?"

She leaned toward him as if they were conspiring together for a great cause. "I haven't yet, but I'm going to."

"What makes you so sure I'm a good guy? You barely know me."

Lana patted his arm. "Oh, please, you ooze goodness."

He narrowed his eyes at her. "I'm certain that's the first time I've ever heard myself described that way. If it's true, why should you have to tell Emalea? She should see it for herself." In fact, he knew Emalea thought *evil* was the perfect word for him.

"That girl can't see a thing where a man like you is concerned. She's wearing blinders." Lana grabbed an eel-skin wallet and flipped through the compartments.

"Maybe it should stay that way."

She tossed the wallet back on the table. "Nope, she'll wake up and see that a man like you doesn't always fit into her little mold."

Jackson crossed his arms in front of his chest. "Woman, you're starting to sound like a learning-impaired parrot. A man like me, a man like me. What the hell kind of man am I supposed to be?"

Lana lost her smile for the first time that day as she touched his forearm. "The kind

Emalea is most afraid of and the kind she needs the most."

She hurried away, leaving that particular riddle unexplained. Not that he wanted it defined. He had no intention of being more to Emalea than a friendly acquaintance. He'd send the dress to his sister; the woman at the booth had said one size fits most.

Thirty minutes later, Jackson sat on his bike waiting for the others to finish shopping. They'd all parked on the edge of the street and beside him shops rattled with overflow business from the market. Historic brick buildings, weathered by the years, housed everything from tattoo parlors to sandwich shops. The three men who left the diner two doors down from him caught his attention. They had their back to him but he stiffened automatically as though his subconscious read the situation and was trying to prepare him. The men crossed the street toward the market. Jackson had swung off the bike and gone two steps into the street before he realized he'd even moved. A car horn blared and he jumped back. On the other side of the one-way street, the three men turned. The shortest man stared at Jackson. Something akin to shock or possibly fear settled on his features, then a smile inched across his stubby face.

His hand rose in the air, a forefinger pointed toward Jackson and his thumb pointed skyward as though his appendage were a weapon. One of the other men laughed, then the three disappeared into the crowded market.

Jackson dropped to the seat of his motorcycle, sitting with both feet on one side, hands on his knees. He tried to remind himself to breathe. DePaulo was in New Orleans. Jackson knew the Mafia family had a business here, had for many years, but it was small time compared to the operations in Chicago. He'd made it his mission to be DePaulo's shadow back in Chicago but DePaulo had disappeared without a trace and Jackson had been left with nowhere to unleash his anger. As soon as he got home, he'd make a call to one of his friends in the bureau. Surely they'd have an explanation.... He stopped thinking and started to run across the street. His hip bumped a vendor's table, sending sunglasses clattering to the ground. The man shouted at him in a foreign language but Jackson moved deeper into the crowd. He had to hurry. DePaulo was in here somewhere and so was Emalea. She stood ten feet away from him holding a bracelet. Sweat dripped into his eyes, and Jackson swiped at it, trying to control his breathing. DePaulo didn't know Emalea. She had nothing to fear from him. Jackson threaded his way through the shoppers back to his motorcycle. Maybe if he stayed out of New Orleans, everyone around him would be safe.

BEHIND HER, THE LIGHTS of Jackson's motorcycle became more distant until they disappeared and Emalea realized he'd taken the road to his house. She'd had a brief, almost girlish thought that he might follow her home. Then what? Certainly they weren't going to fall into each other's arms. Were they? She had no intention of doing that. So why was she having fantasies that were filled with him? A little fantasizing is healthy, she told herself as she steered into her driveway and killed the motorcycle engine.

Admittedly, he'd given her plenty of reason for fantasies this afternoon. She couldn't remember the last time she'd laughed so much. After leaving the French Market they'd ridden back to Jackson Square to spend the rest of the afternoon watching the artists paint and wandering in a variety of unusual stores. If Jackson's goal had been to prove he could be a likable companion, he'd definitely won the prize. Her disappointment must have been evident when he'd told her they had to meet the others, because he'd leaned toward her and whispered, "We'll have to take another trip soon."

Before she could stop herself, she'd blurted, "Really, I'd love to. I've had a great time today." The words hung in the mildly humid air like a smoky cloud, and she wished she could take them back; but in all honesty, she'd meant what she'd said.

Jackson had smiled, no gibes or snide remarks. He'd leaned even closer to add, "I'm glad, because I've had fun today, too, thanks to you." It could have been a meaningless line that a gorgeous man gave a girl he was trying to hit on, but if it had been, he'd made it the most sincere one Emalea had ever heard.

"Give him a chance. He's a nice guy." Lana had taken it upon herself to become Jackson's champion on the ride home that evening. At every stop she had found a reason why he was a very delectable creature.

"See how he held the door for that elderly lady.... Doesn't he have a kind smile and gentle eyes?... Isn't he built like the perfect bodybuilder?" Emalea had finally threatened to inform Lance that his wife was drooling over another man. Then had come Lana's shocker.

"I'm afraid for you, Em. Afraid you'll never get done with the past. That it will dictate your every move, until one day you'll realize you've spent your whole life running from a memory. I don't want you not to live your life because of fear."

Emalea had straddled her bike and been the first to depart from the service station, leaving Lana standing on the oil-splotched concrete. Who exactly held the psychology degree here? The last time she'd truly cared about someone, her feelings had blinded her from seeing what kind of man he really was. She couldn't let that happen again. She hadn't been running scared, just being careful not to repeat past mistakes. And that's what getting involved with Jackson would be…a mistake.

KENT RAYNOR STARED at the ceiling dappled with light from the moon shining in his window. The rumbling of his father's truck drowned out the peaceful chirping of the crickets. He was late coming home, very late. Kent hoped he wasn't drunk. The last few weeks, the atmosphere in this house had been intense. Earl Raynor's role in the militia gave him much more responsibility than many people imagined. Kent wasn't sure exactly what, except that he knew many men listened to his father. Those were probably the only people in the world who would want the opinion of such a man.

Kent refused to join or participate in the militia and he wondered every day when the fact would make his father angry enough to kill him. He knew his father planned for him to become more active when he was older, even though boys his age participated in marksmanship contests all the time. Several weeks ago, Earl had been pushing the issue, trying to make Kent come to a game. It would be fun he said, a game of paintball.

Lots of people enjoyed playing paintball. The guns and pistols shot balls of paint. If you got splattered, well, you considered yourself splattered, as in dead. Under other circumstances, he might have liked the game, but a feeling seemed to get under his skin whenever he was at the camp across the river, a hatred or anger, and he didn't want to feel it. He reserved most of his hatred and anger for his own father, who chose to come home and take out his frustrations on his family, most often his wife. Saying you hated one of your parents had to be wrong, and he figured maybe a part of him might still love Earl Raynor. But that part remained buried for safety.

Earl told him sooner or later he'd have to join, that one day Kent would take his father's place in the family business as well as in the militia. It was his duty. Kent didn't want those things. He'd rather do something with his art, maybe even go to college, an idea his father laughed at.

Kent thought of Ms. LeBlanc. What a cool lady. On his first visit, he'd called her Dr. LeBlanc but she'd said that made her feel like she should be giving him a shot in his butt. She wanted to hear all his problems, but he didn't know where to start and, if he did, where it would end. A list of his problems could take days to compile.

And what if she thought the social worker needed to come because of his father? That had happened once and, when she'd left, the results hadn't been pretty. His mother probably should have gone to the hospital but his father wouldn't allow it. "Only bring that damn social worker here again," he'd growled. The social worker had never come back.

He'd heard a few rumors that Ms. Leblanc had lived through problems of her own when she was younger, that her father had even gone to prison. If he told her just a few things, maybe she could help him find a way to stay alive long enough to graduate from high school. Then he could get away. But one huge problem remained. Who would take care of his mother if he left?

The door banged open and the whole house shook. Kent rolled over in his bed as the sound of shuffling feet paused at his door, but passed on. He moved to sit on the edge of the bed, waiting. If things got bad enough, he'd have to go to his parents' room and try to divert his father's attention, something that always left him in pretty poor shape. In his parents' bedroom, his father started shouting, but quieted by the time Kent reached the hallway. He waited. A few feet away, the door opened a crack and his mother's face, barely visible in the dim light, showed both fear and determination.

He took a half step toward her. "He pass out?"

She nodded, quickly shutting the door. Kent returned to his bed, using the sheet to wipe away the beads of perspiration on his forehead. They were hurtling toward a point he couldn't exactly see. He only hoped they'd survive.

CHAPTER SEVEN

LATE SPRING HAD BEGUN to feel like midsummer. Emalea wiped the perspiration from her upper lip. The air-conditioning she'd had Uncle John install in her truck had been whining and barely blowing cool air all week. To make her Friday a little more interesting, it had died its last death this morning on her way to the prison to do her evaluations.

She pushed the door open with her foot while trying to see through the garage doors of her uncle's shop. If she was lucky, Uncle John would be able to fix the truck's air this evening, although the number of cars parked both in and around the garage didn't seem very promising. Movement at the back of the shop caught her attention, so she set off in that direction only to come to a halt at what she saw.

Her uncle John was bent over a familiar-looking motorcycle. Squatting next to him in a tight red T-shirt with the sleeves cut off was Jackson Cooper. Did the man have no decency? First he showed up at every outing she attended; now he was making himself at home with her aunt and uncle. Even if the only outings she'd attended were the ride last Saturday and a search-and-rescue meeting on Tuesday, wasn't that enough?

Jackson glanced back, noticed her standing there and straightened. "Emalea, Mr. Berteau didn't think you'd come by this evening."

Her uncle stood as well and tapped Jackson's shoulder with a wrench. "I've told you ten times it's no Mr. This or Mr. That. The name's John."

The big man smiled and her uncle grinned right along with him. It was a conspiracy to test her patience. She was going to fail the test.

"Jackson here came by to have me work on this bike of his so you won't be outrunning him anymore."

Jackson managed to look a little sheepish, which had to be hard for such a bear. "I really just came by for a tune-up."

She ignored him, directing her words to her uncle. "My air-conditioning broke this morning. I was hoping you might have time to fix it, but since you're busy, it'll wait."

Uncle John let her take three strides before stopping her. "Emalea!"

When she turned back, the older man's dark gaze told her just how much she sounded like a churlish five-year-old. He paused, wiping his hands on a rag. "I'll be checking on your air right now and you'll start behaving so as not to embarrass your aunt. You and Jackson gonna stay for supper. Your aunt Alice made a big pot of gumbo. She's been trying to call all evening to invite you."

She hung her head. "I was at the prison and I left my cell phone at home."

Uncle John patted her arm, making Emalea feel even worse for her snippy comment. "While I check your truck, take Jackson around to the house. He needs to wash up and you can help Alice get the food ready."

He headed out the front of the garage while Emalea steeled herself to try and be polite for the next few hours.

"I'm not trying to intrude on your family dinner but your aunt and uncle insisted I stay and eat."

"Of course you should stay. Aunt Alice is a great cook and they love to have company."

He moved closer. "What about you? Would you like some company, too?"

"My aunt and uncle can invite whoever they want to eat with them. It's not up to me."

"That's not exactly what I meant. I thought we'd developed a kind of understanding last weekend, but the other night at the meeting you didn't have much to say to me. Has my secret split personality been harassing you again?"

"No, I just had a lot on my mind the other night." She didn't say she'd been trying to remind herself of all the reasons she didn't need to like Jackson Cooper. Unfortunately, she was finding him more likable by the minute.

"Come with me, the house is just through this back door and across the yard." Thankfully, he followed without further comment.

JACKSON TOOK UP the entire kitchen, or at least it felt that way to Emalea. She seemed to bump into him every time she turned around while preparing a loaf of French bread with garlic butter.

Her aunt was all over him. Offering him iced tea and digging into his family history. Emalea learned more in five minutes than she'd heard in all the other time they'd spent together. It was a lot more than she wanted to know. His mother was an elementary school teacher as was his sister. Jackson's father had worked his whole life in the police department and one brother was a lawyer, the other a fireman.

He sounded so normal, but she didn't trust that. If only she could be sure why she was attracted to him. Was it because of how nice he seemed? Or because there was a dangerous side of him that her rotten-man magnet was able to detect? A bad side that she was inevitably drawn to.

By the time she and Jackson had put the last dish in the dishwasher, Emalea had begun to believe she could have been wrong pegging him as a brutish man. She wasn't yet ready to admit to a total error, but the man did deserve further observation. He insisted on straightening the kitchen after their meal and had carefully written her aunt's gumbo recipe on a scrap of paper, although he was under strict orders not to attempt to cook it without returning for a lesson in making the perfect roux. He finished the evening at the table, talking cars and motorcycles with her uncle until even Emalea had had enough. She found her aunt in the living room watching television.

"What a nice boy."

Emalea flopped onto the sofa beside her. "He's hardly a boy, Aunt Alice."

The older woman frowned, which reminded Emalea to be more polite. "He may be a big man on the outside, but he's got the boy's heart."

"You've only just met him, how do you know he's got a boy's heart, whatever that is?"

Her aunt's face stiffened, and Emalea knew she was in for a lecture. She'd seen that look on more than one occasion, many more. "Now, it seems to me, you hardly know him, either, so how can you say he doesn't have the boy's heart? The boy's heart is a good heart, kind and gentle. I like him way better than the man who sells the drugs."

Emalea's eyebrows bunched up as she tried to figure out who her aunt was talking about. "The man who sells... Oh, you mean Paul Jones. You make him sound like a criminal. But it doesn't matter because I'm not dating either one of them."

"Well, you should be."

"What, dating both of them?"

Her aunt slapped her leg lightly. "You know I'm speaking of this man here."

Emalea smoothed a few wrinkles in the linen pants she'd worn all day. "Do you really think he's a good guy? What if he's pretending or hiding something?" She continued to study the material of her pants, not meeting her aunt's gaze.

Firm fingers lifted her chin. "Not all men are like that, Em."

"He reminds me of a few bad men I've known."

Her aunt nodded. "Maybe on the outside that's true, but I don't see it on the inside. If you do, maybe it's because you're wanting so badly to find it."

Emalea grasped her aunt's hand. "Maybe you're right."

In the other room, she heard chairs scooting across the floor and she smiled.

Her uncle entered the small living room with Jackson behind him. "Em, I forgot to tell you earlier, but I already started on your truck. I had to take a few parts out to get to the air, so you'll have to leave it here. I'll run you home when you're ready."

"I'd be glad to take Emalea home," Jackson interrupted. "That is if she wouldn't mind."

Emalea tried not to give Uncle John a look of panic. Maybe her uncle would say, "No stranger's taking my niece home." But he didn't. He only smiled, thanking Jackson for his kind offer and giving Emalea a hard stare that said, "Be nice." In all fairness to Uncle John, it was nearly ten o'clock and Jackson wasn't exactly a stranger. The man was employed by the sheriff's office. No good reason existed for her or her uncle to refuse his offer. If she were honest, which she didn't really want to be, she'd admit Jackson wasn't the one she was afraid of. She was scared of herself and how he made her feel. Alone with him, she might lose control, she might start to fall for him, and the nightmare would begin. However, a small voice deep inside her whispered, a fantasy might begin. For once, it might be wonderful. She stood, thanking Jackson for the offer and, after a quick hug from her aunt and uncle, she followed him through the door.

THE DARK INTERIOR of the truck shadowed Jackson's face as he turned into her driveway, still praising her aunt and uncle. Moonlight shone between the branches of the trees and Emalea leaned forward to peer at the sky.

"Full moon," she said.

"Not afraid of ghosts and goblins, are you?"

"Only on Halloween."

He laughed, bending across the seat in front

of her. The cushions pressed into her back as she tried to widen the distance between them. She wondered what he was thinking. He paused for a moment, smiling as if he knew he had sent her into a panic, then pulled the handle to open the door for her.

"I didn't figure you'd sit in here until I walked around, and my mother did try to teach me manners, like opening doors for ladies."

He climbed out on his side and she realized he was going to follow her to the front door.

"Your place is so peaceful. I know I've only been here at night but I bet you can really relax here."

"I do. I have a screened porch on the back with a daybed and when the weather's good, I'll sleep there, where I can hear the creek running." She almost sighed just thinking about it.

"There's a creek behind your house?"

She smiled. "Sure, do you want to see?"

"Absolutely."

He stayed at her shoulder as she led him around the house and down a slight incline to the creek, where the water flowing among the rocks made a swishing sound that always helped her unwind.

"This is nice." Jackson motioned to the wooden bench with a decorative ironwork inlay in the backrest. In front of the bench was a small wooden table with a stone top. "It's like having your living room outside."

The rush of pleasure his words brought surprised her. It was her special place. She hadn't expected to be happy that he liked it, too.

"I could make coffee, if you'd like to sit for a while."

In the shimmering light, his smile was barely visible. "I'd like that a lot. Do you need help?"

"No, it'll only take a minute."

He sat on the bench and propped his feet up on the table. "I'll wait here."

Throwing coffee into the filter, Emalea didn't even try to analyze what she was doing. She ought to have said goodbye at the truck. *Curiosity killed the cat* was the old saying, and the only memory she had involving a cat wasn't a very good one. Despite the warnings her brain kept giving her, she was curious. So far, Jackson didn't fit the image she'd had of him and, in all honesty, he had enough sex appeal to make her toes tingle.

Frogs and crickets chorused in a never-ending concert as she carried her stainless-steel carafe and two coffee mugs to the creek bank. She'd never sat here at night with a man. This was her sanctuary, but Jackson didn't feel like an intruder.

He took the carafe from her and poured while she held the cups, praying her hands wouldn't shake. Sliding to one side, he made room for her on the bench. "I can see why you would want to sleep on your porch, at least until it gets really hot."

She nodded. "I opt for the air-conditioning as soon as summer sets in."

"Thanks for not being mad at my eating with your aunt and uncle. I went by for the work on my motorcycle, but they really insisted I stay."

"Don't be ridiculous. Why should that make me mad?" The moonlight cast odd shadows across his smiling face, making her chuckle. "All right, I've been a little testy around you, but like I said, it's not personal."

"Hostile is more like it. And it feels very personal to me."

Emalea paused. She'd never spent much time considering how she was making him feel. "I guess what I mean is it's not about you."

"Who is it about then?"

"I really don't think we need to get into all

that now." She might be giving herself room to be interested in Jackson but she wasn't ready to spill her life history right here on the creek bank. A cool breeze lifted her hair into her face, but before she could grab it herself, Jackson caught the wisps between his fingers and tucked them behind her ear.

"I've wanted to do that for a while now."

She pretended not to hear him; instead she concentrated on not noticing how his touch lingered on her cheek.

"You know, you don't have to tell me more than you're comfortable with. I'm not pushing for information, just trying to talk to you."

Emalea watched the wisteria swing back and forth. Comfortable? She didn't think she could be more comfortable with anyone, but it was an ugly story and when told it would probably leave him with a less-than-favorable opinion of her. Holding on to his respect, for at least a little longer, had somehow become important.

"I'm not sure how to say it. I guess I've just had really bad experiences with certain men and you have some of the same central traits."

"What exactly are central traits?"

She rubbed her hand along the wooden

seat. "They are things that influence an outsider's impression of a person, leading to assumptions of the presence of other traits. For instance, big, strong men with that bad-boy appeal. They tend to be overbearing and set on having things their own way."

He studied her face before he responded. "And you think I fall into that group?"

She shrugged, beginning to feel a bit guilty, but she didn't have reason to be, did she? "You do look the part."

"If you didn't make it all sound so negative, I'd say I was flattered, at least by the strong-man, bad-boy part. But you can't actually believe any of the rest of that describes me. You're generalizing."

"Like I said, you look the part." She didn't want to tell him how she'd been duped by that kind before. How she'd believed a man had been special only to find he could hurt her without a second thought.

He sighed. "Haven't you ever heard that appearances can be deceiving? It's a very old adage."

She smiled. "I'm having difficulty deciding what's the appearance part and what's the real you."

He twisted on the bench, closing the distance between them. "How do you mean?"

In the milky light, his eyes appeared dark with occasional glimmers. She wanted to look away, stare at the dirt under her feet, but she couldn't bring herself to break what felt like the beginning of a special connection between the two of them. "I guess I'm not sure if the real you is the nice guy you often seem to be, or the bad boy I see on the surface."

He buried his hand in her hair, grabbing a fistful, letting it drift through his fingers. Her mouth was dry but she couldn't seem to bring her coffee cup to her lips.

"Why can't I be a nice mixture of both? Everyone you meet in life is not going to fit into a prescribed slot."

"I don't expect everyone to. There are people who fall into the slot all by themselves. I don't put them there."

He leaned closer, his breath a whisper against her ear. "You're trying to put me there, but I promise, I'm not going to fit. If you keep hanging around me long enough you'll find that out." His hand covered hers and her fingers intertwined with his of their own accord. The air around her warmed with the heat of his body and he seemed to draw every breath with her. She was afraid he would kiss her, while at the same time dying for him to get on with it.

"I'd like that."

"What?" He seemed distracted as he fingered a strand of hair with his other hand, touching it to his lips.

"To hang around you enough to see the real you."

"I can make that happen, but I have to be honest, you're seeing the real me right now."

His lips touched her cheek, the side of her neck while her hand clung to his with desperation. Then he was gone, walking away from her. "I'll see you at the lake next weekend for SAR dive training, if I don't see you before."

He disappeared into the moonlit night and she didn't move until she heard his truck accelerating onto the highway. If Jackson Cooper was a mistake, she couldn't remember making one before that felt so right.

A STRONG SMELL OF CHEMICALS and cleaning fluid stung his nose. Jackson watched the lab technician hold the plastic bag up to the light and shake it slightly.

"It was crystal methamphetamine, just like we all figured."

He placed the bag into a box with several

other bagged items. Driving all the way to Baton Rouge to the state crime lab hadn't been necessary but he'd wanted to talk to lab personnel firsthand about the results they'd had on the evidence from the shooting. A bag of white powder had been discovered, sealed and completely dry, in the bag with the guns.

"So we're talking about someone who's selling drugs and guns?" He leaned over the counter to take one last look at the bag.

The lab tech shrugged. "Maybe they're trading guns for drugs. Who knows? You're in the middle of a big militia area. Anything's possible. I can run some more tests, but that won't help you trace where the crystal meth came from. It could be anywhere. There's huge operations making this stuff, as well as idiots cooking it up at home. We're talking over-the-counter sinus meds, fertilizer and good old battery acid. Stuff you can get any-where."

Jackson sighed and straightened.

"Sorry I couldn't be more help. Maybe they came up with something on the guns."

Taking his pad, he made a few notes then looked back at the tech. "Yeah, maybe so." He picked up the bag and shook it, staring at the off-white powder. "Battery acid, huh?

Amazing what people will willingly put in their bodies."

The lab technician opened another bag from a different box. "Not much surprises me anymore."

Two hours later, Jackson steered onto the highway toward Cypress Landing. The man in charge of ballistics hadn't been much help, either. None of the guns found in the bag had been used to shoot the guys at the river. No surprise there. Today he officially learned zero. But he felt like he was right on the edge of something and just couldn't quite see it. The whole thing smelled like DePaulo and he didn't like that scent at all.

For the second time this week, Emalea's day had been uncharacteristically quiet. When her two evening appointments canceled, she finished her paperwork and locked the tiny side street office. Afternoon sunlight glinted through her windshield and, before her driveway came into view, she knew exactly what she wanted to do.

Twenty minutes later, wearing a pair of faded jeans and an orange shirt, she pulled her motorcycle onto the highway. With the wind snapping her ponytail, the bike devoured the miles along the country roads.

Here she could feel freedom and hope for her future. Hope that she could find the piece of herself she had lost long ago.

After an hour, a rumbling in her stomach reminded her she hadn't eaten since breakfast and she steered the bike in the direction of Sal's. Going home to cook a meal this late in the evening wasn't exactly appealing, nor was the idea of sitting alone at her kitchen table. Not that solitary dining usually bothered her. She relished the tranquillity, the peace of mind it afforded. But lately, her serenity kept being interrupted by nagging thoughts of Jackson. Sal's was a good place to stop when you were by yourself but didn't want to feel like you were.

Atop a bar stool, Emalea sipped a soda, shouting an order to Mick, who was wiping the counter at the other end of the bar. A deep rumbling outside had her twisting to peer through the door.

Automatically her hand went to her head to make sure she had smoothed her hair after she'd gotten off her bike. Was it possible he had planted a homing device on her? For the second day in a row, Jackson Cooper appeared, seemingly out of thin air. Yesterday morning he'd arrived at her aunt's restaurant five minutes after she'd sat down.

They'd had breakfast together, which had pleased Aunt Alice immensely.

"I'm starting to think you're following me." She wiped drops of sweat off her glass as he slid onto a seat beside her.

"Nah, you're just lucky I've happened by the same places you chose to eat." Jackson waved at Mick, who seemed to know what he wanted and yelled back to the kitchen before filling a mug and setting it in front of him.

She glanced back and forth between the two of them. "Come here a lot, do you? Or let me guess, Mick is lucky enough to be able to read your mind."

"I have to admit I'm a frequent customer. Don't get me wrong, I can cook, but remember, I'm still getting used to all this peace and quiet. Occasionally, it's just a little *too* quiet at my house."

By the time Mick brought them their food and they had managed to eat most of it, Emalea was having a hard time convincing herself that Jackson was remotely like any other man she'd known. Funny, charming and undeniably gorgeous, he put her at ease rather than making her nervous to distraction.

"You two gonna ride some more before it gets dark?"

Emalea glanced at the bartender as he took her plate. "I don't know, Mick. I haven't even considered it."

"You need to take Jackson to the Bluffs. I bet he ain't been there yet."

Jackson leaned against the bar, but Emalea focused on the second button on Mick's shirt. The Bluffs, not really a place she was interested in going with Jackson in tow. Her throat tightened. "I don't know, Mick. It's kind of far and I doubt if he's interested in a bunch of washed-out dirt."

"It's only eight miles from here, Doc."

"Yeah, Doc, and I'd like to see these bluffs." Jackson leaned closer but she continued to ignore him. Mick's mood was evident from the way the second button on his shirt jiggled up and down. But she still couldn't manage to look him in the face. If she looked at either one of them, they'd see her fear. Deep concentration was required to get her fists unclenched. With that accomplished, she wiped her palms on her jeans. How hard could it be?

Dropping money on the bar, she got to her feet. "I guess we're going to the Bluffs."

Jackson gave a little whoop, as though

she'd said they were going on a Caribbean cruise, before following her to their bikes.

THE BLUFFS SOUNDED like an unthreatening place but, judging by the rigid set of Emalea's jaw, Jackson was beginning to believe they might have to do time in purgatory to get there. At the first turn he'd almost shouted to tell her to forget it, but she had shot ahead and he decided to keep going. The woman was hard to get close to, and he wasn't even sure that was what he wanted, except when he was with her. Then he came alive again. A certain amount of risk was involved, especially for his heart. But he hadn't reached the point where he felt he was risking too much, not yet.

Emalea dropped behind him and, before he realized it, she had stopped completely. He glanced back then made a slow turn. Pulling alongside her, he killed the engine and the sound of frogs, crickets and birds filled the air. They were at the end of an overgrown driveway. Grass and weeds had long ago covered all but a few spots of gravel. Through the thicket, he spotted a house nearly obliterated by tree limbs and vines. A porch ran the length of the front and wrapped around one side, but it had rotted and collapsed in several places. Across the roof, a tree limb rested. The hole it had made was clearly visible.

Emalea's hand covered her mouth, and Jackson held his breath for a moment as he noticed the slightest trembling of her fingers. He took her other hand in his and held it. For a few moments she was unaware of him, lost again.

"This is where I lived."

The statement was made without a quiver in her voice. Unsure how to respond or even if he should, Jackson remained quiet. He only knew her mother had died in an accident and her father "hadn't been around." Having dealt with death more closely than he wished, he didn't want to press her. At times, words had a way of bringing ghosts to life, but sometimes talking was the only way to put them to rest.

She turned to him at last with an uncharacteristic sneer. "The place hasn't changed much." With a shrug, she reached toward the start button on her handlebar. He continued to hold her other hand and she paused. "You could say I come from meager beginnings."

"That doesn't mean much to me. From where I'm standing you've done well."

"You couldn't imagine how well."

"So tell me."

She shook her head. "I don't think I have the energy for it." She glanced at the old house again. "Besides, some things are just better left in the woods."

He let go of her hand. Her motorcycle roared to life and she spewed rocks into the weeds in her eagerness to get going.

Within minutes they rounded a curve and the river came into view. They bumped along a dirt road before stopping in an open area where the grass had been worn away from the cars that had parked here. Live oak trees spread their branches wide and several, unable to support their own weight, had wooden braces placed under them to keep the heavy limbs from breaking off. At the river's edge, the clay-rich earth dropped away below their feet. The setting sun sent streaks of pink, yellow and red onto the bank leading to the muddy water below.

"This is spectacular." Jackson found the white cliffs rising from the brown depths to be like a ray of light.

"Yeah, it's hard to describe. You have to see it. We're lucky to be here just as the sun is setting. That's the best time. The colors really come alive. I used to come here when I needed to be alone. It wasn't a bad walk from my house. There was a path." She shaded her eyes from the glare of the sun sinking low on the horizon and pointed to a tree farther up the bank. "I'd climb into that tree and sit for hours. Often, I'd bring a book to read. I couldn't tell you how many sunsets I've seen from that tree."

"Your parents didn't mind you being here by yourself after dark?"

She laughed, a brittle and unhappy sound. "It wasn't your average household. There was a lot more to worry about than whether or not I was home by dark."

For a moment, he thought she shivered as she moved closer toward the rail that had been placed at the edge. No more information would be forthcoming. He could see the wall she'd erected to keep that part of her life private. Stepping behind her, he slipped his arms around her waist, pulling her against his chest. His chin fit nicely on top of her head.

She was stiff against him, and he moved his mouth near her ear. "Relax, I'm not going to throw you over."

The tenseness leaked from her muscles. He held his breath as quietly, slowly her body eased against his. If it were possible, he'd freeze this moment. Her hands rested on top of his, which were still clasped at her waist. He loosened his grip to weave his fingers with hers. Her back pressed closer into him, her bottom fitting tightly against his hardness. Exactly when he'd become so aroused he wasn't sure. Was it when he'd put his arms around her? No, it had been before that. It might have been at Sal's. He was beginning to think he couldn't remember a time since he'd met her that he didn't want her.

From behind him a horn honked. He turned to see three cars loaded with teenagers stopping near their motorcycles. He groaned and Emalea sighed audibly, before stepping away from him.

"We better go. I'll see you at the meeting Thursday and we can finish planning that training program for Saturday."

He nodded and possibly said yes. He wasn't sure if he'd spoken because his mind was busy debating if he should ask her to his house or invite himself to hers. He matched her stride, trying to read her expression. He couldn't—continue this tonight, that is. Reading her expression had been a breeze. It said, "See you later," in really big letters.

He knew he should leave whatever brewed between them alone. If he got closer to her, he'd be responsible for her and he didn't need to be responsible for anyone ever again. He'd proven himself as a failure in that department. With Emalea, he almost felt invincible again. He craved that feeling even though he knew he'd never truly been invincible. Not once.

CHAPTER EIGHT

KENT USUALLY WENT STRAIGHT home on Tuesday or at least to his dad's shop to help. On this particular Tuesday, Mrs. Wright, who taught art part-time at the schools and owned her own art-supply store, Picture Perfect, had asked him to help do odd jobs after school. She would pay him, which had kept his father from complaining when he'd called from school to say he'd be late coming home.

He'd unloaded boxes in Mrs. Wright's storeroom and rearranged several shelves, all with Megan Johnson's help, which made him feel like he was getting paid twice. Right now, on the sidewalk, cleaning the front display-case glass with Megan a few feet away, he almost felt like he'd won a prize.

He heard footsteps approaching and he stiffened. Trouble was coming. He could feel it.

"Megan, what is this backwoods redneck doing here? Is he bothering you?"

Kent took a deep breath, hating Gary Johnson, even if he was Megan's cousin.

"Stop it, Gary! Kent is working for Mrs. Cecile today, so why don't you go away?"

"Why doesn't he tell me to go away?"

Kent tightened his grip on the rag he'd been using to clean the glass. "Save it for another time, Gary. Mrs. Cecile wouldn't want trouble at her shop and she's the sheriff's wife."

Mentioning the sheriff put a damper on Gary's fun, but only briefly. Kent didn't see the punch coming, but it was poorly aimed and glanced off his shoulder, sending him slamming against the glass, which, thankfully, remained intact.

He'd never wanted to hit anyone so much in his life, except his father. It wasn't that he couldn't fight—his dad made sure he knew how to use his fists. But for Kent, hitting people was a last resort. Doing so on the street in the middle of the afternoon was unacceptable. Instead, he stood his ground and Megan stepped between them.

"Go home, Gary. If you want to hit someone, you'll have to hit me."

"You wait till I tell your dad what kind of trash you're hanging around with, then we'll see who gets in trouble."

If Kent had thought this situation bad, worse arrived just when he believed the incident might be over. Appearing as if from nowhere, his two cousins, Randy and Dennis, shouldered their way into the scene.

"Gary, I know you're not over here picking on Kent again after we told you not to." Dennis stood an inch closer to Gary than was polite.

The two boys were tall and lanky, but everyone knew their reputation. They were both two grades behind in school and could care less. They'd likely quit as soon as their mothers stopped holding on to the slim hope that they would turn out better than their fathers. A part of him appreciated their taking up for him, but mostly he wished they'd just go away.

Randy shoved Gary into Dennis and Gary raised his fist. Kent frowned, seeing that violence and stupidity were not confined to poor white trash.

"Randy, Dennis, you guys give it a rest. We don't need this trouble right here on Main Street." Kent might as well have been talking to the sidewalk because his two cousins completely ignored him.

A short bark of squealing tires stopped the three boys poised to fight. A sheriff's car had spun neatly into an empty spot right in front of them. Sheriff Wright himself stepped from behind the wheel and a man Kent had never seen before climbed from the passenger side.

"What's going on here, men?" The sheriff crossed his arms in front of his chest but all the boys cringed when the other man stepped onto the sidewalk. There'd be no arguing with him. The man looked like a Mack truck.

A lot of *nothing*s were mumbled and Randy kept his gaze on the ground. With two visits to juvenile court already, he didn't need a third. A bell tinkled as Cecile Wright pushed through the shop door.

"This boy," she pointed to Gary, "came along and started bothering my employees."

"I just wanted to visit my cousin Megan."

Cecile Wright frowned. "Visit with her when she gets home. Right now she and Kent are supposed to be working for me and I don't want people, cousin or not, coming along bothering them."

Gary hung his head. "Yes, ma'am."

The sheriff narrowed his eyes. "Okay, you guys, go home. I don't want y'all taking this fight elsewhere. If there's more trouble, Mr. Cooper and I will find you, and we won't be in a good mood. I have to tell you, when Mr. Cooper's not in a good mood, it's really bad."

The man appeared ready and willing to break them all into bite-size morsels. The other boys slunk away while Kent focused his attention on a crack in the concrete.

"I'm sorry, Mrs. Cecile. It's all my fault."

"Don't be ridiculous, Kent. I watched the whole thing from inside. Gary wanted to cause trouble. I called the sheriff's office right after he came."

"He never would have stopped if I hadn't been here. Maybe you should get another kid to help you. It might be less trouble for you."

Mrs. Wright gripped his arm, forcing him to look at her. "Kent, I've never been one to worry much over trouble. I want you to work for me every Tuesday."

Kent smiled with relief. "I'd like that."

"Good enough. Now you and Megan go get things ready to close. If we have more problems, I bet Mr. Cooper here can take care of them, don't you think so?"

"Yes, ma'am. I believe he could take care of several at one time."

The big man laughed, and he didn't seem nearly so bad. Kent left with Megan following him, glad that he'd stayed on the right side of the law. He wanted to keep it that way. Maybe he could even be a deputy when he got older.

TAKING A BITE of her chicken-salad sandwich, Emalea listened to Lana reprimand a second grader who had just tossed a roll across the aisle. The elementary cafeteria was not her first choice for lunch, but if she wanted to eat with Lana this was the only place they could do so with school in session.

"Will summer break ever get here?" Lana groaned.

Emalea smiled, admiring her friend's patience. This many kids in one room would send her screaming out the door but Lana seemed to handle it all very well.

"So, have you made plans this weekend with a very large and handsome man we both know?"

Washing her sandwich down with a swig from her bottled water, Emalea tried to remain calm. "Lana, you know I have that training exercise at the lake for new volunteer search-and-rescue divers."

Her friend chewed at her own lunch without speaking and Emalea hoped that there would be no more discussion of Jackson Cooper. But of course Lana had to gnaw that particular bone to death.

"Do you mean to tell me that the sheriff department's SAR coordinator is not even going to ride by and see how things are going and at least make sure you're not drowning one of your students?"

Lana would get to the truth sooner or later on her own, but Emalea still squirmed on the little plastic stool for a few seconds.

"Actually, we've got so many volunteers that he's going to help with the training."

"Woohoo…" A few little heads turned to see what had their teacher shouting.

"Stop it, Lana. It's just work."

"Yeah, that's the kind of job I'd love to have. So tell me, are you going to give this guy a break or what? From everything I've seen, he's a dream."

Emalea's first reaction would be to say Jackson Cooper was more like a nightmare, but it wasn't true. She still felt like she couldn't figure him out and, with her training, she should be able to put the guy in a box and label it. Historically, that kind of problem had often meant trouble for her. She had liked men before and read them completely wrong because of it.

"I wouldn't go that far," she finally responded. Emalea didn't want to admit that she did indeed think Jackson could be dream material, not even to herself.

JACKSON DREW CIRCLES on his notepad as he held the phone to his ear, waiting for Rick Martel to pick up. He'd called his old partner as soon as he'd gotten back from New Orleans. Someone there needed to know DePaulo had surfaced down south. But Rick had been out of town on a case, and Jackson had decided to hold onto the information until his friend returned. The phone clicked on the other end.

"This is Martel."

"Rick, it's Jackson."

"Hey, man, how are things down on the bayou?"

Jackson smiled. Rick, a full-blown city boy, had been horrified at the idea of Jackson moving to someplace as remote as Cypress Landing.

"Actually, things are really good here." A bit of a stretch, but… "I was in New Orleans the other day and you're not going to believe this, but DePaulo was there. He crossed the street right in front of me."

On the other end, Rick was silent for what felt like several minutes. "Did he see you?"

"Oh yeah, he saw me. If his hand would have been a gun he'd have shot me."

Jackson heard Rick's sigh through the phone.

"Tell me you didn't harass him or, worse, try to beat him up."

"Of course not. I told you that's behind me. I was a little crazy for a while, but I…"

Jackson paused and ran the last few minutes of their conversation through his mind. "You knew, didn't you? You knew he was here and didn't tell me."

"Look, Jackson, nobody needed you down there following him and causing trouble again. New Orleans is a big city and far enough away from Cypress Landing, I figured you weren't likely to run into the guy."

"You figured wrong. What's he doing here?" He had to wait patiently as Rick obviously debated whether or not to give him information. He heard his friend's resigned grunt.

"I guess I might as well tell you, or you'll go down there and try to beat an answer out of him. After he skimmed money from his uncle, the old man wasn't going to bring DePaulo back to Chicago and let him sell guns. From what we've gathered so far, it looks like he's down there helping with the purchases of guns to send north. Notice I said helping. I don't think his uncle was willing to let him handle much money. But you stay away from him. The New Orleans office has an eye on what's happening down there."

Jackson shook his head as if Rick could see him. "I'm not going to New Orleans, but I might not have to." He filled Rick in on the guns and the two dead bodies. He could imagine Rick scrambling to take notes and dragging his fingers through his hair.

"I'll check into this on my end, but you stay away from DePaulo. He won't appreciate you causing trouble for him, again. Personally I think he's going to try and build his own little gang and maybe challenge his uncle for a chunk of the business. I believe that's why he risked skimming that money, to make his own working cash. If he thinks you're going to get in the way of that he'll be more than happy to get rid of you."

Jackson stared at his notepad, now covered with marks. He wrote DePaulo's name in the bit of white space left then roughly scratched it out, tearing the paper. "I came here to start my life over, Rick. I'm not looking for trouble, but I'll deal with it if it comes looking for me."

Jackson dropped the phone onto the desk

after he'd said goodbye. He hadn't lied. He wouldn't go after DePaulo, not like he'd done back in Chicago. But DePaulo had better stay out of Cypress Landing because this time Jackson would make sure he didn't get off so easy.

"GUESS YOU HEARD what happened yesterday in front of Mrs. Wright's store." Kent fiddled with the frayed armrest cover on the ancient chair in the counselor's office.

"No, I haven't heard a word." Emalea leaned back in her own equally threadbare chair.

"I figured you being friends with Mrs. Wright and all, she'd tell you."

"Kent, I may be friends with Cecile Wright but neither she nor anyone else except the school counselor knows you're a client of mine. It's confidential and I would never tell unless it was necessary for your safety. So, do you want to tell me what happened?"

Kent shrugged while Emalea waited patiently for the story to come.

When the boy finished retelling the incident, he rested his elbows on his knees. She chewed her lip wondering how deep to dig, right now. "Why didn't you hit Gary back, Kent?"

"It would have been disrespectful to Mrs. Wright. Besides it's not right to be fighting in the middle of town like that."

She wondered how he'd come to that conclusion when his cousins seemed more than happy to break into a fight anywhere, but she had begun to learn that Kent didn't really fit in with his cousins. "You know, Kent, not many guys would have worried that they would be disrespectful for being in a fight if another person threw the first punch."

The boy leaned back and crossed his arms tightly over his chest. "My dad says I'm a chickensh— Well I won't repeat it, but it's not nice. I've had to fight a few times. I'm pretty good at it, but I don't like to hit people. I've seen enough of that to last the rest of my life and I hope..." His voice trailed off as if he realized what he was saying and who he was saying it to.

"Would you like to talk about that?"

"About what?"

"Seeing people get hit." Emalea's stomach quivered slightly as it always did when she had to question a child about abuse. She had hoped she'd been reading too much of her own past into Kent's situation, but now she knew he was very likely living the same nightmare she had suffered.

"If I talk to you, there'll only be more trouble for me."

"How's that?" Honestly, the answer hadn't been a surprise. She could remember feeling the same way, but she wanted to get him to express what he was feeling, in hopes that he might survive the whole thing with fewer scars. He grasped the arms of the chair, his fingers clutching as if holding on for life.

"I won't repeat what you say to me."

"Unless it's to keep me safe, that's what you said." The words came from between tightly pinched lips. "You might think if you told, you'd be helping keep me and my mom safe, but it wouldn't. You can't make life safe for us."

If Emalea could have taken him home with her that instant she would have. She'd even have picked up his mother and carried her away, too. His mother's mindset, which kept her with this man—and kept Kent imprisoned with her—could not be changed in an instant. Sometimes it could never be changed. That kind of emotional connection with an abuser was a survival strategy for a victim.

"Are you afraid for your life, Kent?"

His shimmering eyes met hers. "I'm more

afraid for my mom. For me, I'm mostly afraid I'll end up being just like my dad."

Emalea wanted to make him see that another life waited for him. If he could realize that, see that it was just within his grasp, maybe he'd have a chance. "Is there one thing you can think of that would make your life safe, Kent?"

He stared past her shoulder for so long Emalea thought he might not have heard the question. At last his eyes met hers.

"Only if my dad was dead, but I guess you wouldn't ever understand that."

"You're wrong, Kent. I understand exactly."

Ms. LeBlanc left her chair to stand by the window. He watched her, unsure what to say. "I…I guess you're not supposed to tell me stuff about yourself."

She lifted one slat of a blind and peeked outside. After a minute, she turned to lean against the wall, watching him with narrowed eyes.

"How much time have you got?"

He shrugged. "I'm good for a while longer."

She moved to her chair, resting her elbows on the armrests and leaning her head back. "Get comfortable, Kent, because this won't be pretty."

He almost told her he didn't want to know. His one help in this whole mess sat in front of him, ready to tell him things he'd been afraid to reveal about himself.

Wriggling in his chair, he stayed focused on the bright green eyes across from him, then gave a slight smile. "Okay. Shoot."

EMALEA USED LAKE SEWELL to do dive training because the water was clearer than most other lakes in the area and a large section had been reserved exclusively for swimmers and divers. Her truck sat on the knoll just above the edge of the lake, along with a row of other vehicles, including Jackson's. The group of new volunteers numbered eight. Normally she only trained two or three at a time, so she had been especially appreciative of Jackson's offer to help. She really hadn't been looking forward to dividing the group and using two separate Saturdays.

As the volunteers listened to her give her usual spiel on search-and-rescue diving, Jackson stayed in the back, appearing more than willing to let her run the show.

"You four go with Mr. Cooper." She pointed to four divers on her right. She thought the lone woman in that group might even squeal with joy at being placed under

Jackson's care. The other woman, left with her, wrinkled her brow in apparent protest. Jackson wore an unzipped yellow neoprene vest, revealing much of his impressive body, so she could understand where the two women were coming from. She was having a little difficulty concentrating, too. The vest flapped open, and she saw the flash of a nipple. Her breath caught in her throat and, before she could stop herself, she'd taken a step toward him. With effort, she spun around so she wouldn't have to look directly at him, at least until she could manage a moderate amount of control.

Jackson, completely oblivious to whatever effects he might be having on the women, simply pulled his hands from the pockets of his swim shorts and began prepping his dive gear. Everyone had to pair up with a dive buddy in their group to check each other's gear. When the short blonde sidled up to Jackson, he explained that he and Emalea would be going over their equipment together, just to keep the buddies even among each group. She pouted openly, making Emalea wish for a quick and painless end to this particular training session. Next time there would be no gorgeous, sexy men allowed.

Still wearing shorts and a T-shirt over her swimsuit, Emalea carried her bag next to Jackson's and began attaching her BC jacket and the regulator she would breathe through to the air tank. When the task was completed, she peeled her shorts off, leaving her long T-shirt covering her to mid-thigh. She stepped into her neoprene wet suit, nearly working up a sweat getting the thing to her waist.

"Planning on a drop in temperature?"

She didn't bother to look at him. "The lake is still cool to me this time of year." She spoke while pulling her arms from the sleeves of her shirt. She slipped the wet suit onto her upper body, forcing her arms through the tight sleeves.

When she finished zipping the wet suit up to her neck, she pulled the T-shirt over her head and noticed Jackson staring at her. "What?"

"I don't think I've ever seen a man or woman put a wet suit on and reveal so little skin."

She tossed her T-shirt on top of her bag. "It's a special talent."

He ran a finger down the arm of the gray and black wet suit. "Next time, give a guy a break and don't try so hard. It could easily make my day."

She knew she really couldn't feel through the thick neoprene, but it seemed as if his finger were actually on her skin. She needed a diversion, so he wouldn't see how his touch affected her. A few feet away she spotted one.

Emalea nodded her head to the left where the woman she had assigned to his group had shucked her clothes to reveal a barely there bikini. "Now there's something to make your day."

He sighed. "That'll make my day a pain in the neck. I'll bet you gave her to me on purpose."

"I didn't, but I'm glad she's in your group. If she hadn't been, she might have tried to drown me later for shortchanging her. You could zip that vest up. It would help the situation tremendously."

He rubbed his palm across his bare chest. "Emalea, are you admitting to eyeing my exposed chest?"

"No, I'm saying your little groupie over there is excited because of it."

"Are you sure you're not hoping to see a little more of me?"

She tried to concentrate on setting up her dive gear but he expected a reply. Finally looking up from her equipment, she did her best to frown at him. "No, I'm not trying to see more of you. Right now I'm busy."

"Later?"

His flirting should have made her uncomfortable, but instead she wanted more. He continued to show her he was nothing like she had expected, which made her want to push the limits of their friendship.

"Hmm. I think I would be interested, later."

Fingers closed around her upper arm. "Emalea, I might take you up on that."

"We'll see. But first you have to deal with your little group over there."

Jackson groaned. "I'm only doing this because it's you."

"Yeah, well we're only having this problem because it's you."

A few minutes later, she smiled, watching Jackson pry himself loose from the girl so he could get his group started. She turned to her own trainees and began her instructions. Her group waded into the cool water while, on the bank, Jackson manipulated the blonde's gear trying to get it placed correctly; the three guys with him fell all over themselves hoping to lend a helping hand.

EMALEA HAD JUST FINISHED stowing her dive bag in the back of her truck when Jackson and his four volunteers waded onto the bank for the last time. He yanked his BC jacket loose with the tank still strapped on and dropped the whole contraption in the grass. The fins and mask landed on top of the pile. On his way up the hill, he unzipped the rather tight vest. His expression, though priceless, reminded her of a thundercloud.

He put one hand on the tailgate of her truck. "Do *not*, under any circumstances leave me here alone."

"Afraid of the sharks, Jackson?"

"I've been known as a patient man but, honestly, I can't take much more."

"Jackson!" They both turned in the direction of the female voice.

Emalea snorted. "Your fan club is calling."

He pointed a finger at her. "You heard what I said. Don't leave."

"All right, all right, I'll be over there." She motioned toward the lake. "Maybe I can enjoy a little sunshine and you can finish whatever it is you still have to do."

Spinning on his heel, he strode away, the neoprene booties on his feet making squishing sounds. She almost felt sorry for him, almost. Grabbing a blanket from behind the seat, she found a spot near the lake's edge and tossed her T-shirt and shorts aside. On her back, staring at the blue sky, she couldn't get rid of the smile that kept forming. The busy class had left her tired so she shoved the hem of her silver-gray tankini top under her breasts to sun her stomach. In a matter of minutes she dozed off.

Emalea sat up with a jerk, her hand bumping against Jackson, who sprawled beside her. She didn't know how long she'd been asleep and she didn't remember him lying down on the blanket.

"Is she still here?" Jackson's eyes remained closed and Emalea scanned the grassy area only to see skimpy-bikini girl stretched provocatively on a blanket several yards away.

"Yes, she is. Poor thing's all alone."

"If she is, it's her own choice. Every one of those guys would have paid to stay with her the rest of the evening."

"I believe she had her hook baited for another fish."

His eyes opened and his hand closed around her wrist. "That's too bad because this fish is otherwise occupied. That," he continued as he fingered the hem of her bathing suit top, "is a sexy bathing suit."

"Oh please, how can you say that after having a string bikini in front of you all afternoon?

"Because this is sleek and sexy as opposed to nonexistent." His finger trailed farther down, stopping when his forefinger touched her navel ring. "And this is the thing that would drive a man over the edge."

"A holdover from when I lived in New Orleans. By the way, I think you've made your point, she's leaving."

He continued stroking the silver ring. "Who's leaving?"

"Get real. You know I mean the woman in the little bathing suit."

"I only know what I've been doing and saying has had nothing to do with her and everything to do with you." He rolled onto one elbow, pulling her down beside him.

"What are you trying to do, Jackson?" She feigned an attempt at struggling before she dropped to her side.

"I'm not really sure myself, but I'll keep going until it starts to feel wrong or you say stop."

"Remember we're in a public place." Her imagination played several scenarios of what could happen when they were this close. Things that would likely have gotten Emalea and Jackson arrested if they'd occurred right here.

"I wasn't planning anything that couldn't

be done in public, but if you have other ideas maybe we should consider them."

She tried to decide whether or not Jackson was serious while he rolled up a damp towel for a makeshift pillow and lay face-to-face with her, neither one speaking, bodies only inches apart. Putting away her doubts and misconceptions had been like releasing the floodgates on a dam. For once, she was with a man she was really attracted to and she wasn't afraid.

"Your hair's never going to get dry like that." His sun-warmed skin grazed her arm, as he leaned over her to ease the elastic band from her hair.

She touched a scar at the top of his shoulder.

"What happened?"

"A very uncooperative suspect tried to keep me from arresting him."

"Did he?"

"Stop me with a knife? You've got to be kidding. He managed to cut me just before I took it from him."

Emalea laughed. "Don't think you've escaped to safety down here in small townsville. It's generally quiet but occasionally things get rough and rowdy. And our criminals carry really big knives."

He smiled. "I'll try to be prepared when I make an arrest. Do you consider the recent shootings 'rough and rowdy'?"

She shook her head slightly against the towel, causing a few wet strands of hair to fall across her face. She swept them back, while trying to recall if anything like that had happened in Cypress Landing before. Crimes had occurred, but dead bodies full of bullet holes had never turned up in the river. "No, shootings are unheard of here."

He sighed. "Well, I hope this is the end. I came here to get away from all that."

Emalea studied his profile. He didn't seem to be the kind of man to be bothered by shootings, but then he had left the FBI for this little country town. "I'm glad. That you came here, that is."

She rested her hand on top of his. Turning his hand over, he brought hers to his lips. Fascinated, Emalea could only watch him kiss the palm of her hand. She couldn't recall a man kissing her hand like that, ever.

"If this is a little more than you bargained for when you said you'd take a chance on getting to know me, then say so. I won't mind backing off a bit." He brought her hand to his lips once more. "That's not true. I will mind, but I'll do it, if it's what you want."

She wasn't sure what she wanted. Well, that wasn't exactly true. She could want a lot of things, but they might not be very good for her. "I don't think I had particular expectations, although it's strange how we went from determined to avoid each other to this."

"I thought you were the psychologist here. Surely you can figure that out."

"I guess I'm not very good at analyzing myself." She could have given him the long version of how her ability to help people see their mistakes did not extend to herself, but the story would be much too difficult.

"Here, lie on my couch and I'll do it for you." Before she could argue, he pushed her onto her back and sat up, pretending to a hold a pen and notepad. "Now, Ms. LeBlanc, let me tell you what's happening here. Two people meet and are immediately interested in each other."

"Immediately?" She smothered a laugh at what she deemed a great exaggeration on his part.

"That's what I said, and I'm doing the analyzing here." Pausing, he pretended to write notes on his nonexistent notepad. "There's a connection between them, but they both have a lot of…" He stopped again and appeared to be searching for just the right words.

"Emotional baggage," she suggested.

He frowned. "More like personal junk, in their past. So they think life will be much easier if they stay away from each other, which is very frustrating because there's a voice inside each of them that keeps saying they belong together."

Emalea sat up, her gaze locked on his. "But what made them change their minds and listen to that voice?"

"Maybe they figured there's more important things than an easy life."

"Like what?" she whispered.

"Like a good one." He cupped his hand around her cheek, and she leaned toward him.

The screeching noise that split the air made them both leap to their knees. Emalea twisted her head in all directions trying to locate the source.

Jackson, busy digging in his bag, finally held up the offender. "My pager, I guess I'll have to go. I'm sorry, Emalea, this was really bad timing."

She shrugged, smiling. "I would say that's part of your job, huh?"

"One of my least favorite parts. Maybe I

could call you tonight. We could go to dinner or take an afternoon ride on the bikes tomorrow."

She nodded. "Call me if you get through early, but I've got to drive to New Orleans in the morning to catch a plane to a conference I'm attending in Orlando. I'll be gone until Wednesday."

"You're kidding, right?"

"Nope, I've had this booked for three months. But maybe you should go with me and demonstrate your analyzing."

"Nah, I think it will only work on us."

He watched her for a moment longer, his brown eyes unblinking. Then he bent toward her in a rush, brushing his lips across her forehead.

"I'll call you." He gathered his gear and trotted up the hill to his truck.

She waved and slowly leaned back on the towel, letting go a long breath. When she'd decided to take a chance on getting to know Jackson, she hadn't exactly expected it to go this far. Friends, that was what she'd imagined they would become. But after this, it was evident that much more than friendship brewed between them.

He made it so easy to like him, even though she wasn't really sure she wanted to get involved with a man like him. What if the whole thing ended up in a thousand pieces like china on a brick floor? Of course, she didn't have any china or even a brick floor. So maybe she could afford the risk.

CHAPTER NINE

THE PAIR OF KHAKI SHORTS had green trim that matched her emerald-green henley T-shirt. Satisfied with her appearance, she flipped off the light and left her bedroom. She'd only been home from her trip for a few minutes when Jackson had called to say he was coming by to bring her a present. The skirt and white blouse she'd almost worn were lying on her bed. She'd opted for an outfit she thought was more of a friendly "hello" than one that screamed, "Honey, I'm home." This thing between them could go from good friends to completely downhill or to an unknown point in between, so it was best to play safely for a while.

A knock on the door sent her racing to the living room where she forced herself to slow down. She threw open the door, unable to keep the smile from nearly splitting her face, then she froze.

"What is that?" Emalea didn't even bother

to try and stop her upper lip from grimacing, her smile long gone.

"Why don't you just say, 'Eww, a cat.'" Jackson shifted the ragged creature in his hands and drew his brows together, appearing more than a little disappointed. "It's a kitten. You know, cute, furry animals that purr and love for you to pet them." He shrugged his shoulders. "I thought you might like to have her for company, since you're out here by yourself."

She bit her lower lip, her distaste beginning to fade. So what if she hadn't had a cat since…well, in a really long time. It was a nice gesture on his part, and he didn't know about the other cat. She reached to pet the soft white coat splotched with a black-and-orange patchwork.

In a flash, razor-sharp teeth were bared and a splotchy paw swiped the air.

"What the—" Emalea jerked her hand back and Jackson bent, loosing the little hellion into her living room.

"What are you doing?"

"She's just scared. She'll come around in a minute. I have everything you might need for her in my truck." He tilted his head to one side, squinting at her. "Haven't you ever had a cat before?"

Emalea didn't know if she wanted to bring that particular memory into the open. She blinked once, twice, and squeezed her eyelids shut.

A rough finger thumbed her chin. "I didn't mean to upset you. I can take the kitten back."

Her hair fell into her face as she shook her head. Jackson brushed it behind her ear.

"No, I think I might like the kitten." Her breath caught in her throat as she opened her eyes.

He grinned. "Good. You know I picked her because she kind of reminded me of you, with all the hissing and spitting."

"Ouch. I guess I deserve that. At least you didn't say she looks like me because she's a little on the ugly side."

He didn't laugh or respond immediately. When he did, he'd steered the conversation back to the place she'd wanted to avoid. "You know, Emalea, if you'll invite me in, I'd like to hear you tell me what just happened. You don't have to, but I'm here."

She moved to let him in. "Sorry. I didn't mean to keep you standing on the doorstep. I was just a little shocked."

"If that's what you want to call it."

Shutting the door behind him, she wrapped

her arms around herself. "I'd really rather not get into it right now. I need you to help me in the kitchen."

He stood watching her. "Later, we'll talk."

"Later." She nodded, frowning.

"Lead me to the kitchen then—I'm quite a chef. What are we cooking?"

"Corn-and-crab bisque."

"I don't know that I've ever eaten that."

"You'll love it, come on."

JACKSON HAD TO ADMIT Emalea had been right when she'd said he'd love the corn-and-crab bisque. With the salad and really crusty French bread, it might have been the best meal he'd had in years. Either that or the company was the best he'd had in years. After that night on the creek bank when they'd agreed to quit disagreeing, he'd expected they might have a few friendly conversations. The thought of a full-blown affair had never entered his mind. Well maybe it had entered his mind but he hadn't expected it to happen.

It wasn't a real affair, not yet, but a part of him warmed to the idea. If his beeper hadn't gone off the other day, he didn't know what would have happened. He might have kissed her, and not just a little peck on the forehead, either. He'd definitely wanted to.

The last day or two had given him time to get a better perspective on things. He couldn't rush into this. Though his desire might try to run rampant, he would keep it in check. He went into her living room, dropping onto the middle of an overstuffed sage-green sofa. The kitten, curled in a nearby chair, ignored them. Emalea took a spot next to him. Using the remote to flip on the television, he set the volume to a dull roar.

She leaned forward slightly when he stretched his arm along the back of the sofa behind her neck. "Do you want to tell me why you had that look of horror at the idea of my giving you a kitten?"

A worn spot on the sofa attracted her attention, and she avoided meeting his gaze. Worry raced through him at the thought he might hear something he'd really rather not know. He shook off the feeling. They were going to be friends, which meant talking to her about the parts of her past still haunting her.

"I had—" she stopped to wet her lips before continuing "—a bad experience with a kitten, when I was younger."

His hand, drawn as if by a magnet to her hair, lifted a few strands, letting them trickle between his fingers.

"What kind of experience?"

"Jackson, I doubt you really want to know all this. I left that life behind years ago."

"I'd like to know why you reacted the way you did to the cat first, then maybe we can go from there."

She sighed. "In the end, it's all one story. My dad was not a good guy. He had a cruel streak, and he didn't mind taking out his frustration on anyone or anything. My aunt gave me a kitten once. It was standing at the back door meowing when my dad came home, drunk as usual. I tried to get there before him, to get the kitten before he heard her." She pressed her fingertips to her forehead. "Too late, I was too late. He threw the kitten against the wall of the house and killed it." She swallowed hard before continuing. "I tried to help it, wrapped it in a towel, prayed over it, but nothing helped. I never wanted to have a pet again. I couldn't protect them from him."

Jackson's hand stilled, with strands of Emalea's hair floating against his palm. He was an expert on not being able to protect the ones he loved. Maybe his intuition had been right. This story would likely be much more than he'd expected.

In one smooth motion, she got to her feet

only to kneel on the floor in front of the kitten. She stroked the sleeping animal, and he reminded himself to breath in and out. Watching her, hearing the words, had sucked the air from his lungs. As if they were caught in a vacuum, sealing them off from the world outside. To describe Emalea as tortured would have been like saying it was warm at noon in the middle of the desert. No words described her pain, but he knew what that kind of loss, that kind of helplessness could be like. His gut tightened and he would have gone to her, held her, but the horror he'd seen in her eyes kept him still. Unfortunately, he could tell more would be coming. Her nightmare hadn't ended with the kitten.

After a minute of silence, she continued, and Jackson had to lean forward to hear her. "My father hit us, me and my mom, all the time, but she always stayed with him. The last time she stayed so I could get away. He had fists like hammers, and he'd slam them into you over and over. If you fell, he'd start kicking you. One evening he was especially crazy, asking my mother where she'd been, always thinking she was seeing another man or hiding money from him, or planning to leave. She'd never been guilty of those things, even though I'd wished a million times she'd leave him. I tried to grab his arm, to make him stop hitting her, so he came after me and I ran into the yard. My mother came out behind us, yelling for me to run away. Just as he caught me, she grabbed him. I made it into the trees, and he started hitting her again. From the woods I could see her face, her eyes. She was on the ground, her mouth still moving, telling me to run, even though she made no sound." She gripped the edge of the chair until her knuckles shone white. "So I did. I ran all the way to Cypress Landing. Eight miles through the woods."

"Why didn't you go to a neighbor's house?"

She shook her head, still not looking at him. "We didn't know our neighbors, mostly because they didn't want to know us. I guess I was afraid. But I've always thought, if I'd stayed or stopped to call sooner, my mom might have lived. He'd come so close to killing both of us in the past, I just figured he'd stop before he hurt her too bad. I was wrong, very wrong. He killed her that day." She wiped her hand over her eyes and, though he didn't see the tears, he knew they were there. Maybe not on the outside—those tears went away after a time—but inside she had tears that never quite ended. He knew because he had them, too.

"So you see, I couldn't protect my mom, either. I saved myself, ran away through the woods just like she said. I left her there to die in that ramshackle house." Her voice cracked, then went silent. He didn't move, didn't want to pull her away from her memories, even though they caused her pain.

She sighed. "That's why I went to live with Aunt Alice and Uncle John." She turned to face him and the resolute expression she wore told him how hard she'd worked to be able to say these words. "My mom didn't really die in an accident. At least not the kind of accident you might think. Twelve years of my life, all I knew was surviving one nightmare to get to the next. Why my mother stayed, I'll never really know. I know the book reasons, all the psychological theories. But here—" she tapped her chest "—in my heart, I can't understand why she wouldn't leave, for me."

"What happened to your dad?"

"He went to prison and died there a few years later. I saw him briefly at the trial. I never saw or spoke to him again. I didn't even attend his funeral. My aunt and uncle made the arrangements, but I didn't go. They tried to take me but I refused and they didn't have the heart to force me after all I'd been through."

Emalea scratched at the colored braid on her shorts while Jackson played a thousand responses through his head. None of them were adequate.

"I guess that's more than you wanted to know," she said softly, beginning to stroke the kitten again.

He shook his head. "I wanted you to tell me what felt comfortable for you."

She got to her feet, returning to sit on the sofa beside him, her face pale. "I'm never comfortable with that story, but it's a relief to tell you."

"I assume your dad was a big man, like me."

She nodded. "Exactly like you."

He caught her chin so she had to face him, meet his eyes, and really see him for who he was. "No, not exactly, because I don't use my strength and size to hurt the people I'm supposed to love."

"A lot of men do." The words were so soft he had to strain to hear them.

"Plenty of not-so-big men out there do the same thing. A man's size isn't what matters. It's what kind of person he is that makes a man strike out or not."

Emalea gave him a half smile, and he rubbed his thumb across her cheek. No wonder she could be so guarded. Some people were lucky enough never to know how cruel the world could be. Maybe these hellish memories from the past were why they were drawn to each other when everything in their experience kept telling them to stay away.

His hand had slipped beneath her hair to cup her neck. Exactly when he decided to kiss her, he wasn't sure. One minute her silky hair was brushing the back of his hand and the next he was leaning into her. Maybe it wasn't a decision at all, but the sheer force of his heart searching for hers. She met him halfway, both hands grabbing fistfuls of his shirt. He brushed her lips with his. That would be all, just a light kiss. He wasn't prepared for the storm of desire that hit him when she pulled him closer, her arms slipping around his neck. The weight of it consumed him and all the ugliness he'd seen in the past few years faded to a blur, then disappeared. He could only see, only imagine, Emalea.

His mouth filled with the taste of her. Warm, sweet, spicy. Their tongues touched, tentatively, then hungrily.

Her body moved against him as he slid his

hands under the edge of her shirt to test the softness her skin. Lying back on the sofa, she pulled him with her. When she tugged at his shirt so she could run her hands over his bare skin, a distant part of his mind whispered that this situation was on the verge of blazing out of control, and it felt like pure heaven. He shoved her shirt upward to reveal her smooth stomach and bent to touch his lips to the shiny silver ring at her navel. The next kiss fell an inch above the first and he began a slow sweet trail up her body. Just above him, her breasts, covered in a thin, lacy bra, moved as she arched her body upward. He groaned. Or was it a growl? He couldn't be sure. When the lace slid aside to reveal the silky skin beneath, his breath constricted in his throat. He felt— Inside of him it registered that at last he did feel. Emalea's hand stroked his shoulder, the side of his face.

He wasn't sure why that one particular noise from the television caught his attention. Possibly his subconscious had been trying to protect him, protect both of them from taking this relationship far beyond what they would be happy with later. For whatever reason, he turned toward the screen when the booming sound reverberated in the speakers and he froze. He couldn't control his ragged breathing even though a white-hot pain washed over him like a bucket of ice water. He jerked to a sitting position, and Emalea followed. He pulled away from her, only to stare at the burning wreckage of a car on the screen.

What in the hell had he been thinking? That he could have a relationship, feel what he had been feeling, it was out of the question. How could he ever have forgotten how much it could cost to get that close, to care that much? He shot to his feet and started across the room.

"I've got to go." He escaped through the door and was at his truck in a moment, trying not to look like he was running. But he was, running scared.

Emalea sat stunned. The last thing she'd expected was for Jackson to break and run. Of course, she hadn't really been expecting him to kiss her, either. She'd been incapable of a coherent thought the last few minutes. Losing control was never an option for her, but she just had. He could have hauled her off the couch to her bed and she wouldn't have protested, or even noticed the move as long as he kept touching her.

The image on TV caught her attention.

She watched the smoking car, then sat back with a sigh. Outside she could hear his truck start, then there was a clatter on her front porch. She hurried to peer through the blinds, only to see Jackson striding back to his truck. On her porch was a bag of cat food and every other item she might need for her new pet.

Maybe they could just be friends and forget about all this physical stuff. Obviously neither one of them seemed ready to handle it. And who knew, maybe later they could explore the possibilities. As long as he didn't kiss her anytime soon, everything would be fine and follow a more predictable course. Predictable was good.

CHAPTER TEN

"WHAT IF I USED RED HERE?" Megan pointed to the canvas in front of her.

Kent stepped back to see the overall picture. "Red would be good, but I might add a little brown for a different tone."

Megan moved beside him. "You're right. You've got a good eye for color, Kent."

"Thanks." He quickly went back to his own canvas, reminding himself that Megan was just being polite.

She dabbed her brush in the paint and continued swishing it on the canvas while she talked. "I'm glad Mrs. Wright let us come back here and paint when we finished our work."

"Yeah, I wasn't ready to go home yet." He could have said that he'd just as soon never go home, but he didn't. His mom was there, and he still wanted to see her. Why she stayed with a husband who hurt her, he'd never know. Ms. LeBlanc had tried to explain it to him, using big words like *cogno*...something or other. She'd said this happened when someone was living in something bad, but couldn't admit it to themselves so they just changed their way of thinking. Or at least that's how he remembered it. The whole thing seemed like a lot of mumbo jumbo to him. Once, his mother had told him this was just their way of life. But, if other people's lives could be different, why couldn't his? A hope wriggled inside of him that one day things would be different. He held on to that. It kept him going.

"Is it bad at your house?"

Kent jerked, his paintbrush making a blue streak where there shouldn't have been one. Megan had never mentioned his family or his home life before.

"What I mean is, I've kind of heard your dad is... well, he's hard to get along with."

The corner of his mouth lifted in a sad smile. "He's a lot worse than that."

"Your mom must be really nice."

He glanced at her. "What makes you say that?"

"Because you're really nice, so you must take after her."

Kent dabbed at his painting, not wanting

Megan to see his face getting red. He didn't know what to make of a compliment from her. She was one of those girls whose parents probably told her to stay away from trash like him.

"Yeah, my mom's nice," he mumbled.

She came to stand behind him. She smelled like lemons—fresh and clean. He nearly dropped his paintbrush when she put an arm around his shoulder and gave him a squeeze.

"I'm glad we're friends, Kent. When you finish school you'll be a famous artist or graphic designer. You'll go to all the big cities and wear expensive clothes."

Kent snorted. "I don't need fancy clothes. Just give me a pair of jeans and I'll be fine." He turned toward her and her arm dropped from his shoulder. "My dad says one day I'll have to run his store."

She stared at him then shrugged. "Maybe one day you'll get to do what you want."

Megan went back to her painting and he twisted the brush in his fingers before continuing his own work. From the corner of his eye, he kept watching her. The blond ponytail swung when she moved and her smile was crooked. She was by far the prettiest girl he'd ever seen, maybe even the prettiest in the world, but more than that she was his friend. Not many girls wanted to be his friend, or guys either for that matter.

"Thanks, Megan," he said, continuing to stare at the marred canvas in front of him.

"What for?"

"For hanging out and painting with me."

She didn't answer but suddenly he felt something wet smack against his cheek. His hand flew to his face as he spun around staring at Megan. She grinned and waved her paintbrush while he scrubbed at the blob of paint on his face. Megan squealed as his own brush, full of paint, landed on her nose. He stood still for a second then turned to race across the storeroom with Megan, holding her paintbrush like a sword, in hot pursuit.

HANEY'S STORE ALWAYS made Emalea think of Mayberry. The newer gas stations in town were clean, neat, shiny even, with their pre-packaged goods ready to tempt customers who chose to venture inside rather than just pay for their gas at the pump with a credit card. Haney's had a credit-card machine. It was inside, behind the counter and it didn't connect to a computer or phone line. It made a crunching sound when the clerk shoved the metal piece across to make a copy of the card on bits of carbon paper.

The ever-present Janie, who had been working there for at least thirty years, stood behind the warmer putting Emalea's breakfast in a to go box. The glass-front warmer had been one of the few technological advances brought into the store, if you could call a food warmer technology. Emalea stopped here occasionally if she wanted to know the state of the union or at least the state of the community.

"Heard Wayne Anderson's son got sent to prison for those robberies he did over in Lafayette. Guess you'll be seein' him soon, Emalea."

"Could be, Mr. Redding." Grady Redding was Cecile Wright's grandfather and one of four or five retired men who met at Haney's for breakfast, dominoes and gossip nearly every morning. Of course, they'd never admit to the gossip part. The men all knew Emalea didn't discuss her work, even what she dealt with at the prison. Not that it bothered them. They always seemed to know more than she did about everyone, which occasionally included her own clients.

This morning, Frances Bordeau sat at a table by himself, though still conversing with the four men playing dominoes. His worn clothes and unkempt hair didn't fool Emalea for a minute. He saw and heard everything, mostly because people tended to overlook him. Whether by accident or design, Frances Bordeau could simply blend into the background of wherever he happened to be. In recent years, he'd begun to use this ability to help out the sheriff's office. It might have been that he enjoyed playing a role in the local crime fighting or he just didn't have anything better to do, but Emalea figured that after his wife had died he'd found this was a way to still feel useful and important.

Taking her breakfast, Emalea said a quick goodbye and left. She had just placed the container in the middle of the seat when, behind her, gravel crunched under the tires of a vehicle. A flash of white and green caught her eye, causing her heart to beat erratically. A door slammed, and she knew without looking it was Jackson. Stones rolled under his feet as he rounded the front of his cruiser. More than a week had gone by since he'd brought the kitten to her house. He'd made one phone call to apologize for leaving abruptly and to make sure she was surviving with her new companion.

Gathering her courage, she turned to face him. He strode toward her with a small plastic bag in his hand.

"Before you say anything, I want to apologize for the way I took off the other night."

"You did that already." She wondered briefly if he'd actually forgotten the call he'd made.

"Over the phone, so it doesn't count."

"Since when does apologizing over the phone not count?"

"Since I met you and I know I'm not going to do you that way."

His voice, firm and determined, made Emalea wonder if she wanted to try to continue her friendship with him. She doubted if a simple friendship would even be possible. They'd been dancing around the edges of a fire that was determined to ignite between them.

Paint was peeling off the worn gas tank behind him, and she fixed her gaze there. "Either way, your apology is accepted. As soon as you left, I saw the television and remembered you saying your wife and child had died in an accident. It's a lot to get over and I know you must have loved them very much. So, why don't we just let it go? When you're ready to get close to someone you'll know." She pushed her last words out in a rush. "You and I have lived through a life-time of hurt. Neither one of us is ready for what we started that night. But I hope we can at least be friends." Emalea wanted to pat herself on the back for how perfectly con-trolled her speech had been when her insides quaked.

"I'd like to think we're friends already, Emalea. But we can work on it in Mexico. I'll be going on the scuba diving trip with your group."

She jerked her attention away from the gas tank to focus on his face. He had to be kidding. "Excuse me?"

"One of the guys backed out and Lance asked me to go. We'll have a good time, huh?"

He wasn't kidding. "Uh, yeah. We always have fun. It's a great group." What else could she say?

"Here." He thrust the bag at her. "I wanted to give you this to help say I'm sorry."

She had to concentrate to get her hand to reach out and take the bag. He'd run from her house the other night, and now he smacked her in the face with the news he'd be spend-ing five days with her and her friends in Mexico. To make matters worse, he was trying to give her a gift. Jackson obviously wasn't firing on all cylinders today. She peered in the bag to see brightly colored cloth. Her voice left her, and when she was able to speak again she had to work hard to steady the quiver in her throat. "This...this is the dress from the French Market in New Orleans."

He stuffed his hands in his pockets. "I know. I saw that you liked it, so I got it. I figured I might need a peace offering for you one day. And see? I was right." He glanced toward the front of the store. "I guess I better go now. I'll see you Friday morning at the airport."

He walked away before she could say a word, but he stopped suddenly and stood for a moment with his back to her. When he turned, his eyes had lost most of their shine. "Emalea, what you said before, that I would be able to get close to someone when I'm over the loss of my family."

"Yes." So far this morning Jackson had seemed to jump from one emotion to the next. She couldn't imagine what he was going to say but, judging from his expression, it wouldn't be good.

"I'm not... I can't... What I mean is, that's not going to happen. I won't get close to anyone again, not like that, not enough to marry or have a family. I can't."

The words spewed over her like molten lava from an exploding volcano. She glanced briefly at her chest, half expecting to see burn marks. The idea of Jackson never wanting to develop a lasting relationship should not have bothered her. An hour ago she'd have said she'd be glad, but she wasn't.

When she didn't respond, he continued. "I'm responsible for what happened to them and I won't put anyone else at risk again." He paused as a car pulled in next to them. "This is not the place for us to talk. I could come by tonight."

She wondered if she looked as astonished as she felt. They could be friends, hang out together and nothing more, but he still wanted to talk. She didn't want to be a friend slash therapist. Deep inside she knew she harbored a desire to be a friend slash lover slash wife slash everything, but she couldn't acknowledge it, not when he stood in front of her stating that they'd never have more.

She shook her head. "No, I'll be busy, but it sounds to me as if you've made your decision. Maybe it's for the best, for both of us."

Before he could say a word, she slid behind the wheel of her truck and pulled away. *Get to know the real me,* he'd said. Then he'd come to her house, bringing gifts and practically attacking her on the sofa.

True, she'd been a willing participant. Did he think she wanted to be a one-night stand? Like that was going to happen. She wanted— no, needed—to put a label on him—dangerous, friend or prospect for something more. But she couldn't find a label sticky enough to stay. Now she would have to tolerate him for five days in Mexico, when she should be enjoying her vacation.

IF THE PARKING AREA at Haney's hadn't been covered in rocks he'd be standing in a cloud of dust. Jackson couldn't blame Emalea for being upset with him. It probably wasn't often that a guy tried to make love to her one night, then decided a week later he wasn't interested in a relationship. That's not how it was, but it certainly must look that way to her. He could stop her, say he'd changed his mind. He didn't like the idea of not being close to her again, but what choice did he have? So why did he feel like he'd just made a colossal mistake by letting her go?

Another car pulled in, and Jackson figured he cut a rather silly figure standing by himself in the middle of the parking lot. He'd come here to do business and have breakfast. The small-town pace had begun to grow on him. In fact, he had begun to believe coming to Cypress Landing might have been one of the best moves he'd ever made. He should have done it years ago. Maybe then his family would still be alive. Climbing the steps to the front door, he shoved that thought away. What happened had happened. Hinges creaked as the door opened, and Jackson let another customer by. No use hashing over all that now. He'd found comfort here, in spite of the gun-trade problems and his ongoing dilemma over Emalea. Sort of like putting on an old, soft leather jacket, a perfect fit, with a few worn spots. They'd clear up this gun-trade mess soon enough. He and Emalea could resolve their problems and still be friends, so long as he could keep his libido under control.

He winked at the woman who filled his plate with sausage, eggs and grits, a creamy delicacy he hadn't had since he'd left Arkansas. Once or twice a week he came here for the killer breakfast. He named it that because he imagined the fat and calories would lead straight to a heart attack, although, if the old guys here were an example, he might be able to eat this stuff every day and live to be a hundred.

Carrying his plate and a cup of coffee, he squeezed between the potato-chip rack and slid past the domino table taking the only empty seat available, across from Frances Bordeau.

"Jackson." The old man nodded a greeting. "How's the investigating business?"

"Slow." Jackson sipped his coffee for a moment but when the man remained quiet he dug into his breakfast.

"Jackson, you been fishin' lately?"

He looked at the domino table to see Grady Redding eyeing him while continuing to place his pieces on the table. The other three men at the table with him groaned when he sat back.

"No, sir. I don't do much fishing. I might start, though, now that I'm living in the country."

"You need to. I recommend the bait shop a few miles past the ferry dock. They have good bait there. You could go by tomorrow and check it out."

"I don't know. I've been busy so I might have to wait." Jackson returned to his plate.

"Naw, son, I think the fish'll be bitin', tomorrow."

Still chewing, he looked up from his plate to see Frances watching him. This was new. Were these two really trying to get him to go fishing? It sure didn't seem like it. If the old men wanted to give him information, why didn't they just spit it out, like they normally did? It hadn't taken Frances Bordeau two seconds last week to tell him he needed to check on that Richardson boy if he wanted to find some stolen bicycles. Why the secrecy now?

Jackson glanced to the front of the store where two customers waited in line for their breakfast. Maybe this was a bit bigger than a few stolen bicycles.

"I'm not much good at fishing. If I wanted to catch a lot, when's the best time to go?"

Frances stroked his wiry beard. "Seems like when Grady and I went fishing yesterday we caught fish late in the evening, so I guess if you were gettin' your bait by five o'clock, that'd be right. Don't you think, Grady?"

"Yep, from where I'm sittin' you'd be right on the money at that time."

"I'll be there."

Frances rested his elbows on the table, leaning forward to sip from his cup. He moved a little closer to Jackson. "If I were you, I might take a friend or two with me. Fishin's way better with a few folks along."

Jackson nodded. The older man sat back in his chair and across from them more groans came from the domino table. Grady sat smiling. "I win again."

Swallowing his last bite, Jackson took his empty plate and cup to the trash. "Guess I better get to work. You guys take care."

The men waved while Frances called out, "Good luck with your fishin'."

By the time he got to the county building his mind was spinning with possibilities, most of which involved illegal gun trade. On the way to his office, he spotted Pete and waved for him to follow.

"What's up, Jackson?"

"What if I told you something, I'm not sure what, is going down at the bait shop tomorrow evening? And no, I can't believe I just said that." He shook his head. "I wonder what I've walked into when I have to worry with crimes at the local bait shop."

Pete laughed. "It only sounds weird to you because you don't know the history. The guy who runs the bait shop is one of the top dogs in the militia. There's no telling what's going on over there, guns or possibly drugs. Though most of the drug trade is done by boat on the river. Did you turn up anything tracing the guns that had serial numbers?"

Jackson frowned. After going through the guns in the bag, they'd located several that did have serial numbers, while a few, like the assault rifles, had no number at all. He'd used the computer database to trace the guns with serial numbers to their maker then to the dealer who'd sold them. Unfortunately they'd been purchased legally and reported stolen a few weeks or months later. Which in itself was suspect, but as yet they hadn't been able to prove anything illegal on the part of the seller or buyer. "That's been a dead end so far, but maybe whatever this is at the bait shop will be the break we need. Of course that's if it has anything to do with the guns at all. I need you to find Matt for me so I can let him know what's happening."

"Okay. Did you get a tip on this?"

"Yep," Jackson answered, continuing to study the papers he was thumbing through. "At breakfast this morning." He could still hear laughter as Pete disappeared down the hall.

"WHEN WERE YOU PLANNING on telling me that Jackson Cooper was crashing our dive trip?"

Lana shoved a piece of apple pie toward her then poured coffee in her cup. "Em, I just found out myself this morning. It's not like people planned this for weeks. I told you the other day a guy had dropped out. Lance only invited Jackson this week. What's wrong with you? You guys seemed to get along just fine in New Orleans, after lunch that is."

They had gotten along well, too well. Of course the minute she'd let her guard down, Jackson had decided he wasn't so interested in her. Poking at the pie with her fork, she rested one elbow on Lana's kitchen table. The cheery yellow walls and navy checkered curtains couldn't even make her feel better. This day had been a total bust from the very beginning. Even Kent had canceled on her, just when she'd thought they were making progress.

He had raced into the counselor's office. "I have to go work for my dad today, sorry."

"But doesn't he know you have tutoring on Wednesday?"

"He doesn't care about tutoring. He just wants me at the store because he has stuff to go do."

After that, her mood had soured considerably, so she had come to take it out on her best friend. That's what they were for, right?

"I said, have you two been at it again?"

She realized Lana had been talking to her. "Uh, no, not really. It's just one minute he seems like a nice guy and the next he's Darth Vader."

"Darth Vader? What kind of stupid comparison is that?"

Emalea swallowed a forkful of pie. "It's not stupid. They're both big and have some really funky secrets."

Lana frowned, obviously still championing Jackson. "His wife and child were killed in a car accident. That's no secret."

"I think there's more to it than that."

"Like what?" Lana dropped her fork to the table and leaned forward as if Emalea might have a stunning revelation.

"I don't know what. And besides, you know how I've misjudged men in the past. The minute I get attracted I can't see the most obvious flaws."

Lana's cup followed her fork to the tabletop with a clink. "There you go again, trying to make him a bad guy."

The saucer in front of Emalea held a few crumbs mixed with sticky apple filling. She studied the mixture, wondering why she continued to hang on to the last few crumbs of her past.

"I am not trying to make him a bad guy." She cleared her throat after the words had slipped out in a gravelly whisper.

"You know what I mean. You're doing your damnedest to make him Jean Pierre, but he's not."

Emalea stood so quickly, the chair teetered briefly on its back legs, and she had to catch it with her hand. Once she settled it on all fours, she carried her cup to the counter and refilled it with coffee, then stood in front of the sink staring out the window, her back to Lana. "Jean Pierre has nothing to do with this. I don't know why people keep bringing him up. First Uncle John, now you."

"Em, it's because he's hanging around your stupid neck, everywhere you go. He was a bad guy. He was mean and nasty and he nearly killed you, but he didn't. You survived and got away. You should be proud of that. But you've got to quit thinking every guy you meet will be just like him."

"It's not every guy I meet. It's just the ones I really like."

"You're impossible." Lana leaned back in her chair, holding her coffee cup with both hands. "You make one bad decision that puts you in an awful marriage, with a near psychopath, and you think you're jinxed for life.

Give yourself a break. You're one of the best decision makers I know, trust your stupid gut, for once."

"What if I did trust my gut and it didn't work out?" Wasn't that what she had done when she'd let her guard down and gotten closer to Jackson?

"Then trust it again. You can't possibly expect everything to be like a fairy tale, not with the mess you two have in your past."

Emalea returned to her chair and frowned at Lana. "Well, thank you, Fairy Godmother."

"If I could wave a magic wand and get you to relax and just let things take their natural course, I would."

Emalea shoved her saucer across the table. "I promise to relax, if you'll give me another piece of pie."

Lana picked up the server then glanced at her. "Maybe you should have two more, if it will relax you."

CHAPTER ELEVEN

TEN UNTIL FIVE. Those old guys must have an inside scoop. Jackson rubbed his hand across his chest, his palm bumping against the bulk of the bulletproof vest beneath his shirt. In front of him, an ice truck lumbered into the dirt parking lot.

He and the rest of the department had spent yesterday and this morning trying to dredge up clues. They'd discovered a gun sale would take place at this store today. The owner, a longtime militia member, had left town yesterday at noon. The man had distanced himself from what would happen today and Jackson figured they'd find nothing to tie him to what was about to take place. The employee stood ready to make the sale and take the fall if things went bad. The boy would likely rot in prison before he'd rat out his boss.

Last night, through an anonymous tip, Jackson had stumbled on a girl who'd brought the story together for them. He'd gone into Haney's for a minute, leaving the window down on his cruiser. When he'd returned, a slip of paper had lain on the seat with the girl's name and phone number. The message "You need to call her" was scribbled beneath.

The girl had spent a couple of nights with a guy who worked part-time at the bait shop. She'd heard him on the phone arguing over when the ice should be delivered, only she was certain they were discussing more than a few bags of frozen water. Jackson met with the girl and her face explained her willingness to pass on the information. The guy had banged her around quite a bit before he'd left.

The ice truck rattled to a stop, and a young man in camouflage pants, a worn T-shirt and sporting a very scruffy beard stepped through the front door of the store. He couldn't have been more than twenty-one, and Jackson decided the beard was intended to give the illusion of a much older man.

Snapping the clip to his Glock in place, Jackson glanced over the edge of the bluff where he and three other officers were hidden. Below them, the river swirled in a muddy mess. Fifteen yards away, the driver of the truck stepped to the ground. Jackson's brain started working, and he felt a memory tugging at him. The guy looked familiar. Jackson turned his attention to Pete, who was beside him on the bluff.

"Do you think they'll unload the guns right here in the open, Cooper?"

Jackson glanced back toward the truck. "It's possible. We're way off the beaten path and… Yep, there you are, he's getting a gun from the bag right now."

The young guy had taken a large canvas bag from the back of the truck and unzipped it. He was now brandishing a shiny rifle.

"I'd say you could radio the sheriff to come in now, Pete."

He heard Pete key the radio, then motioned for the others to follow him. He leaped to the top of the embankment, weapon drawn and ready. "Put the gun down!"

Jackson hadn't expected the speed at which the young man would drop to the ground and start firing. Of course he hadn't expected the weapons in the bag to be loaded. He and the deputies scrambled below the embankment, returning fire while trying to remain concealed.

Next to him, Pete cried out, holding his arm.

"Tell me you're not hit," Jackson groaned.

"Sorry, buddy, but I am. I think it's just grazed."

The two men by the ice truck stopped firing as four sheriff's cars fishtailed to a stop in the gravel.

Jackson climbed to level ground. Behind him, Pete protested as another deputy radioed for an ambulance and Jackson stomped to Matt's car where the arriving officers had cuffed the two men. A few cars came around the curve in front of the bait shop, slowing to see what could be causing so much commotion. He was glad they hadn't come through earlier.

Jackson nodded at the deputy standing with the two men. "Looks like we have another bag of guns, same as we found before. At least this time we have a breathing suspect we can question."

"I ain't tellin' you nothin'," the boy from the bait shop shouted. Jackson stepped in front of him, his fist knotted and his breathing controlled by sheer determination. The idiot had managed to shoot Pete, and he really wanted to choke this kid.

He turned his attention to the man he'd recognized earlier. Another one of DePaulo's circle of so-called friends who had made the move south with him.

The corner of the man's lip curled upward, and as he leaned forward, a chill began to settle near the base of Jackson's spine.

"Thought you'd learned your lesson already, back at 434 Oakhaven."

The iciness swept to the top of Jackson's head. "What about 434 Oakhaven?" He could barely get his mouth around the address. It had been his address in Chicago.

"Come on, we both know what I'm talking about. The way I hear it, you got your wife and kid killed diggin' around in other people's business."

BESIDE EMALEA, KENT SAT in the passenger seat staring out the window. She'd picked him up at the edge of town walking to his father's store. As she rounded a curve, Emalea's throat constricted at the sight of sheriff's cars and flashing lights ahead at the bait shop.

"Kent, wait!"

The boy was through the truck door the instant she'd pulled onto the shoulder of the road across from the store, but whether from her voice or fear of what he might find, he stopped short. Jackson towered in front of two men who were standing handcuffed by a patrol car. Sliding across the seat, she got out of the truck and stood behind Kent.

"That's the big guy who was with Sheriff Wright the other day," Kent whispered. "He's... Oh my gosh."

"GOT YOUR WIFE AND KID killed." Like a clanging alarm bell the words echoed in Jackson's head, destroying his resolve, his control. A sheet of frosty rage settled onto him and Jackson slammed the man against the car just before he let his fists fly again and again. A red film blurred his vision. On the edge of his brain, the pain in his knuckles nudged his conscious. The pain felt good, dampening the rage that blinded him. He didn't even notice the spray of blood as the man's nose broke beneath the onslaught.

TO EMALEA, THE SCENE SLOWED until it was like footage from a very bad movie. Only this was happening right in front of her.

Was this the same Jackson she knew delivering such a beating to a man in handcuffs? A man who couldn't fight back or even defend himself. Jackson's fists pounded into flesh again and again while she looked on, unable to turn away but desperately wanting to. Blood splattered across his face and shirt as he repeatedly pounded the man.

Kent broke away from her. "Dad," he said

in a low voice then raced across the road. For an instant she thought he meant the man underneath Jackson's blows. Then she noticed the old truck coming to a stop at the edge of the rutted parking area. She took a step, but couldn't seem to go farther. Two men were on each side of Jackson trying to stop him but he shook them off like pesky flies. It took four deputies to wrestle the raging man to the ground.

Matt shoved the two prisoners into his car, shouting angrily at the deputies before speeding away. When Matt's car had disappeared, the men dragged Jackson to his feet. His head hung low and even from across the road she could see him still shaking with rage. The four men pushed him toward one of the cruisers. Force wasn't necessary. He went with them, docile and apparently dazed. At the car, he lifted his head and Emalea froze as her eyes met his. His mouth moved as if he wanted to speak to her, but she stepped backward until the door handle of her truck pressed against her shoulder. A deputy put a hand to the top of Jackson's head and he ducked low to get in the back seat.

The car had been gone for several minutes before Emalea could move. One of the young deputies she didn't know very well came to the edge of the parking lot. "You need help, ma'am?"

She shook her head, stumbling to the driver's side of her truck. The prisoner could have done nothing to warrant Jackson's actions. He'd wanted her to see the real Jackson Cooper and she feared she just had. She was sure this was a side of him he'd rather keep hidden, at least for a while longer. She hadn't been wrong in her assessment of him. She'd seen that as plainly as she ever would.

"I'M CANCELING MY TRIP in the morning. We're right in the middle of this investigation. I can't afford to leave for five days." Jackson sat in a wooden chair while Matt waited silently behind his desk.

"I'll call the guys and let them know," he continued when Matt didn't respond.

Finally, the sheriff of Cypress Landing shifted in his chair. He took a framed photo from atop his desk, staring at it for what seemed to Jackson like an eternity.

"You'll go on that trip."

"Matt, I'm the lead investigator. I can't leave right when things are starting to come together."

The sheriff's crystal-blue eyes pinned him

to the chair while the room began to feel considerably smaller, as if the walls were crushing in on them.

"Jackson, you are neck deep in a pile of trouble. You're going to get the hell away from here for a few days. What do you think you're going to do? Question the suspect? You've beaten the man to pieces. We'll be lucky if we don't get sued into next week."

"You don't understand, Matt. What he said to me, he knew something about Christa and Connor."

Matt sighed, putting his elbows on his desk and resting his forehead in his hands. He sat quietly for several seconds before looking at Jackson again.

"One of the deputies told me what he said. Believe me, I might have done the same thing in your place, but that wouldn't make it right."

"Does that mean you're placing me on leave and taking me off this case?" Jackson tried not to hold his breath as he waited for Matt to answer.

"No, not unless some suit comes in here and twists my arm. But I think if you aren't hanging around here for the next few days things will go a lot smoother. When you get back, you can work on the case again, just not with this particular suspect. So pack your stuff and go to Mexico. This whole mess will still be here when you get home."

Jackson hung his head. It could have been much worse. Matt could have told him to pack his things and get out.

EMALEA HURRIED ALONG the hallway of the New Orleans airport. Ahead, at the terminal gate, she could see her friends waiting. Lana stood near the edge of the seating area while others milled around.

She tried to smile at her friend but the action fell short of its mark. "I guess we're going to have one less person on the trip after all."

Lana tilted her head. "What do you mean?"

"After what happened yesterday, Jackson won't be going, so we'll be one short."

"Don't be silly, of course Jackson is still going on the trip. He's waiting with everyone else."

Glancing over Lana's head, she could see Jackson in a chair his long legs stretched in front of him.

"I can't believe it. He practically beat a man to death. I saw him."

Lana grabbed her arm. "I haven't heard a

thing. But please tell me you aren't going to treat him like some kind of predator for the entire trip. You'll make everyone uncomfortable."

She glared at her friend. "What about me? What if I'm uncomfortable? He's no different than Jean Pierre or my own damn father."

Lana let go of Emalea and put her hands on her hips. "I don't believe you're saying this. If you'd quit racing back to home plate every other minute you might actually get somewhere."

"I am somewhere." Emalea gritted her teeth and tried to remember exactly when her best friend had turned against her. Her life had been fine before Jackson had come to town.

"Well, we both know it's not going to make you happy."

Did Lana think she would actually overlook what Jackson had done and go chasing after him? "It will make me happy if I can just stay as far away from Jackson Cooper as possible for the next few days."

Lana flipped her hands in the air. "Do what you want. It's your trip."

"If it were my trip he wouldn't be going."

"Maybe, maybe not."

Lana left to grab her bags as their flight was called. Emalea boarded the plane, finding her seat near the front, thankful to see complete strangers in the seats next to her. At least she wasn't stuck sitting next to Jackson for the whole flight.

CHAPTER TWELVE

"NO MORE ROOMS, SORRY."

"You've got to have another room, anything, a broom closet."

The woman behind the desk wrinkled her brow, not really understanding what Emalea meant.

"No more rooms," she repeated.

"I'll go to another hotel." Hoisting one of her bags, Emalea swung round only to bump into Lana.

"Em, you're making a scene. You're only going to be next door to Jackson. It's not like you'll be in the same room. Now get over it."

"Why don't you and Lance trade rooms with me?"

Lana snorted. "Your room and Jackson's have two double beds and ours has a king as do all the rest of the couples on this trip. You two are the only single people. Need I say more?"

A PALM FROND HUNG over the sidewalk and
Emalea slapped it away. Neatly manicured
grass with spots of red, orange and white
flowering plants surrounded her. She wished
she knew their names but she wasn't very
good at identifying plants. Nearby someone
smacked a tennis ball, and she ran her fingers along the meringue-colored stucco
walls of the building as she walked. The
young boy assisting with her luggage didn't
speak English and her Spanish was negligi-
ble so they proceeded in silence while Jackson followed a safe distance behind her.
He'd spoken to her when their luggage had
been put in the cab, but she'd ignored him.
He'd had the good sense to get in the other
cab.

Stopping in front of a red door, the boy
shoved the key into the lock then stepped
back to let her enter. Handing him a tip as
soon as he dropped her luggage, she hurried
to the sliding glass door on the opposite side
of the room, fumbling to get it unlocked,
feeling trapped in this tiny space. On the
small patio, she breathed in the clean salt air.
A concrete divider separated her patio from
Jackson's. She put her hand against it, and
Jackson suddenly appeared, then stepped
into her space. The patio hardly seemed big

enough for both of them, so she moved off the tile onto the grass.

"You don't have to run away, Emalea."

"What makes you think I'm running? I just wanted to go to the dive shop then maybe stick my feet in the water."

"You're running. I'm not trying to ruin your trip or mine. If you'll just let me talk to you, let me explain what you saw yesterday. I know it looked bad."

She spun around. "Bad? You think it looked bad? It was like a nightmare. There's nothing you could tell me that would make what you did right."

He seemed to cringe at her words, but she couldn't feel sorry for him.

"I'm not saying I can make it right. I can't. What I did was wrong. It was stupid and inexcusable. If you'll just listen to me you might understand what could put me into that kind of rage."

"You get so violent because that's the kind of man you are. I'm not interested in hearing excuses from you."

Her feet flew across the grass and then the sand. If Jackson Cooper thought he could give her a lame excuse then try his let's-be-friends act, he was in for a rude awakening. Did he believe what he'd done yesterday would mean nothing to her? She stopped at the sea wall and took several deep breaths, blowing slowly through her nose.

As her tension eased, she tried to make herself think rationally. She banged her fist against the stone. Drawn to the wrong man again. Like a kid who had to touch the burner on the stove just to see if it was hot.

Below her, the water sparkled in the afternoon sun while two small yellow-and-black fish flitted back and forth. She was more than just attracted to him. She'd fallen in love with him. She hadn't wanted to admit it, but it had happened. Kicking herself wouldn't be helpful at this point. She'd done it a thousand times already. This was her destiny, part of her genetic code, to fall in love with a man who was all wrong. She'd prayed her mother hadn't passed that part of herself to her only daughter, but she had. Her education told her that kind of thinking was ludicrous, but what she felt went beyond book learning.

"Emalea."

"Can't you leave me alone?" The words tasted bitter with anger.

His mouth thinned to an angry line, and Jackson lifted his hand. "No, I can't. I—"

He'd stopped in midsentence because

she'd lifted her arm between them and ducked her head away. The automatic response to defend herself against a raised hand remained ingrained. She hated it, but couldn't seem to prevent it.

"Good God, Emalea, I was only going to push your hair away from your face. Just because your dad hit you when he was mad doesn't mean other men will."

"It wasn't just my dad." The words left her mouth without her wanting them to. "I've always tried to consider Jean Pierre as a mistake."

"Who's Jean Pierre?"

"My ex-husband." One look at his shocked face and she realized no one in town had told him.

"I hope you're not going to end this conversation with that," he said when she remained silent.

She shook her head. "I was living in New Orleans when I met him. I fell in love and never recognized what he could be. I like to say he hid his violent side, but maybe I was just too blind to see it. He was the kind of man I knew best, because I'd spent the first twelve years of my life with one just like him. Maybe that was why I gravitated to him, familiarity." She sighed and sat on the rock wall.

"Everything I'd learned as a psychologist couldn't help me. I could counsel others but I couldn't analyze what was happening in my own life. He was my first real boyfriend, the first man I'd ever made love with and the only man, besides my father, to send me to the hospital. I didn't allow him a second opportunity. When I was released, I called Lana. We loaded her dad's truck and hauled everything I owned home to Cypress Landing." She pressed the heel of her hand against her forehead. "I'm afraid I have a problem with being attracted to potentially dangerous men."

She looked up to Jackson's starkly handsome face. No doubt he was the best-looking man she'd ever fallen for. That she'd fallen for him at all was a bad sign.

"I'm not like that, Emalea."

"Aren't you?"

He lifted his hands in exasperation. "I want to tell you what happened yesterday, but you're not ready to hear it. I can't change your past any more than you can change mine. But the future, it's wide open. I'm sorry, but for some reason, I keep seeing you in mine." This time when he reached to brush the hair from her face, she didn't try to stop him. He let his fingers linger an instant on her skin then walked away.

She could chalk up Jean Pierre to being young and ignorant. But she couldn't find a good enough excuse for falling in love with Jackson. Sure, he'd hidden his violence behind kind words, a soft voice and caring gestures. But yesterday she'd seen him unleash the monster within, and she wouldn't put herself in harm's way ever again.

JACKSON PUSHED HIS WET dive gear onto the hooks set in the patio's wall. The group had spent the afternoon exploring a small reef just off the hotel beach. Their last excursion had been made at sunset. They'd used dive lights to view the myriad of colors on the reef, and for a few hours the events of yesterday had been pushed to the back of his mind. Matt had been right. He'd needed to get away. To think over what had happened and realize how wrong he'd been to lose control. He should have walked away, beat on the hood of a cruiser, anything, but he hadn't. Now the price he would pay might be more than he imagined.

If Emalea would just listen to him. She might not care, but his heart kept telling him she would understand. She had to. He'd dealt her a double whammy in two days; fixing that would be more than difficult. Jackson decided his first mistake had been telling Emalea he could never have another relationship. She'd been gone exactly one minute that day when he'd realized he wanted a relationship with her a thousand times more than he was afraid of it. He should have gone after her then and told her he was wrong. But he'd wanted to give her time to cool off. Before he could do anything, though, all hell had broken loose with the gun deal, and he'd kept thinking they'd have this time in Mexico. Finally, he'd done the very thing he'd hoped to prove to her he wasn't capable of. But he *was* capable of being the kind of person she was most afraid of. She had to know he could never be that way with her, that he would never be that way under normal circumstances. But nothing had been normal for him the past two years—until he'd met Emalea.

EMPTY BEER BOTTLES were scattered around the table, and Jackson had lost count of exactly how many belonged to him. After the evening meal, Lance had produced a deck of cards and a box with enough toothpicks to supply a truck stop for at least two years. A pile of the tiny wooden sticks lay in front of him. He wasn't sure how long they'd been in the open-air bar playing poker, but it was late, or was it early?

"Guys," Jackson said while pushing back his chair, "I'm done for tonight." A few groans followed as the others did the same.

He eased along the dimly lit path to his room, occasionally stumbling on an uneven tile. A few beers, even more than a few, hadn't done this to him. His head seemed to float just above his shoulders. An act that caused his stomach a certain amount of concern.

With one foot on the tile of his patio, he dug in his pocket for the key. He didn't want to wake his neighbors, one in particular. His second step onto the patio placed his foot directly in the water that had drained from his wet dive gear and completely thwarted any efforts he'd made at being quiet. As he lost his balance, he grabbed for the patio chair, sending it straight into the patio door. The glass didn't break but the thunderous rattling echoed in the night. His other hand flailed and managed to latch on to his damp dive gear. Unfortunately, the hook in the wall had never been intended to hold a man of his size. Hook and dive gear crashed to the ground on top of him, and he imagined the whole building reverberated with the impact.

He opened his eyes to find a pair of bare feet directly in front of his nose. Flat out on his stomach happened to be a very bad position for meeting people.

"What are you doing?"

The words spoken in a very familiar voice bounced off his head.

"I'm trying to get to my room, but I slipped. This damn tile is slick when it's wet."

"Did you have to bring the whole building down with you?"

"It's not like I had a plan." He got to his knees before climbing to his feet, swaying, and feeling a little shaky.

"Jackson Cooper, you're drunk."

"I've had a few beers, well, maybe more than a few, but I'm not drunk." Resting one hand on the wall, he used the other to wipe away the cold film of sweat coating his forehead. "I don't feel very good, so could you just give it a rest and let me get to bed?"

She made a cackling sound and he tried to focus on her.

"Great, I'm sick and you're laughing at me."

"I can't help it. You're so pale, like the Incredible Hulk after he's spent six hours in a pool of bleach."

"Thanks, I—" He reached for the door but knew it would take too long to unlock. Instead, he bolted for the shrubbery between the building and the sandy beach, unable to finish snidely telling her how much he appreciated her candor. Wave after wave of nausea hit him as he was sick for what felt like an hour. A cold cloth covered the back of his neck, and he heard ice clattering against plastic. He tried to speak but was sick again. Finally, exhausted he sat back on his heels.

"For God's sake, Emalea, what are you doing?"

She squatted beside him holding one cloth to his forehead and one to the back of his neck. "I'm trying to help you while you're sick."

"I'd rather do this in private if you don't mind." He tried to push her away but he swayed and had to steady himself instead.

"Well, I do mind, so get over it."

He sat for a moment without speaking, still fighting his roiling stomach. "I thought you were mad at me, weren't speaking to me."

"I am, but I'm not going to lie in my bed

while you roll around in the grass or your bathroom sick. I've got a couple of tablets if you think you can keep them down. Next time don't drink so much."

"I didn't drink too much."

"What did you eat?"

"I don't know. They brought all kinds of stuff to our table while we were playing cards. I just ate it. Could we not discuss food or drink right now?"

She shook her head. "To be such a big tough guy, you're pretty pathetic when you're sick."

He had a smart comeback, but forgot it as he fell forward and was sick, again.

THE CLOTH ON THE PILLOWS scratched his back, but it beat leaning against the rough, cold wall in the bathroom, where he'd sat after coming inside. When he'd finally been able to stand, he'd found Emalea had set his toothbrush by the sink and fresh towels on the counter so he could take a shower. He'd heard her on the phone earlier, then she'd shouted that a couple of the other guys were sick, too. She had disappeared when he'd finally left the bathroom behind. Now, resting in the bed, he imagined he might survive, and he gave a silent prayer to the porcelain god that he'd paid his last respects.

The door rattled and Emalea blew in. "Can you believe a store was open at this time of the morning?" She set crackers, a lemon-lime soda and a small tablet on his bedside table, then fell onto the other bed. "If you can keep that pill down it should help with the nausea and vomiting. You might want to pass on the crackers till the morning."

He could only nod, swallowing the pill with a few sips of the soda.

"I doubt you'll be able to go on the dive tomorrow, but you can catch one the next day."

"I'm going tomorrow or today, whatever it is."

"Jackson, it's three o'clock in the morning and the boat picks us up at eight."

He slid under the sheet. "That's why I'm going to sleep right now."

She watched him for a minute while he tried to ignore her, then she clicked off the bedside lamp and crawled under the covers of the bed in the shorts and T-shirt she'd worn to the store. His eyes adjusted to the dim light coming from the bathroom.

"Emalea, what are you doing?"

"I'm going to sleep here tonight in case

you get worse or need anything. If you happen to have a bad case of food poisoning, we might be making a trip to the clinic."

He didn't bother to argue with her. Why should he? Less than three feet away, in another bed, was the woman he wanted to have next to him forever. She might as well have been on another continent. He was sick and she was just sick of him.

"Emalea."

"Good grief, Jackson, what is it?" She turned over, her features shadowed but visible.

"Are you still angry at me?"

Her pensive expression didn't give him much hope while he waited for her reply. "I'm not angry at you, Jackson, I just don't think I trust who you are."

"You don't know who I am."

"I know enough."

"You only know what you've made yourself believe. If you think I'm so dangerous and so bad, why did you do all this tonight? Why not just let me wallow on the floor and be sick?"

Her answer was so long in coming he'd begun to think she wouldn't give one. She rolled on her back, eyes open, staring at the ceiling.

"Maybe because I don't know who I am anymore. Now go to sleep."

He lay on his side wanting to tell her everything. But she didn't want to listen, not yet. Maybe tomorrow. Maybe then he could set things right.

"WE'RE NOT IN THE SOUTH and you're still eating food on a stick."

A solitary grilled shrimp coated in tangy barbecue sauce clung to the wooden skewer. Emalea shook it at Jackson. "At least it's not fried and we are south…of the border."

The last rays of the sun sank below the horizon as they finished their meal in the hotel restaurant. In the bar, music hummed and people crammed onto the dance floor.

Jackson turned to answer a question from one of the guys sitting next to him. Emalea had decided to be civil to Jackson after he'd been sick. If she treated him rudely, it would ruin everyone's trip, or at least that's how she'd justified it. Once she'd stopped rebuffing him, he'd managed to show her all the reasons she'd fallen for him in the first place. But she hadn't forgotten what she'd seen him do. She didn't want to get closer to him than she was right now. In fact, she was planning on calling Paul Jones as soon as she got home. A few safe dates with him and this whole Jackson Cooper mess would be a distant memory. In her heart, she knew that wouldn't work. Every time she concocted the perfect plan to forget him, she caught herself trying to get closer to him. The dress she had on tonight only proved that point.

Jackson wanted to explain the incident at the bait shop, but she couldn't hear it. What if it wasn't a good enough explanation for what he had done? Or even worse, what if it was? She didn't imagine he could say anything to make her think differently about what she'd seen, although sitting next to him right now she wished she'd never given Kent a ride, wished the whole thing had never happened.

"Let's go, Em." Jerked away from her thoughts, she found herself alone with Jackson.

Before she could protest, Jackson had pulled her to her feet and was dragging her to the dance floor.

He locked his arms around her waist, and she put her hands flat against his chest. "I don't want to dance with you."

He shook his head. "That's not true and you know it. Just for a minute, forget that you think I'm going to turn into someone horrible when you least expect it. Quit trying to analyze me and let your heart tell you what's right."

"My heart is what led me astray before."

He caught her chin with his fingers, forcing her to meet his gaze. "Not this time."

He let go of her face and returned his hand to her waist. Neither spoke while they danced. The song ended, but was followed by another, and someone yelled his approval.

The hand at her waist moved upward, coming to rest on the back of her neck. He pulled her close, while she tried to hold herself away, her heart shuddering when he whispered her name. He lowered his head until his mouth nuzzled the hair around her rear, causing her tight muscles to give in, and she relaxed against him. His swift intake of breath made her stomach tingle at the idea that she had such an effect on him.

"The dress is perfect on you. I'm glad you wore it."

She kept her head buried near his shoulder. Why she'd even brought the dress he'd given her, she wasn't sure. Tonight she'd automatically reached for it when she'd gotten dressed and had been unable to convince herself not to put it on.

"Please talk to me." Jackson's lips brushed the edge of her ear as he pleaded.

She leaned back. "Can't you just let it go? Let's enjoy this for now, for what it is, a vacation, a time away from our real lives."

He stopped moving. "I don't want being close to you to be a time away from my real life. Why can't it be part of our lives?"

"I seem to recall you telling me just the opposite of that the other day."

"I was wrong."

She tried to shrug under the weight of the hands on her shoulders. "Maybe you were right, maybe it is too much of a risk."

"Maybe there are things worth that kind of risk. Events in my life and how I've handled them have put me where I am right now, just like you. Let me tell you what happened the other day."

She fought with herself but knew what her answer would be, because she couldn't overcome her past. Her head kept telling her to stay away. But inside of her, something, obviously the genetic material inherited from her mother, made her pull closer.

"I'll hear your explanation."

His body slumped against her as if he'd been holding his breath. He glanced around the noisy room. "Not here, let's go out to the beach, by the water, where it's quiet."

She sat on the stiff resin lounge chair,

kicked off her sandals and dug her toes in the sand. Water splashed against the steps that led into the ocean, while underneath the water, Emalea could see people on a night dive, the dim glow of their lights making eerie circles on the surface.

"I should have told you all of this weeks ago. Part of me figured you'd hear it by way of the grapevine and another part of me just wanted to put it in the past."

Not sure what to say, she remained silent. Jackson sat across from her, their knees only inches apart.

"Emalea, my wife and daughter didn't exactly die in a car accident. They were in a car when they died, but there was a bomb in the car." He wiped his hand across his face. To Emalea, the breath he took before continuing resembled a gasp, possibly the last breath of a dying man. "They never left the front drive. The whole car blew up right in front of me and I couldn't do a thing to stop it."

She sat up straighter. "How could that happen? Was someone after you?"

"They were after me, but the bomb wasn't set for me. They intended to kill my family. It was a warning. I'd been working under-cover in a special organized-crime unit in the FBI. We arrested a guy I'd been working with, the nephew of a mob boss. He never went to jail because our witnesses decided not to talk. For him, hurting my family was the best way to tell me to leave him alone." Elbows resting on his knees, he lowered his head to his hands. "It worked. I guess I went a little nuts. I drank too much, too often, and my temper turned worse than nasty. I used to follow the guy whenever I could, openly, so he'd know I was there. I even beat him up once. I was angry at the world and at myself for putting my family in that position. Finally, the FBI wanted me behind a desk. That's the real reason I came to Cypress Landing. But I've put all that behind me now."

"What about the other day?"

Jackson got to his feet, shuffling through the sand to the gray stone seawall. He kept his back to her as he continued.

"We were arresting the two men for illegal gun trade. Only, I knew the guy delivering the guns from my work with the Mafia. He knew me, too." He sat on the rocks, his back to the ocean. "He knew what happened to Christa and Connor, my wife and daughter. He taunted me with it. I lost control. There's no excusing what I did. I know I was wrong, but I can't tell you if the same situation happened again I'd do it differently. They took my family from me, and I couldn't stop them." His voice shook on the last sentence. Emalea moved to the wall, next to him, leaning against the uneven stones and she saw in his eyes unshed tears shimmering in the glow of the night lights.

She covered his hand with her own. "I'm sorry, I guess that also explains what happened at my house that night."

He hung his head. "I should have told you all this then, but I couldn't. What happened to them showed me just how little control I have over what happens to those around me."

"So you decided to strike out at those you thought responsible."

He nodded.

She squeezed his hand. "It's understandable."

"Does that mean you're okay with what happened at the bait shop?"

Emalea wasn't sure how to respond. His story should have hit all her alarm buttons, so why weren't they raising a clamor? He waited without another word and she knew, sooner or later, she'd have to say something. "I don't honestly know how I feel about that. I wouldn't say I'm okay with it, but then it doesn't sound to me like you're okay with it, either. At least now I can understand where that rage I saw came from."

"That's a part of me, Emalea, but it's not all of me."

She slid her arm across his shoulder. "I know, but is it a part you can control?"

"I promise you this, I never had a problem with my temper before this happened and you have nothing to be afraid of from me. I won't hurt you." He leaned forward to kiss her, lightly at first, then with more determination, more passion. Parting her lips, she gasped as his tongue reached to meet hers. She struggled to pull him closer, and he straddled the wall. Then he slid her between his legs. His hand bunched the soft fabric of her dress at her thigh, never breaking their kiss.

She pressed her mouth to his neck while unbuttoning the top two buttons of his shirt. She wanted to touch her lips to his broad chest. He groaned, tossing his head back. His fingers loosened the knot of the halter dress, carefully exposing the swelling flesh the fabric covered. His mouth followed the cloth lower, until he found her aching nipple and closed his mouth over it.

A voice called across the pier, followed by rubber flapping and the clank of metal against stone. Jackson circled his hand lightly around her throat, replacing the strap of her dress.

"It seems the night dive is over."

She brushed her lips against his cheek. "Maybe we should go inside. It's going to be busy here." The words that came out of her mouth didn't surprise her. Though if someone had told her yesterday she'd be considering making love to Jackson today, she'd have laughed. She wasn't laughing now. The hands that covered her body with caresses so soft and tender could become brutal, but she trusted him. Past lessons had taught her not to trust a man who could use his fists against another that way, but how would she have reacted if a man had joked about her family's death. She thought of the times she'd been tempted to lift the barrel of her father's favorite hunting rifle in his direction. The only thing stopping her had been her mother's misguided but constant devotion to the man.

Jackson pushed away from her, cool air rushing between their bodies. "Let's give it a minute. I don't want this to happen in the heat of the moment. I want you to be sure this is what you want."

"I'm almost sure it will be a lot better if there's a certain amount of that heat-of-the-moment thing going on." She tugged at another button on his shirt, smiling, her breathing still ragged. Her reservations concerning a relationship with Jackson had been buried by the passion that erupted every time he touched her. She had to have his touch, needed it.

"That's not what I mean and you know it." His voice rasped, his features taut, lips full, hungry for more of her. She couldn't remember if she'd ever seen a man so consumed with desire for her. It made a band constrict around her chest and for an instant she couldn't breathe. Then the band broke and a warm ocean of something that was probably love but she'd rather label passion filled her.

"Jackson, just because I'm a psychologist doesn't mean I want to analyze every move I make beforehand." She took his hands in hers. "And you? Is this what you want?"

He bent to kiss the back of each hand. "I want this as much as I want to draw my next breath."

She pulled him to his feet. "Me, too."

Leading him across the soft sand to her room, Emalea did what Lana would have advised. Leaving behind her defenses, for the first time in a long time, she let her heart lead the way.

CHAPTER THIRTEEN

THE AIR SMELLED OF SALT WATER, and the sky was filled with brilliant stars. It wasn't that the stars here were different from the ones at home, but they seemed to burn brighter. Being here, away from reminders of real life, made everything a little clearer. Emalea wasn't sure why, but right now she could see herself and her life with a clarity that had escaped her in the past.

"So, you and Jackson are going to dive Barracuda Reef tomorrow."

Glancing at Lana, languishing in a lounge chair much like herself, Emalea smiled. Nearby, at the hotel bar, she could hear the hum of conversations interrupted by an occasional bark of laughter.

"Yep, do you and Lance want to come, too?"

Lana snorted. "I'm no thrill seeker, and I'm definitely not that good of a diver yet, neither is Lance. Remember, we only just learned last year and we don't do all that rescue diving stuff that you do. Of course, I can't believe the other guys stuck with their promise to go sightseeing with their wives when they heard you two were going."

Emalea shifted in her chair, closing her eyes. In the quiet, she tried to discern Jackson's voice among those drifting to them from the bar. Several of the men had decided to try another game of poker. Occasionally his deep voice washed over her.

"It would appear to me that two people I know are getting along much better now."

Emalea put her hands behind her head. "It would appear that way, wouldn't it?"

Lana rolled to one elbow, shaking her head. "You are so tight-lipped. What gives? Are you two sharing one of those beds now?"

"That's none of your business."

"Em, I'm your best friend. If it's not my business, whose is it?" She flopped onto her back. "You don't have to say a word, though, that guy's face tells the whole story."

This time Emalea sat up to stare at Lana. "What is that supposed to mean?"

The woman beside her gave a low chuckle. "He is so eaten up with you." She sat up, so that they were facing each other.

"In fact, it's almost downright sickening to see that puppy-dog expression of his whenever you leave the room."

"You're crazy."

"I'm right and you don't want to admit it. Jackson loves you. Notice how I didn't say he's 'in love with' you, because he's not just in love. He's got that I'm-in-this-boat-for-the-long-haul look."

Emalea lay back again to gaze at the stars. "I don't know if it's to that point. Besides, things could change when we get home."

"They won't change if you don't try to make them change. God, Em, doesn't it just feel right? From where I'm sitting, the two of you together seems so right."

A shiny white light shot across the sky. Emalea raised her hand to point, but the light was gone.

"Shooting star," she whispered. Sliding her feet across the plastic chair, she bent her knees toward her chest.

Lana remained quiet and Emalea turned to her. "It does feel right, like sitting in that big, stuffy chair I always had in my room when we were in school."

Her friend grinned. "I'm glad. Now don't mess it up with a whole lot of analyzing that doesn't amount to spit."

Emalea started to ask what kind of stuff didn't amount to spit but figured that would be better left unsaid. As far as Lana was concerned, it would be anything that made Emalea second-guess Jackson. A burst of laughter from the men made them both look in the direction of the bar.

"Em, don't you think it's time we went in there and showed them how poker is really played?"

Emalea stuck her feet in her leather sandals. "I think so. We can likely have all their little toothpicks in an hour."

"Oh, easily."

They marched through the sand straight to the men's table where they were greeted with groans and a confused expression from Jackson.

Lana glanced at him then leaned toward Emalea. "Bless him, he doesn't know what's about to happen."

"Too bad, he'll have to learn like the rest of them." Emalea said, then proceeded to take the first hand and half of Jackson's toothpicks.

THE EARLY MORNING SUN hung just above the horizon, not yet hot enough to warm the air that whipped across the bow of the small dive boat. Glad that they'd both donned wet suits before leaving the dock, Emalea wrapped her arms around herself, not really cold, but feeling a chill run through her body.

Jackson winked at her, a toothpick bobbing in the corner of his mouth. At poker she'd managed to win his stash, but later that night he'd found ways to win them back. She hadn't minded one bit. Cool, salty spray misted her face, and she closed her eyes, hoping this feeling wouldn't end. Just the thought of how they spent their time alone together brought burning images to her mind. He was perfect. They were perfect together. Surely, she couldn't be misleading herself about that. When she opened her eyes Jackson smiled at her and her bare toes curled into the bottom of the boat.

She chuckled, remembering how he'd sat in a chair facing the bathroom mirror last night and coached her through shaving his head.

"What's so funny?" Jackson shouted above the whine of the outboard motor.

She ran her hand on top of her head.

He smiled then touched his own head. "You did a good job."

Before she could respond, the engine died and the dive guide, who would be leading them on the trip, began to describe their dive plan in slightly broken English. When the instructions were complete, she, Jackson and the guide suited up before rolling backward into the water. The current tugged at her body, sending all three of them flying along the reef. She made a circle with her thumb and forefinger, letting the guide know she wasn't having problems. The current seemed to lessen when they reached the large section of the reef at ninety feet.

Spotting an array of brightly colored coral surrounded by a school of black-gray queen angelfish, she swam deeper to get a closer look. Jackson followed, and she waved to the guide who gave her the okay sign and then swam past the next coral head to hunt for other interesting sites to show them. The current still pushed them along, so Emalea motioned for Jackson to head into the flow and paddle against it. Colorful fish raced past, while a large green eel appeared, snaking its fierce head from among the rocks. She gave Jackson a thumbs-up sign when she saw his eyes widen. Jackson tapped his dive watch, indicating they didn't have much time left.

The deeper they descended, the more air they used due to pressure. At this depth, their trip would be a short one. Ahead of them was the coral head, where she'd last seen their guide, and Emalea went in that direction. He wasn't there so they continued on, letting the current drag them. The dive guide had obviously been pulled along much faster than she had imagined.

After searching for the guide for close to three minutes, Jackson held his air gauge toward her and Emalea realized they needed to start for the surface. The guide might have had trouble and had to get in the boat. The driver of the boat usually followed the bubbles as they broke the surface, easily keeping up with the divers, and beneath the water, the divers could see the bottom of the boat in the crystal-clear water, even from depths of a hundred feet. Tilting her head to locate their ride home, her throat tightened. The boat was nowhere to be seen.

She pointed upward and they began their ascent, slowly, to keep air bubbles that might have accumulated in their bodies from enlarging as the pressure of the water decreased. Boat or no boat, they had to get to the top or they would run out of air. She reassured herself that their ride back to shore had simply gotten too far away from them while following the dive guide. The journey stretched into an eternity as Emalea looked in every direction for the boat.

At the top, they filled their BC jackets with air to keep them floating. An empty blue sea stretched for miles. Jackson shoved his mask from his head jerking the regulator from his mouth.

"What the hell is going on? Where's the boat?"

"I don't know, but we can't sit here like this for long. The current will only keep moving us. We need to try and swim back to the island."

He pointed past her shoulder. "I hope you don't mean that island."

She squinted to see what appeared to be a spit of land getting smaller by the minute. "That would be the one. We'll need to drop our weight belts, tanks, too. Neither one of them has enough air left to do us any good."

Jackson nodded and they both grabbed the plastic release buckles, getting rid of the pieces of lead that had been strapped to their waist to help keep them under the water when making their dive. Then they took turns loosening the straps holding the tanks to each BC jacket. The heavy metal cylinders sank out of sight. With the added weight gone, Emalea set out swimming.

"You're going in the wrong direction, Emalea."

She twisted round to see Jackson better. "I'm trying to swim across this current. There's no possible way we can swim against it and get back."

For nearly a hundred yards they battled the force of the ocean before the pull of the strong current eased. Heading toward the island now, Emalea tried not to clench her teeth. That took energy and they were going to need every bit they had if they were going to make it to shore.

Twice more, currents threatened to push them farther from their goal. Her stomach knotted with apprehension each time they had to swim parallel to the island rather than toward it. The thought that they might not make it tried to nibble its way into her consciousness, but she pushed it away. Occasionally, they lay on their backs paddling with their feet, hoping to rest tired muscles. Emalea longed to stop swimming and let her air-filled jacket keep her afloat. But they couldn't afford to rest completely; the minute they stopped moving, even the slower currents worked against them. The agonizing burning in her legs had long ago faded to numbness. Beside her, Jackson stroked through the water stoically pretending not to feel fatigue, but Emalea knew his strength was waning, along with hers.

In the beginning, they discussed what could have happened. Maybe the boat had had to make an emergency return or maybe the dive guide had been injured and they'd rushed him to the hospital. For Emalea, no answer was sufficient enough to explain being abandoned. When they couldn't decide on a decent solution they talked about whatever came to mind. Eventually they didn't talk at all.

Salt and sun parched the skin on their faces and burned their eyes, but even with her blurred vision, the beach began to loom larger in front of them. Emalea squinted at her watch, shocked to see they'd been in the water for nearly five hours.

"We're almost there."

"Don't get too excited." Jackson pointed toward the shore ahead of them where waves pounded against the sand. "I don't think the air in these jackets will keep us afloat in waves that rough. Can you make it?"

She glanced at Jackson, even as she began to feel the rise and fall of the surf. "Do we have a choice?"

He took hold of a strap on her jacket. "I'm going to hold on to you."

"We could get banged together."

A wave slapped him in the mouth and he coughed. "I don't know what else to do." The next wave closed over their heads and Emalea's knees slammed against the sandy bottom.

Jackson bobbed above the water first, hauling her with him. She gasped in a breath, coughed, gasped once more and they were hammered again. As they crashed to the bottom, Jackson's knee hit Emalea's head, dulling her already foggy brain.

She struggled to get her head above water only to hear Jackson shout, "Oh, no!" Before she went face-first into the sand. One more breath followed by another back-breaking wave and Emalea found shallow water. She crawled and was partially dragged by Jackson onto the beach. At the edge of the surf, she didn't move, but lay on her stomach letting the waves splash to her waist. Just so long as she could breathe, she wasn't moving, not yet.

A hand grabbed her shoulder, flipping her on her back. Salt water splashed near her neck and Jackson's hand pressed on her forehead like a fifty-pound weight.

She grabbed his wrist. "What are you doing? That hurts!"

"Stop it, Emalea. You're bleeding. You must have hit something with your head."

"Yeah, your knee."

He groaned. "I'm sorry. I guess holding on to you wasn't such a good idea."

"No." She kept her lids clamped tight, but pulled his hand away, replacing it with her own. "If you wouldn't have pulled me to the top a few times, I'd have drowned, even with this jacket on."

His arms came around her as best they could with her dive gear still in place. "I love you, Emalea. I'm not going to let you get hurt."

Astonished, she sat on the sand without moving or speaking. Jackson, as if wanting to rush by the words, began to jerk loose her BC jacket, then took off his own, peeling away his wet suit and helping her remove hers.

"Come on." He pulled her to her feet when she tried to sit down. "I've seen a couple of cars going by, just past those hills. There's got to be a road there."

"Jackson, I'm tired. Can't we rest here? Besides, you can't just blurt out what you did then take off."

"I can and I will. I'll carry you if you're too tired."

"Oh, that'll be the day. Like you're not completely whipped yourself."

He continued to tug her along. "We've been gone a long time. The others will be worried. Besides, I want to get to that dive shop and find out what the hell happened. Now let's go see if that road will get us back to town."

"It will."

He paused mid-stride. "How do you know?"

"Because there's only one paved road that goes around this island. And that would be it."

Grabbing her free hand, he set off through the sand, both of them wearing only their swimsuits and dive boots, leaving the rest of their gear behind. Was she concussed or had Jackson just said he loved her? The thought of the words tumbling from his lips caused a strange and unfamiliar quivering deep inside her, but her emotions were too frazzled at the moment to define exactly what it was. She only knew they had both traveled to a place they'd never intended to go. Part of her hoped they'd be able to remain there, the other part of her couldn't imagine the possibility because of the obstacles. Unable to maintain much coherent thinking, Emalea stumbled along behind Jackson, pressing her hand to her head to keep the trickle of blood from running into her eye. Instead, it dripped down her arm.

"MAN, YOU'VE GOT to be kidding."

The young blond guy hailed from California, at least that's what he'd told Jackson when they'd booked the dive trip. He couldn't have been more than twenty-two. He appeared to be a good kid, but Jackson wasn't in the mood for leniency.

Slamming his hand on the glass counter, he dug deep for control. "Do I look like I'm kidding?"

The boy sobered. "No, I guess not. But man, that boat was stolen this morning before we got ready to come get you. Our guide was running a little late. We tried to call, but you weren't in your room, then we went to the hotel but you were gone and no one knew where you were. We just figured you got tired of waiting and went to do something else."

"We were doing something else, bobbing around in the middle of the ocean for hours. And we had a dive guide. Are you telling me he wasn't one of yours?"

"I don't know what to tell you, but no one

that works for this shop was out with you this morning. We reported the missing boat to the police. Maybe you should go tell them what happened to you."

Jackson didn't bother to inform the boy he'd made that his first stop. The police were definitely concerned. The dive trade was a huge business and the last thing they needed were stories circulating of people left in the ocean by a dive boat. They'd said they'd check into the situation, and he knew they would. He'd given them his phone number, not expecting to hear a word. He didn't doubt their efforts or abilities. Instinct told him whoever was behind this hadn't left a trail.

Leaving the store, he stood on the sidewalk, the late evening sun battering the top of his head. Horns blared while he climbed into a cab, giving the driver the name of his hotel. Maybe Emalea would be back from the clinic when he got there. With her head still bleeding steadily, he'd sent her to the small clinic that often served tourists, while he'd gone to the police and the dive shop. Her eye had already begun to develop a black ring before he'd left, even though the cut was well above her eyebrow.

His fault—the black eye, the cut, even

being left there had been his fault. He hadn't said a word to Emalea but he knew, in his gut, that the people who'd left them had been paid to do so. This had DePaulo's name all over it. Jackson couldn't have been more sure if the gangster had seen them off that morning at the dock.

Sweat trickled down his back and his shirt stuck both to him and the dirty vinyl seat. Crammed in the back seat of the older model Honda, his knees nearly bumped his chin. They'd been so busy since leaving the beach, he'd barely exchanged more than a few cursory words with Emalea. But those had been intense words he'd spit at her on the beach earlier. The conditions hadn't been romantic, not with blood pouring from her head and both of them dead tired. He did love her, in a way he'd thought impossible, lost to him forever. But it was a subject they should have approached slowly, with caution. Of course, caution had gone the way of the trade winds since they'd been here.

All that meant nothing compared to his renewed determination to keep her safe. Without knowing how, he'd come to love her. He realized now that still meant danger for Emalea. The thought that he could escape from those who wanted to hurt him and his loved ones had been a short-lived dream. The other day he'd told her that being together was worth the risk. But now, with the real threat of danger closing in, the reasons he'd vowed not to get involved with a woman had returned. He'd keep her safe, even if he had to leave her and Cypress Landing to do it.

THE AIR-CONDITIONING HUMMED, making the dim room cool. On the bed, Emalea was curled under the covers, her hair damp. She stirred as he climbed across the bed to lie behind her. When she faced him, he tried not to cringe, the bandage on her head stark white against her tanned skin, her eye swollen with splotches of purple.

"Hmm, look that good, do I?"

"You're beautiful, especially for someone who's just had a battle with the bottom of the ocean."

"I'm wondering how you made it through this without a scratch and I appear to have gone ten rounds with George Foreman."

"I'm tough."

She sobered then reached to stroke the spiky hair on his chin. "I know. That's what makes you so special. I really—"

"Shhh." He put his fingers to her lips. "Not

now. I'm exhausted and I know you are, too. I'm hoping they've given you some pain medicine for your head." She nodded and he continued. "There'll be time later, for everything."

Under the sheet, she snuggled her back to his chest while he circled his arm over to pull her closer. It was a lie. He wished they could go back in time or that none of this had happened. But if no one ever knew he and Emalea had begun to care about each other, then DePaulo would have no reason to hurt her. He would trade their love for her life. And she did love him. He knew it, could feel it when she touched him. Cypress Landing was supposed to have been a place where no dangers lurked, where he had no one who could be threatened. He'd imagined life would be different there, but it wasn't.

CHAPTER FOURTEEN

MATT'S PEN SCRATCHED ominously on the papers in front of him and Jackson fought the urge to grab the sheriff's hand and tell him to stop already. Waiting to be put on trial, that's what he felt like.

"It's good to have you back, Jackson." Matt put the pen aside. "So far nothing's been said about that incident. Which is a little surprising to me, but let's hope it stays that way."

Jackson tried not to look too relieved. "I assume I'm back on the case."

"I never considered you off it." Matt smiled while gathering papers and placing them in a folder.

"Good. What's been happening while I was gone?"

Matt shook his head. "Not much. Your guy made bail, as did the boy from the bait shop."

"I've got my files on this case with me." Jackson held up several folders. "Why don't we compare what evidence you've come up with so far and see what we get."

Jackson spread the files across the desktop while Matt placed his alongside. "I believe this is all tied in with the crime family I dealt with in Chicago." He hoped Matt wouldn't think he was trying to make the case something it wasn't or at least that his boss wouldn't think he was chasing ghosts. "DePaulo, the boss's nephew, helped sell illegal guns on the street. I know they bought a lot of guns down here and took them north to sell." Jackson couldn't believe he was uttering these words. He thought he'd left organized crime behind but, like clearing weeds from the garden, it appeared chasing the Mafia was a never-ending task.

Matt raked his fingers through his hair. "If you want to have your friends in the bureau bring what they can share on this it would be good."

Jackson nodded. "Consider it done."

Matt leaned back in his chair. "I hear you had a bit of trouble in Mexico. What was that all about?"

"Somebody stole the boat that we were going out on. They took us to the dive site, then left us." Jackson thumbed through a file knowing Matt was watching him. He didn't want to sound paranoid but he needed to bounce his theory off someone.

"A few weeks ago, when I was in New Orleans, I saw DePaulo. We sort of have a history."

Matt shifted toward his desk, shoving papers aside. "He's the one you did all that work to get arrested and then they got him off?"

Jackson nodded. "I called some of my friends in Chicago who still work in organized crime. They believe the uncle sent him down here as a punishment for skimming money."

"I can't believe he didn't kill DePaulo or at least let him go to jail."

Jackson frowned. "He's his sister's child. I guess he wanted to give DePaulo a chance to redeem himself."

Matt tapped his fingers on the desk while Jackson waited. "And you think he's behind this thing in Mexico."

"I can't prove it, but I'll always believe he killed my family because he knew it would make me suffer. Maybe he figures I've suffered so now it's time to kill me. Especially since I've shown up here. He may even think I'm following him."

Matt rubbed a hand across his forehead

and sighed. "First of all you need to be careful, and we better get to work digging up something on this guy before we turn up more dead bodies, namely yours."

"MAN, YOU LOOK WHACKED."

Emalea patted the bandage on her forehead. "I'll assume that's not a compliment."

Kent appeared nonplussed. "I didn't mean it in a bad way, but you look like you mixed it up with that big guy at the sheriff's office. You know, the one we saw hammering that man the other day."

Emalea smiled. "To tell the truth, it was his knee that did this."

"No sh— I mean no kidding?"

"Yep. He was part of the group I went on a trip with. He and I were knocked down by a big wave in the ocean. We were standing too close and when we fell, my head hit his knee."

"Standing too close? Were you kissing or what?" The corner of Kent's lip curled upward, and Emalea wondered if this had been a story best left untold. She should have just said she hit her head on a rock.

"No, it wasn't like that at all. He was trying to help me stay standing."

Kent snorted. "He didn't do a very good job."

For a moment Emalea wasn't sure how to respond. Jackson had saved her life, no matter how often he said it wasn't true.

She realized Kent was watching her, and she had been daydreaming. Recalling what they should be discussing, she smiled. "The odds were against him."

"That does happen sometimes, Ms. LeBlanc."

She tilted her head to one side and studied the boy, then nodded. "It certainly does, Kent."

When she least expected it, Kent exposed tidbits of himself that made her wonder if he might be a much older man wrapped in a kid's skin. "So how's your dad after his help was arrested?"

"Really mad. The sheriff keeps coming by asking questions like they think he's involved."

"Do you think he is?"

Kent shrugged. "He's worried that it's bad for business, might scare people away. Either way it makes life at home not so nice."

She leaned toward him. "What can I do?"

"I guess you're doing it right now."

She'd never wanted to hug one of her clients like she wanted to hug Kent. Professionally, she couldn't allow it. Perhaps it was the fact his life mirrored hers that made the connection between them more than just doctor to patient. She wanted to be sister, mother, guardian, protector, but she was none of those.

"That's good. But you'll let me know if it starts to get out of hand, huh?" She had to clear her throat to hide the slight crack in her voice.

"Yes, ma'am, I will." What else could he say? For just a second, Kent thought Ms. LeBlanc might cry, then it was gone and she was in control. Behind his eyes, tears pooled, but he'd learned long ago to keep them there, no matter how much they wanted to escape. He should have told her that by the time he saw it getting out of hand it would be too late to call anyone, but he didn't. Maybe it was already out of hand and he just couldn't admit it.

JACKSON SCOOTED the almost-too-small-for-him chair away from the table. Three days ago he'd shared his theory with Matt that DePaulo might be responsible for illegal guns showing up in Cypress Landing. Last night, when deputies answered a call for shots fired on the outskirts of town, they'd picked up one suspect while two others had escaped. What they had thought would be a simple dispute between a couple of hotheads had turned into the break he'd been hoping for.

"So, what else you wanna know?"

The man sitting across from him took a long pull from a cigarette and blew the smoke out slowly. Next to him, his lawyer seemed totally engrossed in what he was writing on a legal pad. The man, who called himself Michael, had refused to say a word until his lawyer had shown up from Chicago. The lawyer had arrived after what Jackson could only deem a miraculously quick trip. Once the lawyer had made a deal to save his client's butt in exchange for information on illegal guns being brought into the area, Michael had become a fount of information. Which was what bothered Jackson.

"I'm wondering why you're so eager to give up your boss."

Michael glanced at his lawyer, who nodded then went back to his work. "Look, this DePaulo did some work for my boss, but he's not my boss. He was doing dirty, you know, taking my boss's money. So my boss sent him down here to work in his shipping business, but he had two guys kinda watching over him. These two guys turned up dead, and we want to know what's going on.

I come down here and find out DePaulo is selling guns to some crazy group and before I can get word to my boss the guy has two of his flunkies try to kill me. Why wouldn't I want to turn him in?"

Jackson shook his head. "Shipping business, huh? I know all about what happened between DePaulo and his uncle in Chicago. I was there. And I know his uncle is this boss of yours. So tell me something about the guns that go up north."

This time the lawyer glanced at his client, but Michael only smiled. "Sorry, all I know is DePaulo's selling guns right here—if he's taking them somewhere else, you'll have to get that from him."

Jackson sighed and stood. "I'll be back in a minute." Outside the room, he stopped in front of the tiny one-way glass Matt had installed when he'd turned the storage closet into Cypress Landing's version of an interview room. Matt and three FBI agents, including Rick Martel, Jackson's former partner, all waited.

Rick leaned against the wall. "What do you think?"

"I think he's not going to give up his boss in Chicago, but then I doubt any of us expected that."

Rick frowned. "You're right. But what he's

saying makes sense. DePaulo comes down here, sets up a crystal meth lab and uses the drugs to pay off addicts who buy guns for him. We see that happening all the time and not just with the mob. DePaulo sells these guns for a whopping profit to the militia. That way the guns aren't tied to anyone in DePaulo's gang or the militia and everybody stays clean."

Jackson scratched his head. "You're saying the guns we traced, the ones that were bought legally and reported stolen, were purchased by someone who was being paid with drugs to make the buy?"

Nodding his head, Rick glanced at the man in the room waiting beside his lawyer. "Absolutely. DePaulo gives them just enough money to buy the guns and plenty of drugs as a payoff. He still sends guns up to his uncle but behind his back, he's making all this money for himself, and I'm sure his uncle would want a cut if he knew about it. I think the boss is letting Michael tell all on DePaulo, to make things easier for Michael. But if DePaulo's making money behind his uncle's back again, we better find him quick, because I doubt the old man has any intention of DePaulo getting picked up by the police. He's more likely to be some alligator's lunch."

Thumbing through his notepad as if he'd find an answer there, Jackson sighed. "You're right. We better start trying to track him down."

The three agents walked down the hall toward the office they were sharing with Jackson. Matt caught his arm before he could return to the interview room. "The other day you said you thought this DePaulo guy was behind what happened in Mexico."

Jackson nodded.

"And it was just you and Emalea on this boat, right?"

Leaning against the wall, Jackson nodded again. The sheriff studied him quietly for a minute, but he knew what was coming.

"You've gotten involved with her, haven't you? I know you're not dating her or I'd have heard the gossip, but something happened between the two of you, didn't it?"

Jackson's shoulders sagged. "I never intended it to happen. I fought it, ran from it, even. We just… We worked, like I never knew two people could."

Matt shook his head. "I've been in the same sinking ship before myself, when Cecile and I got together. You can bail water all day, but you're going down."

"I'm afraid I sank completely to the bottom. But that's where it stops."

"What do you mean?"

Jackson stepped away from the wall. He'd made his decision where he and Emalea were concerned. Matt might as well hear it. "I believe what happened in Mexico was meant to happen to me. Emalea would have been collateral damage. Nobody, except possibly our closest friends here in Cypress Landing, have reason to think there's any relationship between us at all. But if I keep seeing her, everyone will know. After they failed in Mexico, they could go after her. If I stay away from Emalea, they'll have no reason to come looking for her."

Matt frowned. "You think if they believe she's important to you, they'll hurt her, because that's what they did before."

Jackson's hands balled into tight fists, and he fought the urge to punch the wall. "Damn right and I can't let it happen again. Not to Emalea."

"Don't you think she has a say in it?" Matt tapped Jackson's chest with a folder he held.

What did Matt want him to say? He had to see that if DePaulo knew Jackson cared about Emalea, loved her, she'd be in danger. Jackson had already proved one time that he couldn't keep his loved ones safe by trying to watch over them. This was the only way. "She can't have a say. I've decided and I'll do whatever it takes to keep her off their radar."

Matt watched him for a moment. "Even break her heart?"

Jackson pinched the bridge of his nose. His boots were dusty. He needed to clean them. He needed… With resignation, he forced himself to break the dull silence.

"Both of ours." Just as he'd expected, the words hurt as much as the thought.

THE SCENT OF DISINFECTANT and wet dog hair filled Emalea's nose as she waited quietly at the counter to pick up Jade. She'd named the cat Jackson had given her Jade, because of the color of her eyes. Although she was beginning to think Lucy-fur would have been more appropriate. The animal was not a poster cat for friendly felines and her hands held the scratches to prove it. The cat had become much better lately, but the slightest change in routine made her unhappy and going to the vet had her positively enraged.

When she gave her name and asked for the cat, the girl at the front desk dropped her pen, her mouth rounding in surprise—or dread—Emalea wasn't sure which. Instead of bringing Jade to the front the way she had other people's pets, the girl took Emalea's cat carrier then marched to the back as if on a mission. After a few minutes, the most awful racket she'd ever heard emanated from the back room. Someone cursed while Emalea tried not to fidget at the counter.

Returning to the waiting area, the girl held the carrier at arm's length, her hands covered with long leather gloves. Emalea lifted the carrier to peer inside. Jade hissed, swiping the small barred window with a splotchy paw.

"We'll send you a bill and she's due back in a month for another set of shots."

Emalea turned her attention back to the girl. "Oh, okay. Do I need to make an appointment now?"

"No, you can come anytime but please call the day before."

"You'll need a day's notice to schedule her?"

"No, I want to know the day before so I can take off."

Emalea didn't have a response for that. Thank goodness Jade didn't understand the words because they surely would have hurt her feelings. Poor kitty, she'd just been traumatized as a kitten so now she was defensive. Inside the cage, the kitten growled. Maybe she was more psycho than defensive, but everyone dealt with trauma in different ways. Time and the right company helped cure the wounds. She smiled, thinking of Jackson as she put the carrier on the seat beside her.

AN HOUR LATER Emalea was leading Jade on a mad chase with a piece of string when she heard a car door slam. Pushing aside the blind, she was surprised to see Jackson striding up the steps.

"Hi!" She threw open the door before he could knock and he stopped short in surprise.

"I got finished at work a little early, so I decided to drop by. Should I have called?"

Her arms went around his neck and she touched her lips to his briefly before pressing harder. He kissed her back gently but not with passion, then set her away from him.

"I need to talk to you."

She frowned. "That doesn't sound good."

"It's not."

He took her by the hand leading her to the couch. Seeing Jade nearby, he bent to pet her only to be rewarded with a hiss and a red scratch on top of his hand.

"She's not a very friendly kitten."

Postponing what was coming, Emalea lifted the animal in her arms. "She's fine when she gets used to you. But they hate to see us coming at the vet's office."

"I can imagine."

Jade growled, not caring to be held, so Emalea set her on the floor and the cat promptly disappeared from the room.

Jackson watched her pad away. "Where's she going?"

"To hide under the bed." She sat on the sofa, but Jackson remained standing in the middle of the room.

"That must be nice," he murmured.

"What?"

"To be able to hide under the bed when you get scared and come out when things are safe."

She pulled at a thread on her cutoffs. "Why do I get the feeling we're not talking about the cat anymore?"

A booted toe rubbed her floor and for a moment he resembled a little boy who was trying to get the nerve to confess to breaking the neighbor's window. She imagined a lot more than a window might be broken before Jackson finished.

After a protracted silence, he spoke. "I guess I'm not just talking about the cat. Emalea, I don't know how to say this except plainly. We can't keep seeing each other."

She laughed. "What is that supposed to mean?"

"That you can't be a part of my life."

When he didn't laugh with her or add an absurd remark to the statement, Emalea's smile faltered then disappeared. "You're serious, aren't you? This isn't a joke."

"I've never been more serious in my life."

More than a few emotions erupted within her, most she didn't want Jackson to see. She hadn't expected he would get home from Mexico after telling her he loved her and just dump her like a pile of dirty clothes.

"I guess it was a vacation fling after all." A harsh note of anger and hurt shook her voice.

"No, that's not it at all. Don't you see that you're in danger by being close to me? I won't let you get hurt."

"You can't always keep people from getting hurt. What makes you think what happened to your wife and daughter will happen to me?"

Jackson wiped his hand over his mouth, smoothing the hair that surrounded it. He repeated the process twice more before he spoke. "It already has. We just got lucky."

"Do you believe people were trying to hurt us in Mexico?" Emalea almost said he must be crazy, but she knew he based his fears on the cold facts from his past.

"I think they wanted me dead and if that meant you had to be dead, too, then so be it."

Emalea stiffened. She'd always been able to take care of herself. Did Jackson think one incident would send her into hiding? "I'm not afraid. Besides, what's to stop them from coming after me even if we're not seeing each other?"

He took a step toward her. "Right now, no one except your closest friends know there's ever been anything between us. We were together on the dive boat, but I could have been with anyone. There's no reason for DePaulo or anyone else to think of hurting you to get to me. I plan to keep it that way. I didn't expect you to be afraid. But I'm afraid, Emalea, not for myself but for you. I won't stand by and let you get hurt or even killed."

She wrapped her arms around herself for a moment, fighting the urge to shiver. She wasn't sure if it was from anger or pain. "It should be my decision."

Jackson shook his head. "You don't realize the danger. If you did, we wouldn't be having this discussion."

"To me it's not sounding like much of a discussion. It appears you've already made the decision for both of us."

"I have. I'm doing everything I can to keep you safe. If that means not seeing you again, then I'll do it."

Emalea leaped to her feet. Crossing the room in long strides, she threw open the door. "If that's the way it's going to be, then I suggest you get started right now. Though I have to tell you, in a town this size, not running into each other could be next to impossible."

He came to the door slowly, pausing to rest one hand on the frame, refusing to meet her eyes. "I'll do whatever it takes."

"Does that include hightailin' it back to Chicago?"

She waited for him to deny it but he didn't. "It might. I'm just sorry it has to be this way."

She lifted her hand, wanting to reach out to him, but let it drop to her side. A heaviness in her chest and her throat made the words stall then explode in a crumbled rush. "It doesn't have to be."

"I'm sorry, but it does."

"You're just using this as an excuse." She found a bit of anger buried deep within the hurt and she pulled at it, using its strength to keep from breaking down in front of him. "It's not me you want to safeguard at all, is it? It's you. You don't want to risk loving and losing again. Well, Jackson, there will always be a risk of losing those you love, even if you weren't in law enforcement. Be honest about who you're trying to protect here."

He shook his head. "I'm sorry, Emalea."

She gave his arm a shove, loosing it from the door frame. "Don't be. I'm glad I learned how wishy-washy you are now rather than a few weeks or months from now."

He crossed the space to his truck in seconds. Pausing, he stood with the door open, staring at her. He leaned away from the door as though he might change his mind and come back. But he hammered his fist against the metal, then climbed behind the wheel.

Not willing to watch him drive away, she slammed the door. For the second time today, tears threatened, but this time she didn't bother to bite them back. They came in a flood. She slid to the floor, leaning her head against her knees. Maybe it just wasn't meant to be. When Lana had said Emalea would find the perfect man one day, she hadn't believed her. But Jackson had proved her wrong. He was perfect for her. He'd shown her every man couldn't be smacked with a label. No man would ever equal Jackson. No one would ever measure up.

CHAPTER FIFTEEN

A BARGE WITH A TUGBOAT hustling behind glided in slow motion atop the brown-black water of the river. Around Jackson, people and events floated along in a languid motion, moving from one day to the next comforted by the near palpable air, while he bounced like the silver ball of a pinball machine, his direction determined by whatever lead he came across. He longed to be a part of the community that surrounded him, to stroll along the streets where his biggest investigations were stolen bicycles and random acts of teenage pranksters.

From Jackson's vantage point, on a bar stool at Sal's, the opposite bank of the Mississippi rose green and dense. What was going on at the militia encampment? Once this case ended, they would still be there. Even though the town would seem quiet, a restlessness would always be brewing just under the surface.

Nursing a lukewarm beer, he wasn't exactly sure if he was off duty or not and at this point he didn't really care. Since he'd gotten back from Mexico, he'd been working around the clock. Not that he minded. Constant work helped him to avoid seeing and thinking of Emalea. It also meant he didn't have to answer the question of whether or not he would remain in Cypress Landing after he closed this case.

The mug in front of him disappeared and was immediately replaced by a full one, its frosty sides releasing vapor into the warm air.

"Havin' a rough day?"

He nodded at Mick, who refilled a bowl of peanuts.

"Been busy out on the river today."

Jackson glanced toward the water where a small boat raced along with the current. He turned back to the big man. "Anything in particular?"

Mick eyed the few customers in the bar then shrugged. "Couldn't say." He walked from behind the bar to carry a drink to one of the tables. When he came back, he slid a bowl of peanuts toward Jackson.

"There—" he tapped the bowl "—that might be good for you."

Staring into the bowl, Jackson imagined

he saw a flash of white among the red-brown husks. He ate several peanuts until a small folded piece of paper was visible. Catching it in his fingers he pretended to brush his hand across his chest, dropping the paper into his shirt pocket. He sat a few moments longer then pushed away from the bar.

"See ya, Mick."

"Yeah, man. Take care a yourself. Seen Doc around lately?"

Jackson paused at the door. "No, I haven't seen her in a while."

Mick shook his head. "Hate that. I thought the two of you might make a couple one day."

Jackson wiped his hand over his head. "I…I guess not." He hurried to his truck before he opened his mouth and started whining about his woman problems to Mick. The whole idea was to keep people from thinking Emalea was important to him. If he stayed in Cypress Landing that might be a difficult task.

MEGAN JOHNSON SPRAYED glass cleaner on the front door at Picture Perfect, then began to wipe it fiercely with a paper towel.

"Hi, Megan."

Emalea wasn't sure how to word what

she needed to ask and not breach confidentiality. "Where's the boy who usually helps you do this?"

The girl stopped, letting drops of cleaner run to the sill. She glanced up and down the street then took a step closer to Emalea. "Ms. LeBlanc, I know Kent comes to talk to you once a week. He told me but said for me not to mention it 'cause his dad would get really mad if he knew. He said his mom had given permission."

"That's true, Megan. You haven't told, have you?"

"No way. I'd never do anything to hurt Kent."

"That's good, because Kent's life isn't always as nice as yours or a lot of the other kids'."

The girl frowned. "I know. Some of the kids give him a hard time at school. He's really nice, though, and I want to help him. I'm afraid for Kent."

Emalea's stomach tightened. "He missed his appointment with me this week and I haven't seen him. Do you think something's wrong?"

"I don't know. He missed the last three days of school, but he could just be sick. A lot of kids are home with a virus. His crummy cousins were at school yesterday, and I asked them if he was sick, but they just said it was none of my business where he was, that I would just mean trouble for him. I'd call and check on him but I don't think they have a regular phone. I mean his dad has a cell phone, but I don't think he lets them have a phone in the house."

"Yeah, he told me his dad keeps the only phone they have." Emalea rubbed the back of her neck. "Let's give it one more day. I'll come by the school tomorrow afternoon to see if Kent showed up."

"I sure hope he's not in trouble."

She squeezed the girl's shoulder. "Me, too, Megan. Me, too."

JACKSON TOOK THE FOLDED white paper from his pocket, staring at the maze of directions he'd just followed. Still straddling his motorcycle, he watched the shadows growing among the low-hanging limbs of the trees. The place where he waited appeared to be a picnic area that had lost favor with the community. The tables were overturned and broken, with grass and weeds growing knee high. He heard a vehicle on the half mile of dirt road he'd just passed to get here. The cold steel of the Glock hanging in his shoulder harness chilled his fingers as he reached underneath the unbuttoned shirt he wore on top of his T-shirt.

Meeting in the middle of the woods like this made him nervous, especially when he wasn't sure if he could find his way back home. The last rays of daylight clung to the battered truck as it rolled to a stop beside him. The driver's side window squeaked against the dried rubber that lined it as it wound down slowly.

"Mick," Jackson greeted the bearded man.

"Sorry to have you come way out here, but it's my hide I gotta watch out for. Yours, too, I guess."

"I appreciate your help. The tip about the girl with that boy from the bait shop sure paid off. We were able to make arrests. We're hoping to get a bigger fish next time."

"Figured out that was me, did ya?" Jackson nodded and the man continued. "I don't know how much this will help, but the militia is buying a load of guns from someone. It should take place real soon."

Jackson rubbed his goatee then ran his fingers across the stubble on the rest of his face and head. When had he shaved last? He wasn't even sure. In the truck, Mick sat tapping his thumb on the steering wheel to the beat of a country song that played softly on the radio.

"You didn't hear all this in the bar, did you?"

Mick grunted. "Nope."

"So where is all your information coming from?"

"You might say I've got a source on the inside."

Jackson leaned toward the open window of the truck. "I'd like to talk to your source myself."

"No way in hell that's gonna happen. I'd like to keep him alive."

Just when he thought this case was coming together, it got more complicated. He'd really like to get the details firsthand rather than passed through someone else. If he didn't know where Mick was getting his information, how could he know if it was reliable? "You think his life's at risk if he talks to us?"

"I think his life's at risk every day."

Jackson slapped the gas tank in exasperation. "All the more reason to let me talk to this person. We can protect him."

Mick leaned out the truck window, his arm swinging against the dusty door. "Cooper, this is my family we're talkin' about here.

He's only talkin' to me because of that. I'll take care of him. You just do your job."

The bartender paused and glanced toward the ground. Jackson thought he might even apologize for the outburst, the big man looked so embarrassed. Instead, Mick straightened behind the steering wheel and cranked the engine. "We better be goin'. I'll call ya tomorrow. I don't know where or when this meetin' is gonna be, but I'll let ya know."

Before Jackson could answer, the old truck lurched into gear, made a circle, then disappeared into the darkness that had fallen among the trees that lined the road. He'd have to follow up on whatever Mick gave him. What choice did he have? It was the first good lead they'd had since they'd arrested Michael. Unfortunately, everything Michael told them was useless unless they could catch DePaulo, and naturally, Michael hadn't been able to give them a clue as to DePaulo's whereabouts.

When the last sounds of the truck had died away, he started his motorcycle, leaving the lights off until he was back on the highway. Along the way, the warm, empty night air hugged him and no other traffic passed. The small-town boredom he'd been expecting hadn't materialized. When he'd first decided to move here it had been part prison sentence and part self-renewal. He hadn't expected to feel so territorial, become so attached. But right now, he would do whatever was necessary to keep DePaulo's toxic business away from Cypress Landing.

CHAPTER SIXTEEN

A PUFF OF POWDERED SUGAR rose in the air as Emalea dusted the hot pastries. Her aunt had called last night to ask if she could help in the diner this morning since one of her employees was out sick. Loading a tray with beignets and mugs of coffee, she hurried from behind the counter to place the breakfast on the table of the waiting customers. The door rattled as it swung open and three men she didn't know entered. Behind them, Jackson followed, pointing to four empty bar stools at the counter.

Hands shaking, she tightened her grip on the tray. If she acted like this every time she saw him, maybe he should leave town. At least her life would be less complicated. Her uncle took their order, stopping long enough to chat with Jackson.

He met her eyes and his smile faded. She should have nodded, spoken, then moved on, but she couldn't. She set the tray on the table, then hurried into the kitchen where she picked up another order and tried to pretend he wasn't there.

Half an hour later, the diner had nearly emptied except for Jackson and his friends.

"Em, go refill the coffee for everyone at the counter."

She stared at her uncle as though he'd just told her to enter a burning building. The only people at the counter were Jackson and the strangers with him. He winked, thumbing her chin. "Go on now. You'll be fine. You can't skitter around here like a scared rabbit."

"What makes you think I'm scared?"

"Come on now, girl. I know you and Jackson are having a problem."

Her eyes widened. "How do you know that?"

He shrugged. "Men talk."

"Then you know how ridiculous he's been."

"It doesn't matter what I know. It's what you two know about each other and yourselves that makes a difference." He pushed a loose hair away from her forehead. "Now go give them the coffee."

Gripping the coffeepot, she went to the counter.

"Emalea, how are you?" Jackson's lips

turned upward in a smile that she didn't see reflected in his eyes. He introduced the three men, whose names she immediately forgot.

"How's Jade?"

Turning back to Jackson, she shrugged. "She's good."

"She hasn't been terrorizing the vet's office lately?"

"Next week."

He glanced past her into the kitchen. "I'd like to speak to your aunt Alice, if you think she's not too busy."

She shook her head. "I'm sure she'd appreciate it."

He went around the counter while she finished refilling the other men's cups.

"Are you what's been keeping Jackson down here?"

She frowned at the man whose name ended in *ick,* which was exactly what she was thinking of him at the moment. "I don't know what you mean."

"I couldn't understand why Jackson didn't come to Chicago the first time our boss called to offer him a probationary period back in our unit, but I guess he was otherwise occupied. Thankfully, he's coming around and will be going back with us when he's done with this case."

She tried not to show her surprise. She wasn't really, was she? Jackson leaving. She had suspected it would happen, but the reality hadn't actually set in.

"I thought he wasn't welcome there," she managed to say.

"It was never like that. Sure, his temper was out of control. He even worked on me one time, but, hey, the man had a right. Rather than lose him completely they'll let him have a second chance, see if he can keep his head after this bit of time off."

Obviously no one had bothered to tell this guy of Jackson's most recent loss of control. Suddenly, she didn't want to stay here another minute, didn't want to talk to these men.

"You all have a nice visit." She turned and hurried into the kitchen.

Jackson paused in mid conversation with Aunt Alice, who gestured vigorously at him with one finger. Emalea breathed a sigh of relief she wasn't the one receiving her aunt's lecture. The coffeepot banged against the counter followed by her apron.

"I've got to go. I'm late, and I have to be at the prison this morning." Someone called her name, but she pretended not to hear, hurrying through the door as fast as she could.

The usually relaxing drive to the prison couldn't settle her rattled nerves. Even the trees, overhanging the highway and dappling the roadway with shadows, didn't afford their usual peacefulness. So, Jackson was running back to Chicago. She tried to convince herself life would be easier this way. But part of her really wanted him to stay, possibly giving him time to reconsider his decision. He'd said he loved her, but it must not be the same kind of love she felt, because no stupid mobsters would stop her from being with Jackson. She couldn't imagine life without him.

For a moment she couldn't breathe and nearly pulled the car to the side of the road. She'd promised herself after her first husband never to get so committed, so involved with a man. Until now it hadn't been a difficult promise to keep. Not once had she ever been tested, ever felt anything. But she'd finally found the right man and given him her heart. If Jackson felt the same, she'd do whatever he wanted, even brave the streets of Chicago. But he didn't feel that way, did he? He hadn't wanted her to go to Chicago. He'd found the very lame excuse that being with him could be dangerous. And that was the end of that.

OCCASIONALLY THE PASSING of time could be interminable. The glare on the clock face from the fluorescent lights made the hands nearly impossible to see. He'd tried to quit staring at his own watch, but Jackson now found himself studying the plastic Earnhardt Jr. NASCAR clock, as though the driver himself might jump in the car and whisk the hands around.

Mick had said he'd call. Already it was nearly noon and not a word from the bartender. A stack of folders waited patiently for Jackson's attention. He just kept avoiding them. When he did open one, his mind strayed, making a simple form feel like a complex exam. They couldn't even make a decent plan to bust the weapons sale and break the whole gun trade wide open until they knew where the meeting would take place. The idea of at last catching DePaulo nearly had him salivating.

The paper in front of him only needed his signature and with a sigh he scratched the pen on the thin black line. Would putting DePaulo behind bars make life safe for him, for those around him? He prayed it could happen. Emalea's aunt Alice had given him a real going-over this morning. She'd wanted to know why he wasn't with Emalea, didn't he care for her? He wished he could have told the woman that he didn't have feelings for her niece, but the lie just wouldn't materialize. The older woman brushed away his fears as though they were nothing but a little flour on her countertop.

"Do you wish you'd never met your first wife, never had your daughter?" she'd asked.

"Hell, no! I wouldn't take anything for the time we did have together. But it was my fault they were killed, and I can't put Emalea at risk like that."

She hadn't responded immediately, only twisted her mouth in an expression that told him how little sense she thought he was making.

"I think that motorcycle ridin' and scuba divin' silliness could kill the child one day. You don't see me lockin' her in a closet, do you now? We better be livin' this life we got. 'Cause death, it's gonna come lookin' for us soon enough and when it does, no amount of protectin' on earth can be stoppin' it."

The woman had gone back to preparing food while he'd returned to his friends from Chicago. At that very moment he'd been caught between two lives, one he'd left behind, the other he'd barely tasted.

As he'd wrestled with the thought, Matt

Wright had entered the diner. All those who lived in Cypress Landing had called a greeting of some sort. They knew their sheriff by his first name and weren't afraid to use it. The man had barely hit his seat before Emalea's aunt had dropped a plateful of beignets in front of him followed by a cup of hot coffee and a hug.

He'd known then, without hesitation, without doubt, the life he'd left behind was just that, behind him. From now on he only wanted to have breakfast in that run-down little store on the edge of town while he got his day's worth of investigative information. Already, Janie knew how he liked his coffee and what he generally wanted for breakfast. It seemed that he'd made a monumental decision sitting on the bar stool of the diner. Then again, why would he have made it anywhere else? This was home. After that, he'd led the other men back to the car for the short trip to the sheriff's office, all the while trying to control the smile that threatened. It was another one of those things that just felt right.

Now, sitting in his office, he tried to imagine how he would see Emalea every day and not have her in his life. Maybe her aunt was right. Maybe sharing his life with her would be worth the danger. This time he could do better. Then he thought of Emalea's words. She had been right, of course. He'd said he wanted to keep her from danger and in doing so he could keep himself from getting too close, caring too much. But he already cared about her. Rolling back from his desk, he punched the number for Emalea's office. After several rings, the machine came on, so he hung up, not bothering to leave a message. He wouldn't have known what to say. He just wanted to talk to her, see if he had completely ruined everything.

"Heard from your guy yet?"

Realizing he was still holding the phone, Jackson dropped it back on its base, glancing at Rick.

"No, not yet. I was just trying to make a call."

"I hope we hear from him early enough to get organized. If the call comes in and we've got twenty minutes to get there we might be in a bit of trouble." Instead of leaving, Rick leaned against the door frame. "How long do you think it'll take you to clear things away after this case is done and haul yourself back to Chicago?"

Jackson didn't answer immediately, unsure that he could make Rick understand.

Rick watched him for a minute then snorted. "You're not coming back, are you?"

"No, I'm not. I don't want what's back there, not anymore." There, he'd said it out loud and he was more certain than ever this was the life he wanted.

"I guess you're going to try and tell me your decision has nothing to do with that chick you were mooning over this morning at breakfast."

"That chick has a Ph.D. in psychology."

Rick rolled his eyes. "So, she's a smart chick."

He didn't bother to try and tell his friend he might have blown any chance he'd had at a relationship with Emalea. Maybe if he didn't say the words, it wouldn't be true. Besides, even without Emalea, he knew he belonged in Cypress Landing.

"As hard as it may be for you to believe, I really like Cypress Landing. There's just a different feeling to life here, like it really matters. I have to say, gathering information during breakfast with a bunch of old guys sure beats harassing a low-life snitch in a dark alley, wondering if you're gonna get a bullet in the back."

"You make it sound—" Rick stopped short as Jackson's phone shrilled.

Mick, his voice muted on the other end, gave the information they'd been waiting for, then ended the call. Dropping the pen he'd been taking notes with, Jackson scratched at the hair on his chin. "We're on for six this evening."

"Where at?"

Jackson shook his head. "A few miles from here, at the house belonging to the owner of the bait shop. I knew he was in on this. We just haven't been able to get a thing on him."

"Looks like that was for the best—if you had him locked up this meeting wouldn't be happening."

Leaning back in his chair, Jackson gripped the armrests. "I guess so. I've just got a really bad feeling about this."

What was it that bothered him? Was it the man who owned the bait store or something else? For an instant, the image of Emalea standing with a teenage boy across the road from the bait shop lodged in his brain. What had she been doing there and who was the boy? He'd never bothered to ask, not with so many other things going on between them. Had she gotten involved in this in a way that had nothing to do with him?

Noticing Rick still standing there, he gathered his folders. "Let's go to the conference room. We've got work to do if we're going to pull this off."

The other man followed him, and Jackson put Emalea from his mind as best he could. He wasn't sure what it would take to make her accept him after what he'd said and done. First of all, he had to face the fact that he wanted to be with her even if he couldn't protect her all the time. What would she say to that? At least then it would be her decision, which was what she had wanted in the first place. If things didn't work out, he could always take up dominoes.

WHEN EMALEA MADE IT to the school after her day's schedule at the prison, kids had already started pouring out of the building. Megan stepped onto the front sidewalk and Emalea spotted her. Waving to one of her friends, Megan hurried to the white truck.

"He still didn't come back today, and I didn't see his cousins. Do you think something could be wrong?"

"I'm sure he's fine, Megan. He's probably home sick with a virus, like you said."

The girl twisted blond hair around her finger. "I hope so. I'd hate for anything to happen to him."

Emalea rubbed the back of her neck to see if the hair was actually standing on end, but it wasn't. Dread settled familiarly in her stomach. "I'll go to his house and check, just to be sure."

"What if his dad's there? What will you tell him so he won't find out Kent's a patient of yours?"

"I've been thinking on that today. I'll tell him I'm helping the attendance officer. Since Kent's missed several days maybe his dad won't think much of it."

"Would you let me know what you find? I'll be working at Picture Perfect until five this evening." She was now chewing on the piece of hair she had wrapped around her finger earlier.

"I will, Megan, and don't worry."

Back in her truck, Emalea steered toward the road that ran parallel to the river, wishing she could follow her own advice and not worry. She'd found Kent's address early on during their meetings and had even ridden past his driveway. The house hadn't been visible from the road. She drove by a rusted mobile home with thick grass growing in the yard; the trees closed in on her and a chill settled on her skin even though the sun still beamed through the truck's side window. Only a few more miles to Kent's house.

She turned on her blinker and pulled the truck into the Raynors' driveway. Occasional spurts of grass grew in the center of the rocks along the rutted gravel road. Braking, she brought her truck to a stop. *Please don't let me cause trouble for Kent,* she prayed. Her body stiffened with memories she'd hoped had been left behind long ago. She needed to help Kent and his mom. She just had to find a way to make it happen.

Slamming her foot on the accelerator, the truck lurched forward. Waiting around wouldn't make this visit easier. Light blue paint peeled on every board of the sagging house, revealing gray weathered wood beneath. Machine parts of no discernable origin littered the half dirt, half grass yard. That was why the shiny black Hummer 2 sitting next to the house had to belong to a rich relative in for a visit, or else the bait shop business was much better than she imagined.

She forced herself to leave the truck and trudge cautiously to the front steps. The first tread sagged underfoot. She stopped as her throat constricted. She closed her eyes. Before her loomed a huge man, his fist hammering her cheek, knocking her off the step.

She grabbed the rickety porch railing and shook her head, fighting back the images of her father that threatened to send her racing to her truck. She wouldn't let the memories of him keep her from helping Kent and his mother avoid what had been so unavoidable for her. Deep down, she had a strength that had seen her through all those years and she called on it now as she crossed the porch and rapped on the door.

She heard movement inside the house and knocked a second time. The door cracked, then a short wiry man appeared. In his worn camouflage pants and faded brown T-shirt, Earl Raynor didn't fit her image of abusive men and she reminded herself, again, that there was no physical mold that they had all sprung from.

"Hi, you must be Mr. Raynor. I'm working with the school's attendance officer. We noticed Kent's been absent a good bit this week. I… They sent me to check on him."

"He's fine." The man began to shut the door.

"Could I see him? It's concerning the schoolwork he's missed."

"He ain't here."

Emalea tried not to clench her fists. "Has he been sick?"

Earl Raynor pushed the door back and stepped onto the porch. "He's been helping me this week. Not that it's any business of yours or the school's. I'll keep my boy home when I feel like it."

"Actually there is an attendance law here." Emalea fought to keep her voice calm and controlled.

He took a step toward her and the anger she felt at this man's unconcern for his wife and child kept her from backing away. He pointed his finger at her, and she thought he meant to poke her with it. "Don't talk to me about the law."

"When will Kent be back? I want to see him." She wouldn't—couldn't back down.

"You get out of here and don't worry about Kent. He'll be back at school in a week or so, when I say he can go back."

Emalea bit at her bottom lip. She'd had enough. This little man wasn't going to scare her. He might be used to tromping all over his family, but he couldn't do that with her. "Mr. Raynor, I'm going to see Kent. If I have to get the sheriff to do it then I will."

His hand caught her ponytail, yanking her head back. The cold metal of a pistol she couldn't see pressed underneath her chin.

"That ain't gonna happen." With his foot,

he shoved open the door, using the hand at the back of her neck to drive her forward.

On the living-room floor was an array of weapons in every size. The sofa and chairs had seen their better days, but cheap slipcovers were thrown over them in an attempt to disguise their shabbiness. The men sitting on that furniture appeared to be the type more accustomed to fine leather than this ragged decor. Their casual polo shirts, neatly creased chinos and smooth leather shoes were as foreign in this house as the expensive vehicle sitting in the yard.

"What's going on, Raynor?" A younger man with a bit of a paunch and jet-black hair leaned forward in his threadbare recliner.

"It's just a woman from the school, wanting to see my boy."

The man grimaced. "And you thought bringing her in here was a good idea?"

"She was threatening to call the sheriff." Raynor gave her hair a jerk and Emalea's head bobbed backward. She sucked in air to help her bite back a yelp of pain.

"What are we supposed to do with her now?" the man in the recliner asked.

Raynor shoved her farther into the room. "I figured you would know how to take care of her, DePaulo."

The man called DePaulo sighed, picking at a nonexistent thread on his pants.

"I've seen her before." Emalea's eyes jerked toward another man across the room. He was sitting on the sofa as he gestured toward her and addressed the man called De-Paulo. She didn't know him, did she? He was slightly familiar, as though they might have bumped into each other.

"That's the woman who was on the boat with Cooper in Mexico."

The man called DePaulo smoothed his slicked-back hair. "So, what you're telling me is, if you'd done your job before, we wouldn't be having this problem right now."

The other man appeared to squirm into the lumpy cushions. "But you said to make it look like an accident. If I'd shot them and the bodies were found, it wouldn't have been much of an accident."

"You should have made sure the bodies wouldn't be found."

The shorter man was quiet now. Jackson had been right when he'd said what had happened in Mexico had been meant for him. She couldn't bring herself to believe that organized crime had made a pit stop in Cypress Landing. Glancing at Kent's father, she realized she had underestimated him. He was more than just an abusive man misled by petty hatreds. He was dangerous.

DePaulo came to stand in front of her. "So you're Jackson Cooper's girlfriend."

Emalea tried to shake her head while Raynor held on to her hair. "No, I just happened to go diving with him that morning."

Flicking a strand of hair away from her cheek, he grinned, then in a quick forceful motion, he slammed his open hand across the side of her face. Grabbing a chair to keep from falling to the floor, Emalea wondered how far she would get if she tried to break and run. As if reading her mind, the man grabbed her upper arm, dragging her upright.

"That's just so you'll know who's in charge here. Maybe you're Cooper's girlfriend and maybe you aren't. It might just pay me to find out. I've had enough of that cop showing up everywhere I go." He shoved her toward Kent's father. "Lock her in the room with your wife and kid. We'll take her with us when we leave. You never know, she might come in handy—" his finger raked across her lips "—for something."

Raynor pulled her toward the hallway. She stumbled along behind him trying to fix every detail in her mind. Surely she could find a way out of here. Her breathing grew difficult as her chest tightened and for the first time since she'd left New Orleans, years ago, she was afraid for her life.

CHAPTER SEVENTEEN

THE DOOR SLAMMED SHUT behind her while she considered telling them the sheriff knew she was here and would be searching for her soon. But that lie might bring trouble down on her faster than keeping quiet and buying time. A movement in the room caught her attention and behind her a dim light appeared. Spinning around she saw Kent and his mother standing against the opposite wall of the windowless room; Kent's hand covered the end of a flashlight. In the murky glow, the cuts and bruises on their faces gave them an eerie, almost ghostlike appearance. Mrs. Raynor radiated fear.

"Ms. LeBlanc, what happened? What are you doing here?"

She shook her head as the boy came to stand in front of her. "I wanted to check on you. I was worried when you missed your appointment and Megan told me you'd missed school most of the week."

The boy was quiet, and Emalea surveyed the room, hoping for a point of escape, but with no windows and not even a stick of furniture the place was worse than a jail cell.

"What is this room?" she asked.

"My dad uses it for a storeroom. He keeps it locked and has the only key. I guess maybe he keeps guns here. I found this flashlight in that stuff in the corner." He swung the beam toward a few dusty boxes before staring at the floor. "I didn't know, Ms. LeBlanc. I suspected he was doing something wrong but I didn't know what, not until the last few weeks."

She touched the boy's shoulder. "It's all right, Kent. Why are you two in here?"

Mrs. Raynor came forward. "My husband said we should go visit my sister in Lafayette. We went, but came home early." She touched her bruised face. "My husband was furious. He threw us in here and locked the door."

"Did you see the other men who are here?"

"No, he was alone."

Emalea twisted her hair behind her head. "We've got to find a way out. You two might be safe, but that guy is going to make sure I stay quiet and I don't think he's going to ask me nicely. I'm just praying the sheriff has an idea what's going on."

"They know."

She watched Kent as he leaned against the wall.

"How can you be so sure?"

"Because I told them, or at least I told someone to tell them."

Mrs. Raynor stepped toward him. "When? How did you do it? How did you know?"

"After they arrested the boy selling guns at the bait shop, Dad acted strange. I hung around when I could listen to his cell-phone calls and his calls at the bait shop. I found out they were selling the guns right before he sent us to Lafayette."

Mrs. Raynor grabbed his arm. "Why did you let me come back, Kent?"

"I didn't know exactly when it would happen or how to tell you or what you would do if you knew. You might have come back anyway, maybe even told him the sheriff knew."

"Kent, you can't believe I would put us in danger like that."

He glanced past his mother at the wall behind her. "We've been in danger for a long time."

Mrs. Raynor could only stare at the boy. Emalea imagined that possibly for the first time, Kent's mother could see the damage her son had suffered in this house. At least if she could recognize it, she might try to change their situation.

After a few moments, Kent continued. "When we got here I heard my dad on the phone. He said they weren't making the sale until six—that's the message I sent the sheriff. I guess after he put us in here they changed the time."

"How did you contact the sheriff?"

"I had a cell phone."

Kent's mother stared at the boy. "Where did you get a cell phone?"

"Never mind that." Emalea grabbed the boy's shoulder. "Where is the phone?"

"I was afraid they'd find it on me and the person I was calling would get in trouble, so I dropped it in the back of the commode when I went to the bathroom earlier."

Emalea spun around banging on the door. "Hey, I need to go to the bathroom." She had no idea if the phone would work but it was worth a try. "Come on, I need to go!"

There was a bumping at the door followed by a loud voice. "DePaulo says you can go on the floor for all he cares, but you're not leaving that room."

She slammed her back against the door.

"I went before those men got here," Kent said softly.

Emalea grasped his shoulders again, spinning him around to face her. "If you told the sheriff six they might be too late."

Kent nodded.

She began a slow circuit of the room. "We've got to try and find a way out."

An hour later, Emalea leaned back, rubbing her raw fingers. She'd spent part of the time peeling back the already curling linoleum. Escape through the floor had been their only option, but they'd been unable to get a board loose. The door was padlocked on the outside. So, short of breaking the thing down, they wouldn't be able to go that way. She wouldn't admit the situation was hopeless, but she could see the despair on Kent's face as well as his mother's.

Outside the door, the lock rattled. She shoved her keys back in her pocket as she bolted to her feet. DePaulo stood in the doorway smiling.

"Time to go, little lady."

As the other two men with him came toward her, she shoved one and kicked her foot in the shin of the other. Kent jumped on the back of the man holding his lower leg, knocking him to the floor. Emalea punched the second man who rushed toward her as she tried to race for the open door. Her cheek met cold steel that pushed her head to one side.

"Don't make me shoot you right here. I'd rather not leave a mess to deal with afterward." The nose of the pistol forced her head back even farther.

"Raynor, you deal with your family. I'll take the lady with me."

With the gun still against her head, DePaulo took hold of Emalea's shoulder, shoving her through the house. Stumbling on the porch steps, she tried to watch for an opportunity to break away, but the gun never wavered. DePaulo slammed her against the door of the Hummer then jerked her hands behind her back. She heard an ominous sound she couldn't distinguish, then a sticky strip of tape bit into the skin of her wrists. *Hopeless* still wasn't a word she was willing to use, not yet, but without her hands free her situation had become dismal.

DePaulo dragged her into the back seat next to him while one of the other men slammed the door. He smiled and bumped her chin with the muzzle of the gun as the vehicle began to move.

"Now for a little deception. We'll—"

"Boss, we got trouble."

The warning from the front seat had both DePaulo and Emalea turning for a better view through the tinted windows. One, no make that three, cruisers pulled into sight on the long gravel drive. They were still several hundred yards away, but relief flooded through her, maybe her chances *had* improved. DePaulo seemed completely unperturbed by the approach of the officers.

"We should follow the plan we established."

The man in front nodded, and the big truck bounced across the yard toward the woods. Just when Emalea had decided their plan was to ram the truck into the trees, a narrow clearing appeared. The driver steered along the path while tree limbs raked the sides of the SUV. Twenty yards in, a small tree lay across the opening. The Hummer never slowed. Emalea's head hit the roof and her shoulder crashed into the door. Behind them sirens wailed, not quite covering the brief thump-thump of gunfire she knew came from the house. She prayed Kent and his mother wouldn't be hurt. She prayed for a way to escape. Even though she knew the sheriff's men were behind them, she couldn't see them. They couldn't keep up with a vehicle made for the very thing they were doing.

The truck slowed to a crawl as the path made a ninety-degree turn, the river just visible through the underbrush. DePaulo took a handful of her hair, threw open the door and jumped, dragging Emalea headfirst behind him.

She tucked her legs under to keep the truck from rolling on top of them, then half ran, half crawled into the trees, with DePaulo still holding her by the hair. Five feet into the woods, he hit her with his full weight in a tackle that sent them both to the ground, his body crushing her into the spongy dirt. The gun banged against her temple.

"Don't even think about moving or I'll kill you right here, on the spot. They think you're in the truck so your stinking body won't be found until I'm long gone."

Fog shrouded her brain and her head ached where he'd hit her. She didn't have time to weigh her chances of drawing attention, as the two sheriff cars and a game warden's truck roared past, tires flinging chunks of dirt while the drivers negotiated the sharp curve.

Dead leaves and dirt clung to her. DePaulo grabbed her shirt and dragged her to her feet.

He pushed her toward the river, but she stumbled, falling to her knees. He pulled her upright by her hair. A formidable-looking man waited beside a small boat. If she could only get away long enough to lose herself in the woods, she would be safe. They'd never follow her. They wouldn't be able to. She knew these woods better than most, certainly better than these city criminals.

She jerked hard, hair ripping from her head, but she was free. Desperate to keep her balance with her hands behind her back, she floundered through the grass and leaves. The neck of her shirt tightened around her throat, and she was jerked backward. This time, when the gun cracked against her skull, the earth tilted and the scent of musty leaves filled her nose, then nothing.

THE SIGHT OF EMALEA'S TRUCK in front of Earl Raynor's house left Jackson numb and slow to react. It was happening again. Even ending their relationship hadn't protected her. He couldn't imagine one good reason for Emalea to be here, but she was. At the edge of the woods, a black Hummer chewed loose grass and sent it flying.

He barked at the young man behind the wheel of the game warden's truck to follow the Hummer. His head thumped against the passenger window as the vehicle jerked forward with more power than he'd anticipated.

When the Hummer entered the trees, they lost sight of it. They followed the torn ground easily, but the big machine left them far behind. They'd trailed the truck through the woods for nearly fifteen minutes when the path opened to a clear field covered in the fresh green grass of late spring. A white-and-red Cessna rolled away from them at full speed, the Hummer abandoned.

Jackson rolled down his window as the young game warden sent his truck roaring after the plane. The wheels of the aircraft lifted off the ground for a few seconds only to return with a bump. Leaning out the window, Jackson unloaded the entire clip of his pistol, even though he knew the plane was too far away. He sat back in the seat for a quick reload while ahead of them the Cessna's wheels left the ground and this time the plane kept rising. His eyes blurred in the waning light reflected off the side of the plane. Then it was gone.

The truck drew to a stop and he jumped out, stomping around the front of the vehicle, kicking at the offending grass. What now? Sure, they could try and have the plane tracked. But they'd just taken off from a cow pasture. They could just as easily land in a field miles from here. And Emalea was with them. Even though he hadn't seen her, he knew. He could hear one of the deputies with them radioing to tell Matt and Rick what had happened.

From his belt, his own radio squawked his name. He nearly threw it into the woods. He sat on the bumper of the truck, wiping his hand across his eyes, before punching the button to talk.

"This is Jackson."

Rick's voice crackled through the speaker. "Cooper, we've got a damn mess at this house. You need to get back here right now."

"Is Emalea there?" He didn't know why he even bothered to ask when he knew in his heart DePaulo would never have left her behind.

"No, she's not here. They took her."

He snapped the radio onto his belt as he climbed into the truck. "You heard 'em, back to the house."

The boy steered the truck toward a nearby road rather than the way they had come. "It'll be quicker," he promised.

Jackson leaned against the headrest. This wasn't the end. He'd find Emalea and if DePaulo had hurt her, the man would pay.

A SOFT SWAYING MOTION almost lulled Emalea to sleep. The smell of leaves had been replaced by clean cool air. Air-conditioning, that's why she was cold. Eyelids that seemed almost glued together kept her from seeing anything, and the gentle rocking threatened to lull her back to sleep. She forced her lids to part, but she could see nothing in the haze that still cloaked her vision. Far away, a nightlight glowed. She almost sighed. Her head ached unbelievably, and her fuzzy brain began to clear, as did her vision. She was lying on the floor of a room on a boat, of course. That was why she kept feeling a rocking sensation. Thick gray tape now bound her feet as well as her hands. She jerked her arms and legs. The tape wouldn't budge. Nausea swelled into her throat but she bit it back. She couldn't afford the luxury of being sick or even afraid. She had to get out of here.

What she'd thought was a night-light was now easily recognizable as simply the shaft of light under the door. Outside of this room, lights were on and people moved, going about the business of...of what? Were they readying the necessary equipment to dispose of her body?

She hauled herself to a sitting position,

squinting into the shadowed darkness. Feet, hands and shoulders worked together as she scooted around the floor. A set of bunk beds was attached to one wall and across from them was a small built-in dresser. Fingers scraped over every surface in the room. Then she found it. On the corner of the bed, a piece of metal hadn't been set properly. She tugged at it, feeling the sharpness in her palm. Thank goodness for poor workmanship. Even a wealthy mafioso's yacht couldn't escape a factory flaw. Guardedly, she moved her arm against the sharp edge, which bit into her skin as she scrubbed the tape across it.

What would she do if she got free? The boat had to be on the Mississippi River. It didn't feel as if it were moving but just sloshing along with the current, possibly anchored. If she jumped into this water she was as likely to drown as not. The current and the river itself were too unpredictable, taking its victims where it wanted; but if her choices were waiting around to see what these men would do or battling against the river, she'd take the river any day. Metal scraped her arm and she twisted her wrists before shoving the tape against the sharp edge with renewed vigor. Outside her room, a door banged and voices grew louder. Someone was coming for her.

CHAPTER EIGHTEEN

FOOTSTEPS STOPPED NEAR the door before it swung silently open. Even the dim light from the interior of the boat blinded Emalea. She held her hands with the frayed gray tape behind her.

DePaulo stood in the door framed by the lights of the other room. "So, I didn't kill you after all. That's good. I wanted you alive, at least until I can get you back to New Orleans."

"The sheriff and FBI will find you before you ever get to New Orleans. The Raynors will tell them where we are."

"The Raynors don't know about this boat and even if they did, they're all dead anyway."

Emalea slumped against the wall. "You're lying."

"When we left, Raynor went back to kill his wife and kid. When he came back, he tried to shoot his way out, but one of those country deputies got him. I saw him go down just as we hit the woods. So you can forget about that little family."

"They'll know I'm here. My truck was at that house." Her voice cracked as she tried to swallow.

"Right now the sheriff is searching for the plane he thinks you're on. So sit back and enjoy what little time you have left. When we get to New Orleans we'll find out just how much you mean to my friend Mr. Cooper. I'm betting he'll run right down there to save you. Then I can finish him off for good."

The door thudded closed, returning Emalea to darkness. Everything had gone so incredibly wrong. Kent and his mother... She bit back a sob and fell onto her side while tears ran into her ear and onto the floor. In an instant the whole world had gone spiraling out of control and the cost of the ticket to end it could be her life and Jackson's. She tried to rub her cheeks against her shoulders as she struggled to a sitting position. Finding the sharp edge on the bed, she began to bump the tape across it. No one could help her now, except herself.

WITH EACH MOVEMENT THE tiny canoe shivered beneath him. Jackson paddled with all his might, wishing he could risk using the small motor. Rick and the others from the FBI were certain the noise of a motor wouldn't be noticed, especially since they'd be stopping on the opposite side of the spit of land between DePaulo's boat and Cypress Landing's side of the river. His boat camouflaged by the tiny island, DePaulo doubtlessly thought his ploy with the plane had worked, but the least sign of trouble could send him and his men running, which was why Jackson chose the quietest approach possible. Right now he could only hope that Emalea was still on the boat, and that she wasn't hurt. He had to be thankful for the information that had sent them here instead of chasing after the plane.

Behind him, Pete shifted, causing the boat to wobble even more. His arm still in a sling, Pete had to be hurting. He couldn't help Jackson paddle but had insisted on coming. The sheriff had agreed.

"He knows the area better than anyone. Besides, there's not a whole lot of solid ground on that little piece of dirt in the middle of the river. But Pete can get you to the other side."

Thankfully, darkness had set in with a vengeance. Clouds chased each other across the sky, sending only patches of milky light onto the water. The canoe, or pirogue, as Pete had called it, thudded against the muddy bottom as they slid through thick grass beneath the drooping arms of a weeping willow. He stepped out with Pete right behind him, both of them sinking to their ankles in mud.

"You sure you know the way across? I don't want to sink neck deep in mud."

Pete snorted. "I know exactly where we need to go. I never said we wouldn't get muddy, though. We're just lucky we found out they were using this boat."

"It was a surprise, but a good one, for sure."

The squish of mud echoed in Jackson's ears, sounding bigger than an alarm bell. What if he was too late? What if… He shook his head. He wouldn't give in to that kind of thinking. Emalea was alive. She had to be because he wouldn't accept the possibility that he might lose her. Not when he'd only just begun to believe he could care again. In truth, he'd long since passed the point of just beginning to care. Totally consumed would be a much better description of the feelings that swamped him at the thought of Emalea, and especially at the thought he might not be able to share his life with her.

The heavy bag bumped against his hip, making him aware of the silence punctuated only by his and Pete's labored breathing. He stopped at the edge of the underbrush, the water swirling, in front of him, the boat's lights giving off a yellowish gleam. De-Paulo wasn't hiding. Confident in his plan to confuse his pursuers, he wasn't concerned that the local sheriff might find him.

Dropping the bag into the mud, Jackson began slipping into his dive gear. He carried no extra gear for Emalea except the octopus or extra breathing piece attached to the air tank along with the regulator he would breathe through. He knew the water was dangerous but they would make it. They had to.

Reading his thoughts, Pete bumped his shoulder. "You should be able to swim straight to the boat from here. The current's not so bad on this side and they're anchored close in. You'll do fine. Em's a strong swimmer, too. When you two get off that boat use your scuba gear to stay deep until the sheriff picks you up. You don't want to be in range of their bullets if they shoot at you from the boat. The SWAT team is ready to go at my signal." Pete paused, looking at the boat calmly floating in the water. "So this is how the rich and unlawful live?"

Jackson snorted. "Yeah, kinda sickening, isn't it?"

"Maybe when you catch the guy, we can impound the boat and take it for a little fishing trip."

He laughed then held out his hand. "Thanks, Pete, for everything."

"Just hurry and get our girl off that boat."

Jackson waded into the river, the mud sucking at his calves. Leaning forward, he dropped into the water, dragging his feet free. He swam just under the surface until he was within twenty feet of the boat. There was no movement on deck, but through a small window he could see three men inside the cabin. No sign of Emalea, not that he expected her to be in the open. Sighting in the boat's anchor line on his compass, he dove deeper and began fighting the current. He'd seen no indication of the sheriff or the SWAT team, but he knew they were there, waiting for him to perform what some thought would be a miracle. The SWAT team and the FBI had wanted to swarm the boat, but Jackson knew DePaulo too well. Emalea wouldn't survive such an attack. DePaulo would make sure of that. At the first sign of trouble he'd kill her and torch the boat. No, this was the only way—quietly, when they were least expecting it.

He had to swim for several minutes to reach the anchor line. With his hand on the line, he swam almost to the bottom then removed a rope from his BC jacket. Next, he removed his gear and tied it to the anchor line with the rope he had brought. He put his mask in one of the loops on the jacket then took several deep breaths before twisting the knob on the air tank to the off position. He said a quick prayer that they'd make it back here and be able to get to the equipment. With both hands on the anchor line, he pulled himself to the surface and began making his way to the small water-level deck on the back of the boat.

BLOOD TRICKLED DOWN her fingers as the tape pulled apart. Her hands were free at last, and within minutes she had her legs free. Muscles aching, Emalea struggled to her feet, edging toward the door, hands stretched in front of her, the darkness only broken by the thin glow on the floor. She'd heard the voices of two other men on the boat. Her chances of survival might not be good, but she wouldn't sit around and wait on DePaulo's time schedule. If he wanted to shoot her and toss her in the river, it would be while she was doing everything in her power to get away. She might not be trained in escape tactics or martial arts but, if motivation counted for anything, she was in good shape because every cell of her body was focused on getting out of here alive.

Listening at the door, she could hear muffled voices in another room. Now was not the time. She'd wait. Maybe they'd at least go on deck, giving her a chance to get out of this room and off the boat. As she settled against the wall, she replaced the tape at her feet in case one of them decided to check in on her.

HER EYELIDS WERE HEAVY, and Emalea began to worry she might fall asleep. Time had begun to have no relevance. Had she only just gotten free of the tape or had it been hours ago? She shook her head, realizing that she had actually dozed for a few minutes. Then she heard something. A scraping noise on deck, then a muffled yelp of pain followed by a splash. Outside her room, feet slapped against the floor as the men ran to the top deck. Ripping the tape off her feet, she floundered to the door and twisted the handle easily. Thank goodness for DePaulo's overconfidence. He hadn't been worried that she would escape.

Above her, shouts split the night air, but she tried not to think too long on what might be taking place. She had one way to stay alive and that way was up the steps in front of her.

The first rush of air touched her skin, but she had no time to revel in it as she slammed into a body blocking her way. She recognized one of DePaulo's men as he stumbled then half fell toward her. With a quick jerk, she drove her knee into his groin, grabbing his wrist to capture the pistol in his now loose grip. She backed away, holding the gun on the two men remaining on the deck.

"Emalea."

In the dark, she could barely distinguish Jackson's face, but his body appeared coiled, prepared to spring in an instant. Three feet away, the muzzle of DePaulo's gun was pointed at Jackson.

"Well, well, I'd say we have a situation here, wouldn't you, Mr. Cooper? I hope your girlfriend's a good shot. Either way, you'll get this bullet."

Emalea took a step toward the man. "I'm a very good shot and I promise, if you even start to pull that trigger, you're done." Her hand was firm on the handle of the pistol. She'd never shot anything except a target, but right now Jackson's life as well as her own depended on how she handled herself.

To her right, the man she'd hit rushed toward her. She spun, squeezing the trigger. The gun spit bullets at him and his eyes widened for a few seconds, before he fell to the deck. DePaulo, distracted by her shots, missed Jackson's leap toward him. The force of his attack sent both men to the ground, fighting for control of the weapon as they rolled on the deck.

Emalea trained her gun on the man on top of Jackson. She pulled the trigger, but the gun didn't fire. The clip was empty.

Jackson punched DePaulo, sending the man's pistol clattering across the deck toward the stairs. She made a step toward it as DePaulo scrambled in the same direction.

Something whizzed past her ear, and she realized it was a bullet. The man she'd shot struggled to his feet and fired another smaller pistol he'd concealed. Fingers closed around her wrist and she felt herself hit with a flying tackle. She had no idea what Jackson was doing as they tumbled over the side of the boat into the dark river while a whirring sound vibrated the water near her head. They were still shooting. She tried for a moment to open her eyes but knew she couldn't see, so she kept them closed. Because they'd gone under with no preparation she hadn't had a chance to get a deep breath and already her lungs were beginning to burn. She wasn't sure if she wanted to drown in this muddy river or risk getting a bullet in the head. She tried to kick her feet, trusting that Jackson had a plan and would let her get a breath in a second. Her back bumped against the bottom of the boat and she realized Jackson was feeling for something. She only wished he'd hurry.

They swam farther, and she began to struggle toward the top, her lungs aching for relief, but he pulled her back. Around them, she could hear bullets ripping through the water and she realized their only safety was in deeper water, but she doubted she could hold her breath long enough to outdistance the bullets.

Jackson shoved a rope into her hand, then a piece of plastic bumped against her mouth. With her free hand she grabbed at the round object, recognizing a regulator. Shoving the mouthpiece between her lips she used the last bit of air in her lungs to blow out the water that had gone in her mouth with the plastic, then she took a shallow breath. When she was certain no water remained, she took a deep breath, concentrating on not breathing through her nose. She was used to having a mask to keep her nose pinched closed and to keep water from entering. She heard a clicking noise that almost sounded like a radio crackling, then they were swimming again as the roaring of boat motors passing overhead made her ears ring.

At last they began to go upward. The night air continued to be riddled with gunfire and when the balmy breeze hit her face, she sucked humid air into her lungs. A light flashed on her while, behind her, men swarmed onto DePaulo's boat. An aluminum motorboat pulled alongside them and hands wrapped around her, dragging her into the bottom of the vessel, which rocked precariously as Jackson climbed over the side. She recognized Matt at the back steering.

"Good to see you, Em," he shouted.

She nodded as Jackson dumped diving gear onto the bottom of the boat. He didn't speak, only pulled her close and held on tightly. It reminded her of that first time he'd held her like this in the back of the sheriff's car, right after she'd found the body. At the time, she'd decided he would be trouble. She had been right, but it was a wonderful kind of trouble. Soon it would be over and he'd be gone.

She burrowed closer to his chest and felt his lips against her forehead. If she could say anything to make him stay in Cypress Landing she would, but she couldn't imagine the exact words it would take. His predictions had come true, which would only solidify his belief that he would bring danger to those he loved. If only she could explain that it was her job that had put her in this position and not him, but she knew he'd never listen. He had a job in Chicago that he obviously missed. A job he was good at. Being the investigator in Cypress Landing certainly couldn't compare to what he'd be doing in the FBI. What had happened today with this case would be an everyday occurrence there. His jaw was tense under her palm when she put her hand against it. He turned his head to kiss her hand, then clasped it between both of his. Eyes closed tightly, she held on to him as the boat bumped along toward the lights of Cypress Landing.

CHAPTER NINETEEN

EMALEA ROLLED OVER in the bed groaning. Aching in every part of her body, she squinted at the morning sun streaming through the window. Pink flowered wallpaper made her smile in spite of the nightmarish events of yesterday and last night. Her aunt had insisted on a girlie room when a young Emalea would have rather had motorcycles and animals. As she'd gotten older, she'd learned to appreciate her aunt's cultivating of her more feminine side. Right now that feminine side and every other side throbbed with pain.

The entire trip on the boat and then the ride in the car to her aunt and uncle's home had taken place without one word between Jackson and herself. He'd cupped her face in his hands and kissed her briefly before getting in the car with Matt to help deal with the arrests they'd made.

Aunt Alice had wanted to take her to the hospital for the ugly cuts on her arms and the bruise on her face, but she'd refused and had cleaned them well when she'd bathed. She'd crawled between the sheets not allowing herself to consider what could have happened to her. She'd made it out alive. She had to be thankful for that no matter what happened next.

Wiping her eyes, she rolled to her side. She was alive, but others hadn't been so lucky. In the end, she hadn't been able to save Kent or his mom. She buried her face in the soft pillow, her tears soaking the cloth, the fresh scent of fabric softener filling her nose. She had failed them, just like she'd failed her own mother. The confidence she'd felt climbing those broken-down steps had been a mistake. No class, no education could teach her how to save someone else. Now she realized how helpless Jackson must have felt after what had happened to his family. At least this time he'd been wrong. She had survived and she would continue to because she had learned the skills at an early age—but what good did that do those she wanted to help? Her shoulders drooped from the weight of her failure as she dug deeper into the mattress.

With slow movements, Emalea left the bed and pulled on the ragged clothes that her aunt had laundered. Later, when she got home, they'd go straight in the garbage. For now she made her way along the side street to the restaurant.

Inside, breakfast was booming as usual. Everything was so normal. She could almost forget that people had died yesterday. There was a difference, though, inside her, where everything that could remotely be called normal had gone into hiding. The people of Cypress Landing weren't going to let her forget yesterday. It seemed to be the topic of everyone's conversation. At least six questions were hurled at her before she got past the first two tables. Managing to escape by shaking her head, she slipped into the kitchen where her aunt and uncle were busy putting together orders.

"Your help out sick again?"

Her aunt waved a spatula at her. "Yes, but you don't need to be in here. You should have stayed in bed."

"I prefer to keep busy, it helps me to keep from thinking too much."

Her aunt nodded then tossed her an apron. "Better that you work in here. You'll get nothin' but the nosies there." She bobbed her head toward the dining area.

Emalea didn't want to discuss what had

happened to Kent and his family. People had died. It was just too much. Tying on the apron, she stepped in front of the hot stove, pushing pans aside to make the next order.

An hour later, she found a moment to take a break and fixed herself a cup of coffee while glancing through the opening between the kitchen and dining area. Matt sat at the bar finishing his breakfast. She stepped in front of him, placing her cup on the counter. A wet spot on the smooth surface caught her attention and she wiped it with a napkin.

"You're looking much better this morning." He tapped his own cheek. "Got a bit of bruise right there, but you'll be fine."

She gripped the napkin in her fist. "I wish I could say the same for the Raynor family." Her throat knotted as she thought of Kent and what his future might have held, if he'd only had half a chance.

"Yeah, it's a shame. They'll have an adjustment, but in the end I think Mr. Raynor wasn't much of a husband or a father."

"No, he wasn't. Have you talked to the family about what happened yesterday? I was wondering if…well, if arrangements had been made."

Matt looked at her skeptically. "You aren't going to the service, are you? I mean you didn't really know the man and he almost got you killed."

"It's not Earl Raynor that I'd be going for. But Kent and his mother deserve my respect, for all they lived through."

He tilted his head to one side watching her, then shrugged. "I don't know Mrs. Raynor's family. I haven't seen either one of them since the boy told us where to find you and I had to tell them Mr. Raynor had been killed."

Emalea's cup thudded against the counter, coffee sloshing over the sides. "What are you talking about?"

Matt leaned back. "You didn't know the boy was the one feeding us information the whole time? It was through a relative but that was how we knew there would be a meeting at Raynor's place."

She shook her head. "I knew Kent was helping you, but I thought that Raynor had killed his wife and son. That's what DePaulo told me."

Matt brushed at the powdered sugar left on his mouth. "Nope, the boy and his mother are fine. I'm sure they're still feeling the loss, no matter what kind of man Earl Raynor was, but physically they were only banged up. They'll need help getting their lives together. You all right, Em?"

Her knees shook and she bent forward resting her head on the edge of the counter. For a minute she couldn't respond. Straightening and rubbing her forehead, she sniffed then wiped at her eyes with the damp napkin. "I'm just so relieved. I've been thinking all this time they'd been killed. I need to go to the house and see them."

"Are you sure? That could bring back a few ugly memories."

She threw the napkin in the garbage. "I'm sure. I went there to try and protect them and I was the one who got in the most trouble. Either way, they need help and I want to do whatever I can."

"They'll be glad to see you I'm sure. They were really worried about what would happen to you. I hear from Jackson you handled yourself like a pro."

She shoved her hair away from her face, not really interested in recalling the events of last night. "I doubt I was very professional. That was sheer terror and desperation on my part."

Matt took a drink of his coffee. "Jackson seems to think he would have been in trouble if you hadn't been, as he put it, 'about to get away all by herself.'"

She shrugged. "As far as I knew, no one was coming to help me. That guy said they were going to use me as bait to lure Jackson into a setup so he'd be killed, too, I imagine. I figured I was the only one to get myself out of there."

Matt wadded up his napkin. "I better get to the station. We've still got a load of paperwork." He slid off the stool. "You seen Jackson this morning?"

She shrugged. "I imagine he's busy."

"He'll be by later. I think he's leaving for Chicago with his friends from the FBI this evening."

"That's what I heard."

The sheriff stood for a moment longer, as if he might say something more. Instead, he pushed open the door and left. What else was there to say? She hadn't planned on falling for Jackson and now those in town who knew how she felt would be feeling sorry for her. She didn't need sympathy or pity. At least she'd put an end to the distrust she'd felt in herself. She'd finally learned she wasn't always attracted to men like her father. Sure, Jackson had shown unrestrained anger, but she had to admit that in his place she would have done the same. He'd shown her nothing but gentleness. She might have to suffer the pain of losing Jackson, but along the way she'd managed to salvage a piece of herself she hadn't even known was missing. That had to be a good thing.

The coffee in her cup was cold. She had lost interest in it anyway. She dumped it in the nearest sink, putting the cup in with the rest of the dirty dishes.

"I'm going to the Raynors'."

Aunt Alice stopped in the middle of cracking an egg, the white leaking onto the countertop. "What in the world you wanna go and do that for?"

"I need to check on Kent and his mother." She paused, glancing around the kitchen. "I should take some food with me."

Her aunt helped her load a box with containers of rolls, a casserole from the freezer and meats and cheeses for sandwiches.

Halfway to the door, Emalea stopped. "I don't have my truck. Matt brought me home last night and my truck's still at the Raynors'."

Her aunt smiled. "Your truck's at the garage. Jackson got your uncle's spare key and had a deputy bring it by."

She wanted to tell her aunt all the kind deeds in the world weren't going to change the fact that Jackson would be living in Chicago again before the month was finished. At the moment, she just didn't have the heart to broach the subject. Her aunt would be disappointed and Emalea would be a lot more than that.

JACKSON PUSHED PAPERS aside on his desk as Matt eased into the chair across from him. "It seems your man, DePaulo, will be locked up for good."

"I'm glad, even though it's taken some time to catch him. And his uncle won't get him off this time. Not after DePaulo was going behind his back selling guns to the militia and pocketing the money himself."

Matt nodded and sat watching him for a moment before he spoke. "Rick tells me he's trying to convince you to come to Chicago. He says the agency has offered you a probationary period at your old position."

"Yep, he's been persistent."

"He doesn't seem to think he's convinced you yet, says he's hoping when you go with them for a few days you won't be able to leave."

Jackson leaned back in his chair, trying not to smile at Matt so obviously fishing for information.

"You're my boss. Don't you think I'd have told you if I planned on leaving?"

Matt shrugged.

"What do you think I'm going to do?"

"I think you'll do whatever makes you happy," Matt said.

Jackson laughed, tossing his pen onto the

desktop. "Then I'm sure you know I won't be staying in Chicago. Cypress Landing is home for me now."

Looking a little relieved, Matt grinned. "Found something about this place you like, huh?"

Jackson rubbed his chin. "You could say that."

Matt leaned forward and picked up a small crystal paperweight from Jackson's desk, tapping it lightly against the scarred wood. "I'm glad. I'd hate to see you leave, and I'm sure I wouldn't be the only one."

Jackson sighed. Matt didn't have a clue how complicated things were with Emalea. "I might have to work on that, but I'm going to be here and I'll give her all the time she needs."

"My wife always tells me I give bad romantic advice. In your case I sure did. Thank goodness you didn't listen to me when I told you to stay away from Emalea." Matt dropped the paperweight on the desk and Jackson could only shake his head.

"Part of me thought you were right. This thing with Emalea just seemed to have a life of its own."

"The best things always do." Matt got to

his feet. "You think you'll see her before you go to Chicago?"

He rested his elbows on his desk. He wasn't sure if he could face Emalea, not yet. "I don't know. We're leaving in a few hours."

"Just don't go to Chicago and change your mind," Matt shouted on his way down the hall.

"It's not my mind that would have to be changed," Jackson whispered.

LOOKING AT THE RUTTED gravel drive and battered house brought a weird sensation to Emalea's stomach. Mr. Raynor's truck shimmered in the mid-morning heat and she tried to remember if it had been sitting exactly like that when she'd been here before. She parked and got out of the truck, leaving the food on the seat for the moment.

Hinges squealed on the front door as it swung open before she could get to the steps. Kent let the door bang shut behind him. He appeared unharmed except for the bruises he'd had yesterday and relief rushed through her. Like an animal, unsure of its welcome, he hesitated at the top of the steps. He shivered as if a cold wind had hit him. Emalea opened her mouth to speak, but the words she wanted to say stopped in her throat. It didn't really matter. Nothing she could say would touch what he was feeling now. If it had been her father who had died all those years ago instead of her mother, what would she have felt the next day? What would her life have been like? Kent and his mother would have to start a new life, a whole new way of thinking. Would he let her be a part of that? He still teetered on the edge of the sagging porch.

A whoosh of air escaped from his mouth that became a whine at the very end, then he lunged, completely missing the steps and nearly knocked her off her feet when he threw his arms around her with an abandon and desperation he would have said he'd outgrown. She closed her eyes tightly but a tear leaked out as she hugged him close.

"I'm so sorry, Kent, about your dad, about everything."

Against her shoulder, his head moved from side to side, his words muffled. "It wasn't your fault, none of it. My fault, it was all my fault that you got in the middle. If it hadn't been for me, you wouldn't have come here yesterday."

"Who's to say my being here didn't keep you or your mother from being hurt?" She remembered DePaulo's words that Earl Raynor had been going to kill his wife and son. "It's all over now and you and your mom will be fine."

He stepped away from her, his head bowed. "Maybe. My mom is… Well, this is the only life she knows. What if she meets a man and gets in this same mess?"

She caught Kent's hand in hers. "Then we'll just have to show her another way."

"Do you think we can? Do you think she can learn to be different?"

"The important question is do you believe it? If you can make that new life for yourself then maybe we can help your mom do it, too."

Kent straightened his shoulders. "You changed your life, Ms. LeBlanc, so can I. I know they say kids who get beat up learn to beat their own kids later. I read an article in a magazine once." He raked his unruly hair away from his forehead. "But I don't feel that way inside. I don't feel like hurting people when I get mad. I just get mad, then it's over."

She put her hands on his shoulders and squeezed. "You know what, Kent? I don't think you need to change at all."

An engine groaned from the direction of the highway and a battered truck lumbered into view. Emalea squinted, trying to iden- tify the unexpected visitor.

"Mick!" Kent broke away from her hand, loping toward the slowing vehicle.

"How do you know Mick?"

"He was my dad's cousin."

Another bout of anxiety threatened her. She'd known Mick for years but she hadn't known he was related to Earl Raynor. Would he hold her in some way culpable for his cousin's death? That she knew of, Mick had never participated in the militia, but maybe she was wrong. She watched as he hugged the boy then headed in her direction.

"Doc." He pulled her into a smothering bear hug. She wasn't sure why, but he obviously harbored no vengeance where his cousin was concerned. "Thanks for everything you've done for Kent. Earl never let me have much contact with his family because I'd never joined the militia and he didn't want me leadin' Kent here down the wrong path. As if joining that damn group of his was the right path. All that's gonna change now." He grasped Kent's neck and gave him a gentle shake.

"You know Kent's the one you gotta thank for the sheriff finding you last night, Doc. If it weren't for him, the sheriff wouldn't have even known what was going on here."

Confused, Emalea studied the big man and the bony kid. "I'm lost, Mick. I mean,

Kent told me he had the phone last night, but how do you know?"

Kent scuffed the toe of his worn sneaker in the dirt and Mick smiled at him, then at Emalea.

"Kent called me at the bar a few weeks ago from school. Wanted me to meet him that afternoon. I couldn't recall him ever bein' allowed to call me before, so I kept it quiet and met him outside of school. That's when he got to tellin' me all the mess my cousin was into. He was afraid to tell you 'cause he didn't want you to get in it and get hurt." He winked at her. "But I guess you did that anyway. I went that afternoon and bought a cell phone for him to hide and use when he needed it. After that, he called me with all sorts of information and I kinda passed it right along to that investigator, Jackson."

"So the two of you were helping the sheriff."

Kent grinned and Emalea was thankful for the gruff bartender, who'd decided not to buy into his cousin's hatred.

"Mick!"

All three turned to the source of the voice. Kent's mother stepped onto the porch, her face bruised and swollen. She noticed Mick flinch at the sight. The bartender's gentle side had always been at odds with his rough-and-tumble appearance. These two, mother and son, their lives devastated, could certainly use a friend with a little softness. Kent's mother came down the steps.

"I brought some food for you." Emalea motioned toward her truck. "I don't know what I can do to help, Mrs. Raynor, but if you think of anything, please let me know." Emalea paused. "I'd be glad to recommend someone for counseling for both you and Kent."

"But, Ms. LeBlanc, I already see you. Why can't my mother come, too?"

Emalea put a hand on the boy's shoulder. She hated doing this. Part of her wanted to have Kent and his mother at a counseling session every week. But she'd gotten too close. The boy had become more than just her client and she knew she couldn't be objective; too much had happened.

"You can still come by to see me anytime, Kent, but as a friend now."

The sadness in his eyes lifted briefly. "I guess, that'll be good, if you have time."

"I'll definitely have time."

Mick pulled his truck keys from his pocket. "I think I'll go down to the bait shop.

You wanna come, Kent?" The boy nodded, following the big man.

Mrs. Raynor watched them go.

"What will you do now?"

The woman glanced at Emalea and shrugged. "I don't know. We may move to Lafayette with my sister, but then Kent would have to change schools and I hate to put him through any more. I've never been on my own." She sighed without continuing and to Emalea she appeared lost without the fear and violence that had been her companion for so long.

"I meant what I said about helping you get a counselor. It would be at no cost and I know someone who specializes in family therapy." The woman stared at her and Emalea was glad she'd used her cell phone on the way over to call and get a friend to offer free service.

"I think that would be good for us. I just don't know what's next."

Emalea caught the woman's hand and squeezed it. "You'll figure it out. It just takes a little time and a few good friends. Now let's get that food inside." Mrs. Raynor followed her to the truck and Emalea knew there were plenty of people in Cypress Landing who would help these two get back on track.

"I HEAR YOU AND YOUR MOM might move."

Kent paused in the middle of unpacking glass for framing from a large box. He wasn't sure what to say or at what point he might do something really stupid like cry.

He glanced at Megan and she was watching him. "I don't know yet. My mom isn't sure what she's going to do."

"Are you guys making it okay without… I mean now that your dad's gone?"

His throat thickened. "We'll do fine." The words escaped from his lips all whispery and he hung his head.

Megan squatted beside him, putting her arm across his shoulders. She didn't say a word, just sat there beside him until he felt his chest start to relax and his eyes cleared.

He tilted his head to look at her. "Thanks."

She smiled, then she gave him a shove. "Now get that box empty before I have to help you and you know how clumsy I am. I'd likely break everything that's left."

He returned to his work, relieved to have a friend like Megan. She'd been really nice to him even when things were at their worst, like at his dad's funeral. They'd buried his dad a few days ago. He and his mother had both cried at the funeral attended by many fishermen and even more militia members. Kent figured his dad had caused them both plenty of tears along the way, but he was still his dad and now he was gone, which was really scary. His mom had never dealt with money or paying bills so he was already helping her manage her bank account. He'd learned that in school. They'd get by, though. He had this job at Picture Perfect and his mom would find something. Every day he gave a small prayer they could stay in Cypress Landing. He should have wanted to get as far from here as possible. But he didn't. It wasn't the town or the people that had made his life bad. His mom was seeing the therapist Ms. LeBlanc had gotten for them. Sometimes he went with her. Twice he'd been by Ms. LeBlanc's office, just to visit. If his mom would find a job here and if he could get her to leave that old house behind... If... If... He guessed the two of them still had a long way to go, but at least now he believed they'd get there, wherever that might be. Yeah, he still cried sometimes, when he thought about his dad, but he often wondered if part of it was from relief.

CHAPTER TWENTY

In a way, he was right back where he had started, at Sal's. The once-frosty mug had turned lukewarm in his grasp. Behind the bar, Mick rinsed glasses, his back to Jackson. At least this time he knew that in Cypress Landing he'd found a home. The French doors had been closed in favor of the air-conditioning, but the river was still visible between the panes. The physical aspects were the only part of him that were the same as the first day he'd sat on this stool. His insides had been scrambled then realigned to form a new-and-improved Jackson Cooper, or at least he thought so. Still, one piece was missing and, because of it, the whole of him didn't run as smoothly.

"You gonna drink that thing or hug it the rest of the evening?"

Jackson took his eyes off the amber liquid in his glass. "Drink it, I guess."

"You guess? Man, what are you doin'

here? Isn't there a lady you need to be chasin' after?"

Would chasing Emalea do him any good? He doubted it. After he'd left without calling, she wasn't likely to speak to him, much less continue a relationship.

"I don't think it'll help, Mick."

"You won't know unless you try, right?" Jackson took a drink of the barely cool beer, while Mick continued to stand in front of him. "What is it?"

"Man, I have to tell ya, I didn't much look for you to come back after you went off to Chicago with those FBI people."

"This is home now, Mick. It's a whole different kind of life in Chicago than in Cypress Landing. I like this better."

"Plenty of people around here thought you was gone for good. I know one in particular who thought so, and she was kinda down about it."

Jackson's eyes narrowed. "Really? I didn't tell her I was staying in Chicago."

Mick ran a rag over the bar top. "Didn't tell her you weren't, either."

"Well, no, I didn't."

Jackson watched the big man continue wiping down the bar. Mick tossed the damp cloth in a box then returned to stand in front of him. "She was by here just before you came. Ridin' her bike. Had a burger then said she was headed to the Bluffs. Don't know why."

Jackson thought of Emalea sitting alone near the river, staring at the water, maybe missing him. "How long has she been gone?"

"Not so long before you came." Mick began putting glasses on a shelf.

"But I've been here for a while. Why didn't you tell me sooner?"

Mick frowned. "I don't recall you askin'. I ain't no mind reader. You gonna have to take care of this business on your own. Nobody can do it for you."

"You're right, Mick, I only hope I can help myself."

Before the bartender could reply, Jackson threw a few bills on the bar and raced to his motorcycle while Mick shouted something about change.

The old house had been sold or the previous owners had decided to do major renovations. Jackson didn't see Emalea at the place she'd once called home, but sheer amazement impelled him to stop and stare. Chips of ancient paint lay scattered around the house, while the weathered planks of the outside walls shone smooth from a recent sanding. No longer sagging beneath the weight of the tree limb, the roof sloped solidly skyward, the hole nonexistent. Grass and weeds were raked into dried, brown piles, some waist high. It was as though the place had been reborn. He was hopeful, excited even, but he wasn't sure why. Spraying gravel as he pulled onto the pavement, Jackson prayed Emalea would still be at her special place.

A PIECE OF GRAY-AND-BLACK BARK broke off in her hand. Undaunted, Emalea stretched upward, pulling herself onto the lowest branch of the tree. Just like old times, the river rolled by not noticing her. Here and there, through the years, the bank had slipped into the water, making the currents change ever so slightly. At least she wasn't the only one affected by the passing of time. Today, the child she had once been was not forgotten, but she had been put to rest in a way Emalea had thought impossible. She'd given her best effort to save Kent and his mother, and though their lives had been spared, she couldn't take credit for it. Kent had done it. He'd saved himself and his mother in a way she'd been unable to save hers, but only because they'd wanted to be saved. Her mother had not. Emalea realized now that even if she had been able to stop her father's beating that day, sooner or later, he'd have finished the job.

All the restraining orders and visits from the sheriff hadn't kept Emalea's mother from deciding to stay with her father. She'd made a choice to remain in that environment. The situation her mother had put herself in had led her to form a bond with the man who would eventually kill her, thus sealing her fate.

Emalea's future stretched in front of her, clearer and brighter than ever before. Just like the old house, she'd been gutted of her guilt at last.

The distinctive rumbling of a Harley had her looking toward the road. Fingers bit into the bark as she recognized Jackson. He must have come for the rest of his things and decided to say goodbye, although how he'd found her she didn't know. Then she almost laughed. That was ridiculous. How could he not find her in Cypress Landing? After all, he had been the investigator. Emalea stayed in her tree. He parked his bike and strode toward her. Let him come to her, say his goodbyes then go. She'd still have a life after he was gone, albeit not one as full as it could have been with him.

"Not reliving old times are you?" He stopped with his head even with her knees.

"No, I've completely given that up. I'm making new times now."

"Good. I saw the house when I came by. It looks like someone's doing an excellent makeover."

"It needed it." Her fingers loosed from the tree and she wiped her palms on her jeans. "So, how's Chicago?"

"Too loud, too busy and generally annoying."

She leaned forward to look at him more closely. "You don't sound very happy to be there."

"If I were living there I'd be miserable." He placed a hand on each of her legs. "Emalea, I'm not going back to Chicago. I never was. I don't know how you got that idea, I'm only sorry I didn't let you know differently. The only thing I can say on my behalf is that I really didn't think you cared whether I stayed or went. In truth, I sorta figured you'd rather I left."

Her eyes were locked on his hands while her body registered the warm sensations that were spreading through her at his touch.

"You have to admit it's going to be awkward working on search and rescue and just being around each other after—" she was unsure how to phrase what had happened between them, but hurried on "—well, after everything. You know what I mean."

His hands slid to her hips then with one smooth movement, he pulled her out of the tree. Standing on the ground in front of him, she felt overwhelmed, not with fear or hatred, but with love for the man who hadn't fit any of her labels.

"It doesn't have to be awkward." His hands traveled up her body to cup the sides of her face. "It could be perfect, like it was before."

"But what about me being in danger?"

"If you're willing to take a chance, then I'm ready to do the same. I know that there will always be one threat or another. DePaulo's in jail and Raynor is dead, but others will step right in to take their place. I'm leaving the decision up to you this time. Besides, from what I've seen, you can hold your own."

"You're serious, aren't you?"

"I'm serious about you, about us. Yes, I'm scared of the dangers the future might hold, but I'm ten times, no, a billion times more afraid of not having you in my life."

She wrapped her hands around the back of his head, pulling him to her until she could touch her lips to his. She feathered a light kiss over his mouth then hungrily pressed her lips against his until they parted and she tasted the warmth of him with her tongue.

Just when she thought she might fall, he broke away. "Is that a yes?" His breath rushed against her face and she reached forward to kiss him again.

"What was the question?"

He went completely still for a moment. "Well, damn, Emalea. You went and kissed me and I got the whole thing messed up." He dropped to one knee. "Marry me, please. I don't want to go through this life without you."

Dropping to her knees, she wrapped her arms around him. "Then the answer is yes. I don't want to do anything without you in my life." It was true. She wanted to spend every minute of her life with Jackson Cooper. She smiled as he pulled her closer. It had happened for her, just like Lana had said. She'd found the perfect man.

* * * *

Don't miss the next in the COUNT ON A COP *series.* The Runaway Daughter *by Anna DeStefano is available March 2007.*

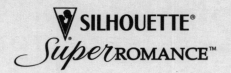

BACK IN TEXAS by Roxanne Rustand
Home To Stay

Kristin Cantrell leapt at the chance to return to her home town and be part of revitalising the dying town. But her reputation had been tarnished by a crime her dead father had supposedly committed. And Ryan Gallagher, her old love, was back too. Now she had to prove not only her father's innocence, but her own.

TO PROTECT HIS OWN by Brenda Mott
Single Father

All Alex wanted was to be left alone on the ranch with his daughter so he could make a better life for them, far away from the city and the drive-by shooting that had changed everything. But he can't turn his back on his new neighbour, Caitlin Kramer, a woman struggling to recover from her own shattered past...

NOT WITHOUT THE TRUTH by Kay David
The Operatives

Lauren Stanley, a woman afraid of almost everything, has no choice but to go to Peru to find a mysterious man named Armando Torres. It's the only way to discover the truth about her past. But before she can, an 'accident' has her forgetting everything that she once knew...

A FAMILY UNITED by Anna Adams

Isabel Barker's life came apart after her husband confessed he loved Isabel's sister—and that they'd had a son together. No one else, including her sister's husband, Ben Jordan, knew the truth about baby Tony. Following a fatal accident, Isabel is torn between letting Tony stay with the only father he's ever known and telling the truth...

On sale from 15th December 2006

Available at WHSmith, Tesco, ASDA, Borders, Eason,
Sainsbury's and most bookshops

www.silhouette.co.uk

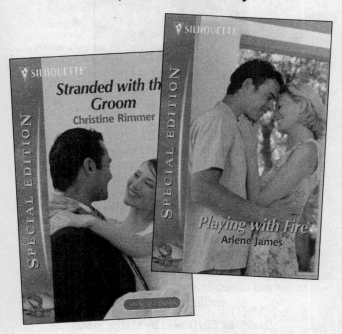

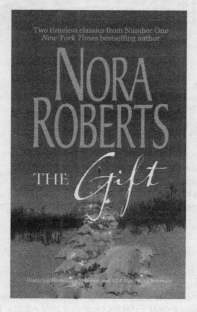
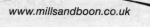

FREE!

2 Books
and a surprise gift!

We would like to take this opportunity to thank you for reading this Silhouette® book by offering you the chance to take TWO more specially selected titles from the Superromance™ series absolutely FREE! We're also making this offer to introduce you to the benefits of the Mills & Boon® Reader Service™—

- ★ **FREE home delivery**
- ★ **FREE gifts and competitions**
- ★ **FREE monthly Newsletter**
- ★ **Exclusive Reader Service offers**
- ★ **Books available before they're in the shops**

Accepting these FREE books and gift places you under no obligation to buy, you may cancel at any time, even after receiving your free shipment. Simply complete your details below and return the entire page to the address below. You don't even need a stamp!

YES! Please send me 2 free Superromance books and a surprise gift. I understand that unless you hear from me, I will receive 4 superb new titles every month for just £3.69 each, postage and packing free. I am under no obligation to purchase any books and may cancel my subscription at any time. The free books and gift will be mine to keep in any case.

U6ZEF

Ms/Mrs/Miss/Mr ....Initials.................................
BLOCK CAPITALS PLEASE

Surname ....

Address ....

....

....Postcode.............................

Send this whole page to:
UK: FREEPOST CN81, Croydon, CR9 3WZ